Manatee Soul

by

Terry Segan

The Marni Legend Series, Book 2

This is a work of fiction. Names, characters, places, and incidents are either the product of the author's imagination or are used fictitiously, and any resemblance to actual persons living or dead, business establishments, events, or locales, is entirely coincidental.

Manatee Soul

Cover Art by *Jennifer Greeff*

The Wild Rose Press, Inc.
PO Box 708
Adams Basin, NY 14410-0708
Visit us at www.thewildrosepress.com

Publishing History
First Edition, 2023
Trade Paperback ISBN 978-1-5092-5152-0
Digital ISBN 978-1-5092-5153-7

The Marni Legend Series, Book 2
Published in the United States of America

"What's wrong? Can't hold your liquor?" Phil quirked from beside the outer rail.

"You are not allowed to comment," Gloria rasped.

"Why not? This is terribly amusing." Phil stood with arms crossed.

"We went to the bar because of you," Gloria said.

"And did I make you down several beers and shots of tequila?" Phil asked.

Gloria put a palm to her forehead. "Can you talk quieter? I can't handle shouting right now."

Phil snickered.

"Phil, give her a break. She's not used to playing the wild girl."

"And I'm not used to playing the dead guy. Guess we all have our issues. At least she'll recover from hers."

She sucked down more soda. "Why is he still here?"

"Because you haven't helped me to move on. You really are slacking on your responsibilities." He shook his head.

Letting out a loud gasp, Gloria said, "I don't mean here, like still on this planet. I mean why are you still here on our balcony? If you don't stop prattling, my head will explode."

Phil rubbed his hands together. "Now that would be fun to watch. And by the way, I do not *prattle*."

"Just let me die in peace." Did she end that comment with a growl?

"If that were to happen, then we'd be together for eternity." Phil clapped his hands together like an excited toddler. "Marni, quick, more tequila."

Dedication

This book is dedicated to my daughter, Bree, whose wandering spirit rivals my own. Always be looking for your next adventure!

Chapter 1

Gloria gripped the side rail of the boat as she peered over the edge. Her knuckles whitened from squeezing the cold metal. "Marni, do we really get in the water with those things? They're huge. And what about the crocodiles?"

I murmured a brief prayer, holding back the expletives. Dragging my older sister out of her sedate life would either be a screaming success or a harrowing nightmare—for both of us. I hoped for the former. Gloria had been the one to suggest a girls' trip to bond over her new-found powers, but I feared it meant mani-pedis in some she-she salon. Walking on my lips would be preferable to stepping into a place of high couture. Sure, who didn't like a few hours of pampering, but crafting a whole trip around a spa day? No thank you.

"Gloria," I reasoned, "swimming with manatees is like walking through a herd of cows. They're docile creatures and quite playful." Those words I'd pulled from the brochure, not first-hand experience, but I didn't need to disclose my source.

"Cows are docile. Aren't there bulls too? They must procreate somehow." She aimed her widened eyes at me while pulling and tugging at the thick rubber of her wetsuit.

Behind her, a mother covered her daughter's ears and glared. The kid looked about thirteen. Certainly old

1

enough to learn about the birds and bees. Or frisky manatees.

"And technically, it would be alligators not crocodiles. But they don't come around the manatees. I think. Well, they're not supposed to be in this section of the river...or so I've heard." Yeah, I suck at pep talks. "Do you think the tour guides would risk their lives every day just for the sake of placating the whims of a few tourists? No. They expect to live beyond puberty and into their twenties," I said.

"Our guides are children? Do you really think they're that young?" She waved her hands in the air like a deranged bingo winner at the senior center.

"I'm sure there are child labor laws, even in Florida. Be glad it won't be some blue-hair with wrap-around cataract glasses looking to supplement her social security. But then if the gators did show up, we know who they'd catch first." I gave her a gleeful thumbs up.

Gloria opened and closed her mouth. "You're playing with me, aren't you?"

"Yup."

"I promised myself to be more accepting of new things." Her shoulders slumped. "I'm failing miserably, aren't I?"

A grin spread across my face. "You're holding your own. Just stay open to something beyond your well-ordered life. Look, we're already here on Crystal River in the tour boat. We've had an adventure and a half squeezing our bodies into these damn wetsuits. They kinda suck in the tummy muscles, huh?" I struck a pose in my black and pink neoprene onesie. A passing boat jostled ours with its wake, and I grabbed the rail to steady myself.

Gloria put a hand on the bench as the deck tilted back and forth. "You got that right. I won't have to go to yoga for a week." She picked up her snorkel gear, placed the mask over her face, and tucked back her short brunette locks as she adjusted the strap to fit.

Our tour guide waited by the ladder. The girl didn't look a day past sixteen. Her sister, maybe a year older, handed out pool noodles.

The younger girl raised her voice. "Listen up, everyone. We're a small group today, so it shouldn't be hard to get in close to the manatees. You'll each get a foam noodle to make it easier for you to stay buoyant. Remember the video you saw back at the shop. Please, for their health and safety, do not touch the manatees."

Out of the side of her mouth, Gloria asked, "What about *our* health and safety?"

"Don't worry," I said. "The alligators only take small bites. Kind of like a snack."

She swatted me on the head with her noodle.

Climbing over the side of the boat, I stopped on the last rung and nodded for my sister to follow. "Come on, Glo. Adventure awaits."

Her hands rested on top of the ladder with arms stiffened. I couldn't tell if she was bracing for entry or hyperventilating. The fog forming on the inside of her mask made it difficult to see her face. "You go ahead. I'm still preparing myself for this river safari."

Preparing? We weren't about to dive into a waterway in the Congo dodging hippos and piranhas. Did she think she would get carried away by one of these things?

Looking at our guide, I said, "Don't let her back

out. I don't care if you have to put your foot on her ass and shove her overboard. She's getting in the water."

Panic crossed the girl's face as she stuttered, "Everyone needs to go at their own pace. Besides, we wouldn't want to spook these gentle creatures." She looked to her sister, who shrugged and signaled for her to start the tour.

With a quiet splash, I released the rungs and slipped into the river, bobbing with the current. The brackish water didn't have the visibility I'd hoped for, but at least I didn't have to touch the murky bottom. In all my research, the internet indicated the water in this Florida river remained a steady seventy-two degrees year-round. They weren't kidding. I had my doubts about coming here in January, but it felt as if I'd plunged into a warm bath. Securing the noodle underneath my arms, I kicked my way toward the four other people in our group, then turned back to watch for my travel companion.

Gloria backed away from the exit and sat next to a man wearing a Hawaiian shirt and khaki shorts, the official uniform of a Floridian retiree. The only thing missing were knee socks with his sandals.

One minute my sister smiled, the next found her bolting up and scurrying for the ladder. As she squatted to plunk herself into the water, she bounced back upright letting out a startled *Oh*. Her head moved back and forth scanning the water. She tried again. This time she made it in, then leaned on her flotation device, wildly kicking to propel herself in my direction.

"Smaller kicks, please." Our guide's blonde ponytail bounced above her dive mask. "You'll spook the manatees with big movements."

Gloria's mask had cleared, and she wore a scowl. She didn't take direction from others well, especially teenagers. Another thing she'd need to work on if she were going to hang with me. Our inherited gift of assisting souls to move on often required good people skills when dealing with the living.

Reaching me, Gloria spouted, "I think I sat on one getting into the water. It felt like a moving couch." She angled her head toward our leader. "Don't tell Susie-Q over there. She might report me to the ranger for abuse of an endangered species."

"It happened under cover of a gloomy surface. I think you'll skate around the law on this one." We swam behind the others, moving closer to the roped off area protecting the habitat.

"Marni, did you see the guy I spoke with?" She glanced behind her at the boat. "Where'd he go? He didn't have a wetsuit on."

"Uh-huh."

She looked back to me. "What a perv! He made a comment about how pretty our young guides looked. The man has to be three times their age. A real sicko."

Great. We came here for a girls' trip and now may need to deal with a dirty old man. "Forget about him. We're here to play with the manatees." I wrapped my mouth around the snorkel and stuck my face into the water. Gloria followed suit floating beside me as we hovered above a small herd where they slept on the bottom. A couple drifted closer to the surface, barely moving.

Out of nowhere, one of the larger mammals swam directly at us, moving faster than the others. As it approached, I saw a jagged scar across its face just below an eye. Gloria released her float and flailed her arms trying to propel herself backward, but only managed to disturb the silt-filled water around us. Her head dipped below the surface, and her snorkel filled with water. She spit out the mouthpiece, coughing and sputtering, taking in more of the brackish swill. Swirling her arms, she sank toward the bottom. I yanked her closer to me and pulled her up to the surface. The creature ducked underneath our bodies, nearly brushing us with its back.

Gloria continued coughing, in between gulping for air. I retrieved her float and shoved it toward her.

Our blonde leader swam up. "Everything okay, ladies? You didn't try to touch one, did you?" Her eyes narrowed.

"That beast tried to ram us." Gloria shoved her mask atop her head. "How is it that thing is the victim?"

"Please remember the guidelines you agreed to before starting the tour. Now, try to keep up with the rest of the group." She spun and effortlessly glided over to the others.

Gloria flashed her eyes at me. "I am so going to trash this place on their website. We nearly got eaten, and she's worried about us *touching* one of her precious mammals."

Helping adjust her mask back over her face, I said, "Look, Neoprene Nancy is too young to understand not everyone is out to ruin the habitat or break the rules. She's gotten a little bit of power as a leader, and her teenaged ego can't handle it. Relax. Breathe. We're here to have fun."

"Easy for you to say. You weren't the one who'd nearly gotten torpedoed by a speeding sea creature."

"Um, Glo, the thing came at both of us. And it probably wanted to be playful but missed the mark. Let's catch up. You good?"

She shoved the end of the snorkel into her mouth. "Rets gro," she mumbled over the plastic and rubber, then kicked away from me.

****

Forty-five minutes later we sat wrapped in blankets, sipping hot cocoa, as our boat motored back to the dock. I elbowed my sister. "Was it worth the contortionist maneuvers getting into these outfits?"

With a big grin, she agreed. "And no alligators. Though, if there had been, I would have offered up the jerk in the flowered shirt as our first sacrifice. Guess he hopped onto another boat."

I loved the fact my sister acquired a sense of humor along with her renewed gifts of being able to see and hear ghosts. Imagine how much fun growing up could have been had she kept them to begin with, instead of Grandma shutting her down at age six.

On second thought, Mom might not have appreciated *two* wise-cracking sarcastic kids. Probably the reason her spirit finally moved on shortly after Gloria got her abilities back. Having our dead mother show up in my kitchen from time to time grew to be annoying, especially with her snarky remarks about my lack of housekeeping skills. Not to mention a damper on my sex life.

We peeled off our second skins at the tour shop, another feat requiring flexibility. I'd left that skill behind in grade school. We went back to the hotel to shower and find lunch.

While Gloria preferred the big box hotels, I

convinced her to forgo her comfort zone and stay in one of the quirky little establishments on the water. Not that she'd had a choice once we'd arrived and checked into the Harbor Inn, but I thought she might decide to sleep in the car after seeing our room. The outdated shag carpet, worn in more than a few places, and faded bedding had caused her to wrinkle her nose as she'd voiced her dismay.

The restaurant had an expansive outdoor patio, giving us views of the bay and preserve we'd been splashing around in all morning. From the brightly colored tables and chairs, the place had a Caribbean vibe with smells of jerk chicken and steaming seafood. I decided to wait until she had a full belly before springing our next tour lined up for tomorrow—kayaking.

Chapter 2

My sister powered down her tablet then waded through the sea of brown and orange shag carpeting between her and the bottle of wine atop our mini fridge. The last vestiges of sunset glimmered through the balcony doors in shades of orange and yellow, almost complementing the rug. "How did you find this hotel anyway? I think they quit updating in the seventies. Do they even make rugs this color anymore?"

"The hotel staff probably smokes a bowl then time warps the furnishings in every evening. I read quite a few positive reviews on the place." All of them focused on the location, where the property sat on the river. Most were unimpressed with the dated décor, but I didn't want to stay in one of the name brand hotels. I find the stand-alone establishments more immersive in local ambiance when visiting someplace. Though I had to admit, the color scheme here could use updating. The bad reviews consisted of lethal warnings about drinking the coffee served in the front office. One rater likened it to primordial ooze. We'd be seeking out the nearest barista come morning as we'd already sampled the sad excuse for coffee found in our room this morning. I neglected to share this info with my sister. She'd insisted this trip be a chance for her to glimpse into my world and allowed me to handle all the arrangements. Not one of her wiser decisions.

Gloria stooped to retrieve the wine cork, which had rolled onto the floor. "Ewww. I hope we won't need to put this back in the bottle." Her fingers brushed at the fuzz sticking to it.

I held out my empty glass. "We won't."

With a refill and half a bag of chips at my side, I settled against the headboard on my bed and opened the mystery novel I'd begun reading on the plane ride here.

Gloria carried her wine out onto the balcony, overlooking the small bay. "That weirdo from the boat is down there waving at me like he wants me to come down. Do they have security here?" she called in through the open doors.

"Unless he can levitate, I think we're safe on the second floor. Wave back. He's probably one of the locals being friendly." I knew he wasn't, but she needed to figure it out herself.

Running inside, she slammed the door, locked it, and drew the curtains.

"What's wrong?" Glancing up, I brushed a lock of brown hair out of my eyes. Does my sister not know the meaning of the word *chill*?

"He dove into the water, popped back up, and waved again. I think we should contact the police. The man could be a lunatic or a deranged killer!"

"Or an Olympic hopeful who enjoys swimming at night."

She sat on the edge of my bed. "How can you be so glib?"

"Glib. Good word. I'll have to work it into my next historical romance." If her eyes had the same properties as a laser, I'd have a gaping hole in my forehead by now. "Look, Glo. The guy may be acting a little…off…but there's no reason to panic. You said he swam away, right?"

"Well…yes…but…" She blew air through her nostrils. "I'm overreacting again, aren't I?"

"Yup."

She stood and sipped her wine. "You could sugar-coat it a bit."

"Okay, I'll work on my tact if you promise to calm down and try to enjoy yourself. Relax. Finish your wine and look forward to our adventure tomorrow. Remember, you said this is what you wanted."

Opening a drawer, she pulled out her cotton pajamas. "Yes, I know I did. Maybe I'm still on edge after the last two souls we helped. You recognized them immediately as being among the dead. It took me a few days and having to see them walk through a solid wall to realize what they were. Now I wonder every time I meet a stranger if they're alive or dead."

"It's only been eight months since you got your powers back. Remember, I've been doing this my whole life. You skipped out on it forty-six years ago. You've got some catching up to do is all."

"I suppose." She slipped on a pair of flip-flops, picked up her oversized cosmetic bag, and headed for the bathroom.

"Glo, I'm confused. You go barefoot onto the balcony, but put on shoes to use the bathroom?"

She huffed. "Have you seen the floor in there? I don't believe garbage-can gray is the original color of those tiles. At least the balcony gets rainwater washing across it almost daily."

I laughed. "Guess I didn't want to look too closely."

She went inside, closing the door behind her. Judging by the arsenal of products stuffed into her case, she'd probably be in there awhile.

As soon as I heard the door click shut, I hopped off my bed and ran onto the balcony. The lights along the walkway weren't very bright, and I could only see a few feet into the bay with the falling dusk. Nothing moved, so whoever—or whatever—Gloria saw, must've gone. Or swam away as she claimed. I'd done my best teaching her how to assist lost spirits move on to the next world. Despite her claim at being ready to do her part, a healthy dose of fear swirled inside of her. Maybe Grandma didn't do her any favors removing my sister's abilities. Now the responsibility fell to me to teach her. *Thanks, Gram.*

Chapter 3

I woke at five to the sound of snarling animals echoing off the walls. Palms sweating, I bolted upright and scanned the room—then realized the sound emanated from the bed beside me. My sister mentioned drinking wine caused her to snore but neglected to say she imitated a feral hyena on the hunt. My God, how did her husband ever sleep?

After staring at the ceiling for half an hour, I decided more shut eye wouldn't happen this morning. I filled the coffee maker with water, threw in the pre-measured packet, dubious about the results, and hit the button. When it finished brewing, and I took the first sip, my nightmare continued. It hadn't improved since yesterday morning. The swill spit out by the offending machine was worse than weak tea. I added a shot of Irish Cream and hoped for the best as I let myself out onto the patio.

Imbibing my marinated brew, I enjoyed the tranquility of the bay. The man in the flowered shirt, who plagued my sister, strolled along the sidewalk. She still needed to develop better perception. He wasn't among the living. For whatever reason, the guy ignored me when I waved.

Sometimes spirits fixated on one person who could help them and discounted all others. Apparently, Glo would be the chosen one for this episode. I didn't have high hopes for either of them given her introduction to the assignment. We might require more wine.

He leaned over the water and a manatee rose to meet his outstretched hand. Even from this distance I could see the scar ravaging the mammal's face—the same one who tried to ram us yesterday. I sprang to the railing, sloshing coffee on the floor, and strained for a better look. Well, that's a new twist. I'd never come across a ghost animal before. The idea had never crossed my mind, but I guess if there are lost human souls, why not animals too?

Now, my dilemma presented itself. *Do I tell Gloria the perv she met is her next task, and he's got a mammal for a sidekick?* Obviously, the man had attached himself to Gloria for help. Would he show up on our kayak tour today? Let's hope he didn't associate with ghost alligators too. That would be enough to send her packing.

I settled back into my chair resting my feet on the little table. The lightweight plastic couldn't hold the weight and tipped sideways. I cussed as hot liquid spilled over the rim of my cup onto my thigh.

"Damn you get up early. How long have you been out here?" Gloria stood in the doorway. She took a sip from her cup then ran to the rail and spat it out. Looking down, she gave a sheepish wave. "Sorry. It spilled." Turning back to me with her shoulders hunched, she asked, "Do you think they have a Clyde's Coffee Shop nearby? This stuff tastes like crap."

"Add Irish Cream. It helps. A little."

She went inside then returned a moment later. "Emphasis on the *little*. At least it's a jolt of caffeine to get us started. What time is our next tour?"

"Nine o'clock."

"Dolphin dancing, right? From a big tour boat? We don tutus and dive in?" She curved her free arm up in the air, lifted onto her toes, and circled once.

"Now you're embracing the spirit of the trip." I chuckled. "Actually, we'll be kayaking and viewing more manatees. At least this time we'll be out of torpedo range."

Gloria flopped into the chair beside me. "Well, that's a relief! I probably kayak as slowly as I swim. At least Manatee Princess won't be there to chastise me about touching the critters."

"Different tour company. Probably find a new herd of teenage know-it-alls." I drank from my cup and grimaced. "But who am I to judge? By the way, did you just spit on someone?"

****

After breakfast in the hotel restaurant, we dressed for our kayak adventure. "You ready?" I waited by the door.

"I can't find my hoodie." She pulled open dresser drawers one at a time then slammed them shut. "I might've left it in the dressing room when I changed out of my wetsuit yesterday. Can we swing by the tour shop on our way?"

"Sure. There's a coffee place nearby too if you require more caffeine. Can we go now?"

She grabbed her backpack and stood by the door. "You mentioned the operative word—coffee."

After a short drive, we entered the J & P Manatee Adventure shop and found one of our teenage guides behind the counter. "Can I help you?" she asked in an overly perky voice. Her high ponytail swished back and forth with the motion of her head.

"We were on your tour yesterday," I said.

Her brows knitted. "Oh?"

"Yes. My sister left her sweatshirt in the dressing room when we changed back into our street clothes."

"Can you describe the garment?" she asked, arching her brows and pursing her lips. Small wonder she didn't whip out a pad and pen to jot down the details.

My sister stepped forward. "It's forest green with the logo of a bank printed on the front. Did you find it?"

"Let me check our Lost and Found bin." She walked into the office and closed the door.

"Why is this hard?" My sister raised her arms up and looked at me with wide eyes.

I pressed my hands down. "Chill, Glo. She'll find it."

Gloria wandered the shop, scanning the pictures on the wall. Most featured manatees or people in wetsuits and snorkels. Stopping in front of one, she waved me over. "Marni, look at this! This is the perv." She pointed while whispering.

The photo depicted a man, the one who'd shown up on our boat and near the hotel. He wore the same outfit in the picture as he did when appearing to us.

"That's my Uncle Phil." The girl from the counter stood behind us offering Gloria her sweatshirt. "Is this yours?"

Gloria took it. "Thanks for finding it. Does he work here?"

The girl sniffled. "He and my mom started this business." She wiped at her eyes. "My uncle died last year. They found his body floating in the river. The authorities believed he ran out of air while diving and drowned."

My sister sucked in a breath. "I'm so sorry. Had he been leading a tour?"

I smacked her on the arm and motioned for us to leave. At least she hadn't asked if he had alligator bites.

"No." The girl rubbed her cheek with a knuckle. "He did a bit of treasure hunting on the side. My mom misses him a lot."

"Thanks for finding the shirt." I pulled Gloria toward the exit. When I glanced back, I saw the teen staring at the picture. Her mom wasn't the only one who missed him.

"Why did you drag me out of there so fast? He's a lost soul who came to us for help. We could have gotten more information about him."

I stopped. "You need sensitivity training!" I pointed at the door. "She got upset telling us the little bit we heard. At least we know he wasn't making inappropriate comments about our guides yesterday. They're his nieces, so his comments were innocent." I nudged her outside and down the steps. "Now, you can't ask questions all willy-nilly. The dead won't get any deader if we take a few days instead of rapid firing questions at their loved ones."

She smirked. "Deader? Is that a word?"

"That's all you picked up from my little tirade? My misuse of adjectives?" Chirping the lock on the car, I pulled open the door. "Get in, or we won't have time to drink our java before the next tour."

Chapter 4

We arrived at Crystal River Kayak Adventures with plenty of time to peruse the gift shop. Why does every tour company need to have *Adventures* as part of the name? Makes it sound like we're trekking across the Serengeti chasing giraffes.

Gloria had a hard time understanding why we couldn't grill the niece of our latest spirit-in-need. Guess I acted the same way at first. When I began helping spirits, I probably offended a few loved ones of the deceased until I acquired more finesse. Might have to sign her up for a crash course in People Skills 101—I pity the instructor.

Our guide, another teen working for his family business, fitted us for our paddles. Uncle Phil joined us. Well, I should say he joined Gloria. She bore his presence with more understanding than she'd done when she thought he was a living felon. Who am I kidding? She ignored him.

"I don't get why he only talks to me," Gloria said.

"Must be your sparkling personality. You do have a certain glow about you."

"Don't make me flip you off, Marni." She held her paddle, practicing a stroke through the air. "At least this tour doesn't involve squeezing my body into a neoprene straight jacket. I think I pulled a muscle tugging the last one over my calves."

It turned out we were the only ones signed up for the nine o'clock slot. Justin, our guide, had more confidence than the two girls leading yesterday's outing. He didn't display a need to lecture us on respecting the environment. We launched our kayaks while Justin climbed atop a stand-up paddle board. From his higher vantage point, he could spot sea life easier.

"Do you see many alligators on your tours?" Gloria floated into the bay poised to begin stroking.

"Really, Glo? You're going there again?" I dug in with my paddle and caught up to Justin.

"Don't you want to know? We are kinda on our own in these things." She gripped her paddle tighter.

"Justin, please assure my sister none of your tour participants has ever been eaten by alligators." *And if anyone has, please lie.*

"No, ma'am. You'll be safe from them critters." Justin assured her.

"I just wanted…" Gloria stopped as a scar-faced manatee hopped onto the bow of her boat. Had it been alive, her kayak would have been dipped below the surface, threatening her buoyancy. Unfortunately, Gloria didn't recognize the beast wasn't among the living. Leaning backward and to the side, her boat flipped, spilling her into the river.

Laughing hysterically, I rocked my own kayak too hard and tipped. Swimming to Gloria while clutching my paddle in one hand, I wrapped my arm around her with the other, and we both gasped for breath in between laughter.

Our guide glided over with my sister's paddle across his board. His face flushed, and his voice rose a few octaves. "Are you ladies okay?" His discomfort made me feel sorry for him. We hadn't gotten five minutes into our trip, and we were both water-logged. I'm sure he had visions of calling Search and Rescue before our excursion ended.

Trying to get back into our boats, and failing, we burst into another fit of giggles.

"We're fine," I said. "Just consider this the safety portion of our trip. Did we pass?"

Regaining his composure, he chuckled along with us. "Glad nothing got injured but your pride. Push your kayaks closer to shore. It'll be easier to remount them."

"Remount?" Gloria whispered. "Sounds like we're climbing onto a camel. By the way, I think that scar-faced creature has it in for me. He's dead, isn't he?"

I shoved my boat toward shore and Gloria did the same. "Was wondering when you'd pick up on him." Standing in shallow water, I slid onto the seat of my kayak.

"How many times have you dealt with ghost animals? You've never mentioned any before."

I tapped my chin. "Hmmmm. Let me think. Ahhh…never."

"What?" She almost tipped her boat again.

"Glo, you really need to quit doing that. You'll send poor Justin into cardiac arrest if he has to fish you out of the brink in deep water."

"You're telling me this ghost manatee is a new twist?" She dug deep with her strokes, propelling the kayak faster.

"Well, it certainly puts a new spin on things. My guess is the creature is connected to Uncle Phil. He did turn up at the same time as our colorfully clothed spirit." The Florida humidity weighed heavily on my stamina. I may not run marathons, but I considered myself in decent shape.

Uncle Phil, whom we'd left on shore, appeared on the bow of Gloria's kayak facing her. "Actually, the manatee is a *she*, who goes by Rosie. At least that's the name I gave her years ago when I rescued her after being mutilated by a careless boater." Rosie surfaced, and he stroked her head.

Gloria stopped paddling. "What is with you showing up on our tours? Can't you be civil about this and come by when we're not busy? This is my vacation."

"I am soooo sorry to interrupt your fun times with my death. Isn't it your obligation to help me?" Phil asked, his hands on his hips.

"You are a testy one, aren't you?" I asked.

He looked at me as if he'd not seen me before. "I only want to deal with *her*." Phil pointed at my sister.

"Both my sister and I have the gift," I said.

"Yeah, but she's feisty. I like her." He winked at Gloria.

My sister resumed paddling. "Look Phil, or should I call you Uncle Perv? If you want my help, zip it with the inappropriate remarks. You won't win points with me." Her anger fueled her paddling, and she pulled ahead, catching up with our guide.

Justin didn't appear to hear our lopsided conversation with a participant he couldn't see. Instead, he rattled off a litany of local wildlife we were passing. I'd never met someone his age so knowledgeable about the environment. He listed off names of more birds than I knew existed in this part of Florida, or the whole country for that matter.

"Lighten up, Glo. This isn't an intervention. Sometimes the deceased get confused and fall back on old habits."

"Old habits? The actions he displays tell me he was an incorrigible flirt who didn't know when to back off. Do we really have to help this guy?"

"You do realize I'm still here?" Phil asked, his arms raised in the air. "Nothing wrong with my hearing."

My sister glared at her uninvited passenger. "Fine. What's your deal, *Phil*? You know you're dead. You know your little swimming friend is dead. How'd it happen? You die in each other's arms?"

"Gloria, we have our gifts to *help* souls, not piss them off." We'd fallen behind our guide, who didn't seem to mind.

Phil pointed at Gloria with his thumb. "She's funny." Turning her way, he said, "And for your information, I have no idea. Yes, we're both dead. No, I don't know if it happened during a quiet dinner out or in a mosh pit at a rock concert."

This next soul definitely had my admiration. On a sarcasm scale of one to ten, this guy hit a twelve. Gloria had point on this assignment, but I'd get to go along for the ride. *Buckle up, and let the insults begin.*

"I'll leave you girls to your touring. But remember—don't touch the manatees." He laughed as he faded from view.

"Are we obligated to help *every* soul who appears to us?" Gloria puffed out a breath.

I got where she's coming from. Sometimes I wanted to tell my current rescue to wait for the next clairvoyant candidate. To date I had helped most. Some who passed by didn't stay long enough for me to give aid. They probably weren't ready for resolution. This guy, however, had hooked into my sister, and we'd be dealing with him until the bitter end. Let's hope it came before we left Florida. Having him appear in my kitchen with a manatee would be awkward.

Chapter 5

After three hours of paddling, sight-seeing, and manatee spotting, we were ready to hang up our life jackets and have lunch. The last half hour of our tour brought wind and rain. It made the journey back more of a challenge. At least Uncle Phil stayed gone. Once we'd beached the kayaks both of us were happy to say so long to the river for the day.

We crawled into the tour van with sore muscles and wet clothes. After leaving a generous tip for our guide and changing into dry outfits, we found Libations, a local winery, a couple of blocks away. With a wine flight in front of me, I perused the menu.

"You know the charcuterie plate is perfect with a flight of reds." The man sitting across from the bar toasted us and pointed to his plate. "I'm happy to share if you ladies would like some." The hand cupping his wine glass sported a wedding ring.

"Thank you for the offer." Gloria fielded this one. "But we're about to order something ourselves."

Did he grimace at the slight? Not to be put off, he persisted. "May I recommend something?" Didn't he already do that, and we turned him down? He was either stepping out on wifey, or she pushed him out the door to annoy the public.

"Hal, I told you to leave the tourists alone. They can read menus and pick food for themselves." Our bartender, Lulu, scolded the man, then turned to us. "He's harmless and faithful to his wife, but don't start a conversation unless you want to be here for hours."

"Noted." Looking over my shoulder, then leaning in, I asked, "So, what would you recommend?"

"Are you looking for lunch or snacks?" she asked.

"Snacks," Gloria said.

At the same time, I blurted out, "Lunch."

"You must be sisters." Lulu flashed a smile.

I laughed. "That obvious?"

"Uh huh. My sister and I never agreed on anything. Except men. We both fell for the same guys in high school. That probably would have continued after graduation, but fortunately, she married her high school sweetheart, leaving me with less competition for dates."

Forgoing recommendations, I ordered a burger and Gloria got the antipasto salad. We toasted with our second glass in the flight, and Uncle Phil materialized on the stool next to her. I looked around for his sidekick. *This could get interesting.*

"How I miss a good cabernet." He sighed.

Gloria jumped, almost falling off her stool. "What is *wrong* with you? Can't you see we're enjoying lunch?"

"I'm sorry, I didn't mean to offend," Hal said. "Please, allow me to pick up your tab."

"Calm down," I mouthed silently. Turning to the local, I replied, "That won't be necessary. The door slamming startled her; it wasn't anything you did."

"It's really no trouble," he offered.

Gloria's eyes widened at me. She had to control her outbursts in public before we got locked up for disturbing the peace. Looking over her shoulder at Phil,

I said, "Perhaps we could continue this conversation later."

Without turning around, my sister chimed in. "Yes, I believe that's the best plan."

"I disagree." Phil crossed his arms. "Why can't we talk now? You don't know anyone here. What do you care if they think you're nuts?"

Continuing to face me, Gloria said, "Because only the living will be involved in our current conversation. You will have to wait."

"Well, pardon me, Miss Snooty Pants. When did propriety take precedence over speaking to a lost soul? I really can be quite charming." Phil leaned closer, sniffing at her wine flight. "Oh, how I miss wine."

Resorting to her signature quirk of speaking without moving her lips—she could have been a ventriloquist—she murmured, "If you know you're a lost soul, you're halfway there. Now scram."

Phil sat up straight and spoke directly to me. "Is she always this difficult?"

Gloria spun around in her chair. "Difficult? I am not difficult. You, sir, are simply being impertinent."

Hal threw cash on the table without waiting for the bill. Leaving his wine half drunk, he slunk out the front door.

Lulu strolled over and leaned on the bar. "I'll have to remember your tactics the next time Hal grates on my nerves. Which will probably be his next visit." She chuckled. "Really, though, he's harmless. Married to a sweetheart of a lady, but I hear she's been housebound for the last few months."

"Believe me, it wasn't anything he did." I leaned in conspiratorially, and stage-whispered, "My sister can be a little high-strung sometimes."

"You know I can hear you, right? I'm sitting right here." Gloria play-slapped me on the shoulder.

Lulu snickered. "Yup. Definitely sisters! Your food should be right up. Try not to scare off any more of the locals while I'm gone. The majority are friendly and tip well." She nodded toward my sister.

"You know, Marni, I'm not sure I'm cut out for this whole spirit assistance program. Maybe I made a mistake telling you about my having the same abilities as you."

Picking up my third taste in the flight, I said, "Are you kidding me? If you hadn't come clean, Mom would still be bugging me."

She snorted. "You think she's really gone?"

"Lord, I hope so! I don't think I could ever have sex again in my apartment if she stuck around."

"Did she show up when you and Kendall were...?"

"No. Kendall and I never...well...she saw another guy in all his glory."

Lulu placed our plates in front of us. "Sounds like you two are having a juicy conversation."

Gloria flushed and swiveled her head to see if anyone else nearby had been listening. "We were just...well..."

"No worries, honey." Lulu patted her hand. "Nobody listens as well as the bartender."

We finished our wine and meals. By this time most of the lunch crowd had gone and only a few patrons remained in the restaurant. After paying the bill, Lulu brought our change, then looked right and left. "I hope one of you can help Phil. He's shown up from time to time but won't interact with me. Gloria, he appears to have taken a liking to you. Give it your best. Phil was a good guy, and the reports of his death stunned the community."

We must've looked like fools with our jaws on the ground. I found my voice first. "You can see him?"

"Yes. Been helping souls most of my life. Phil is one of the few who haven't acknowledged me."

I looked from Gloria to Lulu. It never occurred to me I'd ever meet someone outside of our family with the gift. "Have you seen him near the water? There's a manatee with a scar across her face who accompanies him. He calls her Rosie."

"That makes so much sense." Lulu slapped the counter. "I've seen him with a manatee but never realized the creature wasn't alive. Have you seen ghost animals before?"

"Rosie is my first. Look, do you think we can get together, and have you fill us in on Phil's circumstances? We went on a tour with his nieces, which gave us our first experience with him. Might save us some time getting background from family who might look at us as nosy tourists."

Lulu nodded. "I know what you mean. Sometimes it's difficult not having a playbook. Tell you what. There's a local place over on Fifth called the Crystal Bar. Meet me there at eight and I'll fill you in on what I know. It won't be much. The official report states his tanks ran out of air while on a dive. The fact he hasn't moved on tells me there's more."

"We would appreciate any help. See you at eight," I said.

We went back to the hotel and spent some quality time in the Jacuzzi with a bottle of wine we'd purchased at the winery. The bar Lulu wanted to meet us at was a short three-block stroll, so we could enjoy ourselves and not worry about driving later. Dinner would be at the hotel restaurant.

Since the Harbor Inn didn't allow glass in the pool area, we lounged in the hot tub sipping from red plastic cups. Can you say *redneck*?

Chapter 6

After stuffing ourselves with steamed clams and fresh fish, we walked to the Crystal Bar. A block before arriving, we concluded that allowing Lulu to pick the place might have been a mistake. How well did we really know her?

Engines revved as motorcycles zoomed past us and pulled into the parking lot ahead. Our new friend neglected to mention we'd be meeting at a biker bar. Not my first, but it had been a while. Probably Gloria's first and last, if I even convinced her to venture inside tonight. Might be a hard sell by the way she clutched her purse and shifted her eyes back and forth as she teetered on her chunky wedge heels.

"Maybe we should meet up with Lulu tomorrow at Libations." She clung to the strap of her bag as if she carried the Crown Jewels through a back alley of London.

"I don't have her number. Guess we'll be going in." I led Gloria across the parking lot.

"You've got to be kidding. Let's wait by the street and flag her down before she drives in." She shifted direction and tried to drag me with her.

Shaking her grip off my arm, I stood my ground. "C'mon, Glo. Think of the great story you can tell your kids—their mom drank a beer in a biker bar. Your *cool* rating will be off the charts."

"I don't need to be the cool mom. I'm the responsible mom." She halted in her tracks.

I gave her a sidewise glance. "By that you mean I'm not responsible?"

"No…I mean…oh…you know what I mean. Being cool has never been a goal I've strived to achieve. Honestly, my preference right now is survival." She eyed a large man wearing a black leather vest over a sleeveless T-shirt as he dismounted a bike with gorilla handlebars.

"This from a woman who swam with alligators? Glo, you're braver than you think. If anyone hassles you, stare him or her down. I've seen you take down a snooty maître d' with a few well-placed sneers. These guys don't even compare."

Gloria looked from me to the entrance then back at me before squaring her shoulders. "You're right. This is all part of the new me. The brave me. The adventurous me." She stood poised as if about to spring on an unsuspecting shopper who reached for the last purse on the sale rack. My sister could definitely be a contender. Let's hope the new Gloria didn't involve starting a brawl in this bar.

As we walked toward the entrance, a teal blue motorcycle cut in front of us, flipped a U-turn, then the rider backed it into a space. The new Gloria huffed, and I feared her thoughts were about to be verbalized in a very unladylike manner.

The biker removed both gloves and glasses and stowed them in the saddle bag. When my sister opened her mouth to object to the near-miss the driver had done on us, the rider whipped off her helmet, and long red hair spilled out. Lulu re-buckled the strap and hung it off the hand grip. Spotting us, she waved before pulling her purse from the compartment.

"Sorry, girls. I wanted to snag this spot before one of those macho jerks grabbed it. Have you been inside yet?"

"No. We just arrived and were admiring the rows of...vehicles." My esteem for our new friend went up several pegs. Neither my sister nor I would ever measure up. Drinking would be the only way to get over this. At least we'd arrived at the right place to handle the task.

"Well, let's find a spot to perch and get a round of beers. They have a great selection here."

Lulu pushed through the door, and we followed close behind. The stench of stale beer and cigarette smoke slapped me in the face. It reminded me of The Corner Bar in Northport where I lived.

Gloria's face morphed into a grimace. This trip might break her permanently out of her princess aspirations.

"How...rugged," Gloria stammered.

"It's a bit rough looking, but believe me, this is one of the most popular drinking venues around. There's a table over there. Let's grab it." She made a beeline for an empty high top next to the pool table.

We sat and looked around for a server. Gloria still had a death grip on her bag.

The big man we saw in the parking lot stopped by. "Hey, Lulu. Sweet ride! That new?"

"Nah, I put new pipes on her, so she's got a louder purr. Sounds good, huh?"

He nodded. "Who're your cute friends?" The man winked at Gloria.

I waited for her to run away screaming.

"Down, boy," she said. "This is Marni and Gloria. They're tourists from Long Island. Ladies, this is Tiny. We ride together sometimes."

He extended his hand to my sister. "Nice to meet you."

Tentatively, Gloria stuck out her hand. "Pleasure."

He grabbed it in a hearty shake.

I got the same treatment sans the wink.

"You ladies interested in seeing the area by bike? I know a couple guys who'd be happy to let you ride backseat. Of course, I'd be happy to take one of you with me." He looked directly at my sister.

Why hadn't I thought to film this excursion? The range of emotions playing across Gloria's face rivaled that of a melodrama actress. From where I sat, she struggled between indignation and disgust. Personally, I thought his suggestion could be a fun way to see the area.

"Thank you for the offer, Tiny." His name almost stuck in my throat. The man stood at least six foot three and had to weigh upward of two hundred pounds. Maybe he had small feet?

"Why don't we exchange numbers, and we can set it up?" He looked like a puppy hoping for his owner to drop a bite of steak from his fork.

Gloria glared at me, transmitting her displeasure. Party pooper.

"It's so sweet of you to want to show us around, but we've already got our days scheduled. Maybe another trip?" I suggested.

"You got it. Let Lulu know when you come back, and we can set it up. Until then," he said, not taking his eyes off Gloria.

By this time my sister's lips formed a straight line while her eyes bugged wide. Speechless wasn't an emotion she hit too often. *Damn, this turned out to be a fun night.*

Lulu's large friend moved on to a group of guys at the bar. "So how do you like the place?" she asked.

"It's quaint. Reminds me of a bar at home. Minus the motorcycles. And the leather vests."

She laughed. "Guess it takes getting used to."

A woman in a miniskirt and tank top ran up to the table. "Hey, Lulu. What're you drinking?" She had to be pushing forty, yet her body screamed barely out of high school. Tips must be plentiful for her.

"Hi, Tiff. What IPAs you got on tap tonight?" Lulu asked.

"The usual locals from Crystal Brewery. One's a regular and the other is a double."

"Oooh, gimme the double IPA."

"And for you?" Tiff looked our way.

"What's an IPA? And what's a double IPA?" Gloria asked.

Lulu smirked. "Tiff, bring us three." Looking toward us, she added, "You'll love it! Drinks are on me tonight."

Without objecting, I nodded, relieved we'd be walking back to the hotel. Gloria didn't normally drink beer and had no idea an India Pale Ale had an elevated alcohol percentage, let alone one with twice the punch. *I might be dragging her ass home tonight. Hell, she'd be so out of it I might even ask Tiny for help. Fun times.*

"Why is this place called the Crystal Bar? The name has the connotation of someplace...classier."

Gloria looked around and winced.

With a laugh, Lulu explained. "This building used to be an illegal crystal meth lab. The old proprietors are now serving time, and the new owner has a great sense of humor. Most tourists think it's named for the river."

"Damn, that's good," I said. "The symmetry is downright hysterical."

Almost on cue, a scrawny twenty-something with stringy brown hair stood by our table before wandering into the crowd and disappearing.

"Her name is Gina." Lulu indicated the girl. "She OD'd here. Finding her body is what shut down the lab. I've tried to talk to her, but she won't respond. Not ready, I guess."

Seeing the poor girl made me sad. A tortured life cut short by her own hand. "What can you tell us about Phil?"

"He frequented the wine bar. Good tipper. He and his sister opened the snorkel tour shop. It had been a dream of their parents, who died in a car accident. When the siblings made their parents' dream a reality, the community embraced the business. His sister, Jana, is a sweetheart. Lots of tragedy followed the family. Her husband died of cancer shortly after her parents."

"How awful." Gloria placed a hand to her chest.

"Her daughters were our tour guides," I said. "How old were they when their dad died?"

"They were eleven and twelve. He's been gone five years. Phil passed about a year ago. He'd never married, but he had a steady gal for the last few months of his life. Another weird thing with her. As far as everyone knew, he'd never proposed. But when he turned up dead, she claimed he had asked her to marry him and tried to claim his half of the business. Having no legal documents to back her up, it never went to court."

Tiff arrived with pint-sized glasses for all of us. I fully expected Gloria to fall off her stool before the evening ended. *Maybe Lulu could tie her to the back of the motorcycle and ride her to the hotel.*

"Might that be our angle?" I asked. "A girlfriend claiming legal rights she's not entitled to. Do you think she had anything to do with his demise?"

Lulu sat back and drank her beer. "The authorities believed he'd been diving alone. Gloria, next time he shows up, maybe you could ask him if he had company or where he'd intended to go."

"I still don't know why he won't talk to either one of you. You'd think he'd want someone with experience." Gloria lifted the mug to her lips and sipped. Then she took a longer drink.

Yeah, I'd be calling on reinforcements to get her back to the hotel tonight. "Well, you're the lucky winner, so deal with it."

Lulu arched her brows. "What do you mean someone with more experience? Aren't you older than Marni?"

Gloria bugged her eyes at me, and I nodded for her to continue. "I couldn't handle the burden when I was young. Our grandmother made my powers go dormant with the warning I'd have to regain them when Marni needed help. That only happened several months ago. I still can't differentiate between the living and the dead."

"Wow. I didn't know it was possible to shut off our gifts. Or restart them. Your grandma must've been some kind of grand master at this stuff."

"She did have a lot of knowledge. Maybe there's different levels, and she achieved a high one," I said. "Lulu, if Phil was murdered, he may not remember everything."

Lulu placed her mug on the table. "Yeah, I've found cases like this to be true. Maybe that's why Phil has had a hard time connecting to someone who's able to help him. He may be confused because he died violently."

"Tell me more about his girlfriend. Would she have a reason to want him dead?"

"I didn't know her well enough to say," Lulu said. "The way I heard it she'd been a tourist who'd signed up for one of his manatee tours. Next thing you know, she extended her stay and then a month later moved to Crystal River."

Gloria gulped her beer. "This is *really* tasty. What did you call it again?"

"It's from a local brewery. A Crystal Double IPA." Lulu smirked. "You might want to go easy. The alcohol content is pretty high."

My sister sucked down more. "Don't worry about me. I've been known to have a couple beers and be fine." She downed the rest of her mug. "I'd love another, please."

Lulu and I exchanged a knowing look. Gloria would have a hangover in the morning. I shrugged.

When Tiff came, Lulu pointed at my half drank beer, and I waved her off. Gloria, on the other hand, nodded vigorously. Our server returned with another for both Lulu and my sister. I hated when I had to be the responsible one.

"What do you know about the girlfriend? Maybe start with her name?" I asked.

"Holly. Don't know her last name. He brought her into the winery from time to time. She wasn't what I'd call friendly."

I laughed. "You're welcome to use the *B* word if it applies. At least I'd know who we were dealing with."

"Yeah," Lulu said. "You nailed that one. She really was a bitch to everyone except Phil. Made me wonder what kind of hold she had on him."

"Some women are like that. They can charm the guy they're with, but everyone else around can recognize her for who she really is." I sipped my beer.

Our new friend took a long pull at her mug. "Who wants to do shots?" She waived Tiff down.

"Um, I'm good, thanks." I feared we'd bitten off more than we could chew this evening. *Maybe we should have stuck to meeting at Libations.*

"Sure. What're we drinking?" Gloria asked.

On second thought, this would be more entertaining than a day visit to Lulu's work. Let's hope this town had ride share vehicles available. We definitely weren't walking back, otherwise Gloria would have scrapes down her body from my dragging her along the sidewalk.

Tiff came by and Lulu ordered two tequila shots. I had only two nemeses on the planet and they both came in liquid form—the second being gin. In my book, gin was evil. At least she picked the lesser of the two.

Our server brought two tiny glasses with amber liquid and our host made a toast. "Here's to comrades in the profession of assisting souls." She lifted her glass, and we clinked ours to hers, me with my mug and my sister with her shot.

Gloria dumped it down her throat like a pro. "Next one is on me." She waved for Tiff to bring another round.

"Don't you think you should slow down, Glo? You're not in college anymore." *And you won't be recovering like a twenty-one-year-old either.*

"I'm fine." She swatted a hand in the air and almost fell off her seat. I shot my arm out to steady her, and she giggled.

"Lulu, do you have anything else you can tell us about Phil?" I asked. With Gloria's rapid consumption of alcohol, our remaining time dwindled.

She put a finger to her lips. "Hmmm. He did tell me about his latest quest. Something about a little-known ship out of Spain in the sixteen hundreds called the *Santiago*. Supposedly it carried a stash of jewels stolen from one of the finest houses in Madrid. The one you need to find and talk to is Holly. She comes into the wine bar once in a while with a new guy named Lawrence. Why don't you give me your cell number, and I'll text if she shows up?"

"That'd be great. Hopefully she'll turn up before we leave for home. We're only here four more nights." I looked at my sister, who had a fresh mug of beer in front of her. "Where did that come from?"

Gloria drank heartily before slurring, "While you two were chit-chatting, I flagged down Tiff. She's a great waitress." Her head bobbed back and forth, and her eyelids drooped. I wondered how I'd even get her out the door, let alone up to a second story room with no elevator.

I took out cash from my purse and gave it to Lulu.

"This should cover the damages. I better get Miss Party Animal back to the hotel while she's still conscious."

"Too late." Lulu jerked her head in Gloria's direction.

My sister's forehead rested on the table next to her mostly finished beer. At least she hadn't fallen off the stool. Yet.

Checking my cell phone for any rideshare vehicles in the area, I couldn't get a hit. "What's the local taxi service here?" I asked Lulu.

"You'll die of old age waiting for one." Lulu placed her elbow on the table and rested her chin in her palm.

Gloria listed to the side and slid off her seat. Before she hit the floor, a pair of meaty arms caught her.

"Need some assistance, ladies?" Tiny asked as he held my sister like she weighed no more than a bag of feathers.

"They're staying at the Harbor Inn." Lulu volunteered.

"If you could help get her outside, we can wait for a taxi." I gestured toward the exit.

"Harbor Inn? That's only a couple blocks away. Let's go. I got this. Catch you later, Lulu." Tiny nodded her way.

I looked at our new friend. "Lulu, what does he mean by, 'I got this?' He's not going to bungie her to the back of his bike, is he? Not that it wouldn't be funny, especially when I film the trip with my phone."

She laughed. "He'll get her home safely. Just follow him."

Tiny hefted my sister over his shoulder and headed for the door. Her dangling arms jostled across his backside. All I could do was trail after them, thinking what a great story this would make. Too bad I wrote historical romances and not romantic comedies. Tonight could've gone under "best first date ever.'"

He strode across the parking lot and onto the street.

"Are you going to carry her to the hotel?"

"Why not? She doesn't weigh much. Besides, you'll never get a taxi anytime soon."

Snapping a few pictures with my phone—yeah, I had an evil streak—I walked behind them. They'd be needed to convince Gloria how she got back to the room. "I have to warn you, Tiny, we're on the second floor, and there isn't an elevator."

"Like I said, I got this."

Ten minutes later I unlocked our room, and he gently placed her onto the bed. Wishing me a good night, he left. On the chivalry scale, I had to admit this man rated high.

After removing Gloria's shoes, I got the extra blanket from the closet and draped it over her. Looking down at my unconscious sister, I sighed, fearing the painful morning ahead of her.

Chapter 7

Late the next morning I lounged against my pillow messaging my daughter. A groan emanated from the other bed.

"Do you have to pound so loudly?" Gloria asked me.

"Good morning, Sunshine. All I'm doing is texting." My fingers stopped moving. "You can hear that?"

Her head dropped back onto the pillow with her eyes pinched shut. "I can hear snails crawl." Placing a hand on her stomach, she fingered the fabric of her top. With a slight tilt of her head, she cracked open one eye. "Why am I wearing my clothes from yesterday?"

A grin slid across my lips. "What's the last thing you remember?"

She lay there not responding. I assumed she'd fallen back asleep, but she finally said, "Having a beer with Libby."

"You mean Lulu?"

"Yeah. Her. We were at that crystal place. There were motorcycles. And people in leather. Lots of leather. How many of those things did I drink?"

"Are we only counting beers, or should I include the tequila shots you downed as well?" I chirped with more enthusiasm than necessary. One of us would be having hours of fun with this scenario. The other would be plotting my slow and painful death.

Attempting to prop herself up, she slipped, adjusted the pillows, then tried again. Achieving an upright position, she turned her head toward me. "I drank tequila? I don't drink tequila."

"You did last night." Covering my mouth, I stifled a chuckle.

"Ahhhh. Someone *please* tell the man with the jackhammer to get out of my head," she moaned. "How did we get home?" She looked at her feet. "Did I lose my shoes?"

"Um…we had help from a friend."

"Lulu was on a motorcycle. She couldn't have given us a ride."

I moved to the edge of my bed. "Lulu didn't give us a ride."

"You called a taxi?"

"Nope."

"You're enjoying this way too much." She covered her eyes with her hands.

While she went through her list of questions, I scrolled through my cell to the pictures. Selecting one of our trek from the bar, I handed her the phone. This one showed a clear shot of Gloria hanging over Tiny's shoulder, her arms dangling down his back.

Her eyes widened as she stared at the screen. Without warning, she threw my phone onto the blanket, covered her mouth while jumping from the bed, and ran for the bathroom.

I called after her, "Don't you want to put your flip flops on first?"

A slamming door was her only response.

Carrying a diet soda, I went onto our balcony and

watched the manatee tour boats floating near the preserve. The one we'd been on lay anchored with tourists climbing aboard.

Moving like a sloth, my sister came outside and sat beside me. Her pallor looked several shades lighter than usual, and she wore sunglasses.

I went inside and returned with a can of soda. Popping it open I handed her the cold beverage. "Drink this. It'll help."

Her dark lenses hid her eyes. "What is it?"

"Ginger beer."

"I don't think more alcohol is what I need. That whole hair-of-the-dog thing never worked for me."

Amusement exuded from my voice. "It's non-alcoholic like root beer. Trust me. The ginger will calm your stomach."

She took the can and raised it to her mouth. I hoped what went down wouldn't come back up and go over the edge of the balcony. Our downstairs neighbors wouldn't take kindly to being "spilled on" twice. After a couple of sips, she rested her head against the wall behind her chair.

"What's wrong? Can't hold your liquor?" Phil quirked from beside the outer rail.

"You are not allowed to comment," Gloria rasped.

"Why not? This is terribly amusing." Phil stood with arms crossed.

"We went to the bar because of you," Gloria said.

"And did I make you down several beers and shots of tequila?" Phil asked.

Gloria put a palm to her forehead. "Can you talk quieter? I can't handle shouting right now."

Phil snickered.

"Phil, give her a break. She's not used to playing the wild girl."

"And I'm not used to playing the dead guy. Guess we all have our issues. At least she'll recover from hers."

She sucked down more soda. "Why is he still here?"

"Because you haven't helped me to move on. You really are slacking on your responsibilities." He shook his head.

Letting out a loud gasp, Gloria said, "I don't mean here, like still on this planet. I mean why are you still here on our balcony? If you don't stop prattling, my head will explode."

Phil rubbed his hands together. "Now that would be fun to watch. And by the way, I do not *prattle*."

"Just let me die in peace." Did she end that comment with a growl?

"If that were to happen, then we'd be together for eternity." Phil clapped his hands together like an excited toddler. "Marni, quick, more tequila."

"Okay, Phil. You've had your fun. Now let Gloria suffer in silence, and we'll catch up with you and your pet manatee later. Deal?"

"I don't see how you're actually going to help if you keep sending me away."

Gloria put her hands up and shielded her glasses.

"Well, perhaps I could give you an hour or two. She really is no good to me in her current condition." Phil huffed and disappeared.

"Make it more like three or four hours," she whispered.

"He's gone, Glo. Negotiations are closed."

"Swell." She arose, went inside, and the springs on the mattress squeaked.

****

A few hours later when my sister achieved mobility as opposed to the fetal position on the bed, we drove to the local animal preserve. This had been one of the few things on Gloria's list to visit while here. Taking a stroll on shaded paths stretching beside streams and observing local wildlife and fauna were the right speed for the day.

We purchased tickets and waited for the next tour boat that would take us along the waterway to the entrance. Gloria moved at a slow gait but, for the most part, had recovered from her night of ill judgement. Her sunglasses remained shielding her bloodshot eyes. Maybe I should have picked her up a pair of those wrap around cataract glasses and a big floppy hat.

The guide directed us to a bench at the back of the flat-bottomed boat. Before we launched into the stream, a large man wearing a staff uniform called for the skiff to wait, and he jumped aboard.

He came to the back and sat next to us. "Hello, ladies. How are you this afternoon?"

My sister mumbled, "Fine."

I did a double take. "Tiny?"

He gave a crooked grin. "Here they call me Doc Christopher."

Gloria removed her shades and studied him closer. "You're a doctor? But you're…you're…"

"An Aquatic Veterinarian actually. I tend to most of the aquatic mammals here at the park."

I motioned toward Gloria with my thumb. "My sister referred to your off-duty activities as a man in leather. Not to mention rescuing damsels."

Tiny laughed.

Gloria scowled and replaced the glasses. "That's not what I meant. Now that you mention it, though, I guess I owe you thanks for getting me home."

"You're quite welcome. Glad to assist a beautiful lady in distress." Tiny removed his hat and bowed his head.

"I wouldn't have described my condition as distressed." Gloria squared her shoulders.

"Glo, you were inebriated and passed out. The man carried you home over his shoulder. I think *distressed* fits. You want to review the pictures again, just to be sure?" I pulled my phone from my purse.

Her lips thinned. "Not necessary."

"Gloria, your secret is safe with me. Nobody will know about your rescue." He winked at her.

"Thank you, Tiny. I mean, Doc Christopher. It's good to know *some* people know how to be discreet."

I could feel the heat of her gaze. "I'm discreet. You didn't see any of those pics popping up on your social media feed, did you?" I thought about sending them to her husband, Robert, to print up a few nine by twelve glossies for when she returned home, but he possessed excellent survival skills when it came to dealing with his wife. He would have deleted them and reported the email as spam.

The flat-bottomed boat moved through the water at a sedate pace, allowing the passengers to view the canal's surroundings. A sweet fragrance filled the air from the plants on the shore. Our guide pointed out flora, waterfowl, and the occasional turtle. We motored along for fifteen minutes until docking at the main entrance to the walkway.

We were the last to disembark with Tiny trailing behind us. Gloria got off before me and walked toward the trailhead. As I stepped from the boat, my toe caught the bottom edge of the dock, and I slammed down onto the boards. Did I mention my middle name should have been Grace?

Gloria turned and asked, "Marni, what are you doing down there? Did you drop something?"

Large hands closed around my waist and lifted me to a standing position. "Are you all right?" Tiny towered over me. "No, you're not. You're bleeding."

My chin stung. Gingerly patting it, I found blood on my fingers when I pulled them away. "Let's hope it doesn't leave a scar. Not the look I'd be going for. Guess I could make up a good story to explain it, though."

"Let's get you over to the clinic where I can clean that up." Tiny led me with a hand on my shoulder.

"I hope she won't need stitches." Gloria followed behind us. "We may need to file a claim with the park's insurance."

"Chill out, Glo. It's a scratch. I tripped. Completely self-inflicted." I palmed my chin, hoping I was right about it being minor.

He led us down the path to a one-story building beside a large pond. A cool gust of air wafted past us when the automatic doors swished open. The typical hospital smell of antiseptic hit me immediately.

"Let's go into exam room three." Tiny pointed down the hall.

"Isn't this an animal hospital? You can't treat my sister here." Gloria stopped walking.

The man let out a large belly laugh. "It's not like I'm going to perform surgery on her. Both animals and humans have skin and blood that can be cleaned with the same chemicals and bandaged. Don't worry. I'll take good care of her. Does blood make you squeamish?"

Gloria sputtered. "Why would you think that?"

"Don't mind her. She's always this high strung, Tiny. I mean, Doc. You'll get used to it."

"I am not high strung." She stomped her foot.

My jaw dropped toward the floor as I stared at her, which sent a jolt of pain where the broken skin stretched.

"Okay. Maybe I do go a little...overboard. Occasionally. Let's get you into the exam room." She grasped my arm and led me to the door.

"There's a reception area with chairs at the end of the hall." Tiny indicated to Gloria. "You can wait for your sister there. We'll only be a few minutes."

She lingered a moment longer.

"I'll take good care of her." His voice softened.

I sat on the edge of the exam table blocking out thoughts of what might have occupied this space before me. Hopefully it hadn't been something slimy or with scales.

My rescuer set out gauze and antiseptic, then proceeded to clean the cut. Despite his girth, his touch was light and his movements fluid. Once the blood got removed, it had already stopped bleeding, so he smeared ointment on the wound and finished with a bandage. "It's not going to look pretty but should heal nicely. At least you won't need stiches."

I pulled a cosmetic mirror from my purse and

examined his work. "Yeah, doesn't that look attractive. I'll have men beating down my door for dates."

"I'd be the first in line." He mugged while waggling his eyebrows.

"Alas, I'm not one for long-distance romances. We'll have to control ourselves."

He helped me off the table, and we went to get my sister. We found her examining a wall full of animal photos. The one directly in front of her featured the now familiar scarred face of Rosie.

"I see you've discovered our memory wall." Tiny stood beside her.

She pointed a trembling finger at Rosie. "Did this one die of its facial wound?"

I poked Gloria in the ribs to get her to stop acting weird. Her nerves were already fragile, and the last thing we needed was unwanted attention into our investigation.

"She was a sweetheart. We had a local patron named Phil who named her Rosie. He rescued her after a reckless boater ran over her and didn't even stop to help. After calling us to send a team and retrieve her, we nursed her back to health. Then about a year ago, she was found floating dead in the bay. Kind of a weird coincidence since Phil had been found dead the day before."

Gloria squeezed my arm, but I couldn't look at her. She asked, "What did she die of?"

"We didn't examine her. Since she died in the wild, we didn't autopsy the mammal."

At least we now knew Rosie's timeline, and maybe why her ghost was hanging around with Phil. We needed to find Holly and see if she could shed any light on what happened to her boyfriend. Unless she had a hand in it?

Chapter 8

Once Tiny, I mean Doc Christopher, released me from his care, Gloria and I wandered the park on our own. By the time we returned to the car a couple of hours later, my sister had made a full recovery. She'd even ditched the sunglasses. Well, she tried anyway, but the bright Florida sunshine proved too much for her.

"Let's hit the pool for a couple of hours before dinner. Where do you want to eat?" I asked.

"Hmmmm. I'm feeling Italian right now. You good with that?" She tilted her head.

"Carbo-loading works for me. With all the exercise we've had lately, I feel like I'm wasting away." I touched the back of my hand to my forehead.

"Please don't swoon. The other drivers may not take kindly to you swerving into their lane."

"Sometimes you can be such a party-pooper, Glo. I think we should put their quick reflexes to the test."

She unbuckled her seat belt. "Let me out first. I'll film your little experiment so the insurance company will have proof that it wasn't foul play."

"Okay. Okay. I wouldn't want to scratch our rental car anyway."

"Do you think they'd notice?" Gloria asked. "For a vehicle that had supposedly been cleaned, more bugs splattered the outside than I thought existed in the whole state. We should have made them run it through the car wash—again."

"And arrive even later at our hotel? It really doesn't—" The ringing of my phone interrupted. Fishing my cell out of my purse, the caller ID read "Lulu." I handed it to Gloria. "Answer this. She's probably checking up on your level of consciousness anyway."

"Very funny." Gloria swished her finger across the screen. "Hi, Lulu. It's Gloria. Marni's driving."

She listened a moment. "Yes, I'm fine. No, I didn't remember how I got home, but my sister was kind enough to document it with photos."

Another moment.

"Hang on," Gloria said. "Let me put you on speaker so Marni can hear this too." She tapped a button and set the phone in a cupholder in the center console. "Can you hear me?"

"Loud and clear. Hey, Marni. How's it going?" Lulu's voice came out of the cell.

"I'm good. You make it home all right last night?" I asked.

Lulu chuckled. "Yeah. I was fine. Remember how I told you Holly shows up at the winery once in a while?"

"Is she there?" Gloria shouted.

"Glo, she can hear you fine. You don't have to yell."

My sister clucked her tongue. "How do you know? I find it very hard to hear when people have me on speaker phone."

"I can hear you fine, Gloria. And so can the people sitting at the bar."

"You have us on speaker too? Aren't we supposed

to just run into, *you know who*, instead of her knowing about us?" Gloria bugged her eyes.

"Relax. I was kidding. You make it too easy." Lulu laughed. She lowered her voice. "Anyway, the guy she's usually with is here and saving a seat. I expect her to show up any time. Why don't you two roll on over here and do some investigating? I'll reserve the two stools next to them, but I can't hold the seats for long. Look, it's getting busy, and I gotta get back to work." She ended the call before either of us could answer.

"Guess we're skipping the pool." I turned onto the main roadway.

"Darn! I wanted to see what you ladies looked like in your bikinis. Couldn't you go for a quick dip?" Phil appeared leaning forward between our two seats.

Gloria screamed. I kept driving.

"My you are a jumpy one," he said.

"What is *wrong* with you?" Gloria glared at our visiting specter.

He raised his hands in the air. "You want the list?"

"No. What I want is for you to stop popping up like a nefarious groundhog. Were your manners this bad when you were alive? If they were, it's hard to believe you had any friends at all."

Phil sat back. "I'll have you know I was quite popular. People liked me. Which is more than I can say for you with that sour attitude. Are you sure you're supposed to be *helping* spirits, because you're not very good at it?"

If I didn't intervene soon, there might be a rumble. While neither could hurt the other, it could still get loud. The comments grew more amusing by the minute though. I supposed, as the more experienced ghost-whisperer, it would be up to me to turn this in a more productive direction. Have I mentioned how I hate being the responsible one? "Don't make me pull this car over. You two need to stop arguing and work together." Or we'd never be rid of Uncle Phil and his endless barrage of snarky remarks.

Both stopped talking. Phil's image centered in my rearview mirror. *Was he sticking his tongue out at me?*

"Not nice, Phil," I chastised.

His tongue disappeared. "You can see me? I didn't know I had a reflection."

"You're a spirit not a vampire. Now, if the two of you are done bickering, maybe Phil can tell us about Holly."

Gloria remained silent with her arms crossed and looked straight ahead. No pouting here.

"Oh, my Holly. Such a lovely lady-friend if ever there was one. Even comparable to you, my beautiful, Gloria."

"Hmpf." My sister needed to not take this so personally.

"Anyway, what would you like to know about her?" he asked.

Since he remembered Holly with fondness, I couldn't tell if his death wiped out any memory of wrongdoing on her part, or if she had nothing to do with his demise. "For starters, had you proposed to her before you died?"

"Proposed? Why would you think that? I'd made it clear there would be no nuptials between us. While I'd been happy for her to move in, I wasn't giving up my bachelor status."

Gloria uncrossed her arms and mouthed the words,

"She lied?"

"I couldn't quite hear you, Gloria." Phil leaned closer.

She turned to him. "We were told she'd claimed you had proposed and demanded your half of the tour shop."

For once the man remained speechless. Sadly, it didn't last long. "That's odd. I don't remember asking for her hand."

We'd almost arrived at Libations. Without knowing how long Holly and her new companion would stick around, I needed to wrap up this conversation for now. "It's possible you don't remember. When a person dies violently, the spirit gets confused and can't recall everything. Is there anything you can say about Holly that could be useful in flushing out her true intentions? She's supposed to be at the bar right now, and we're going to lure her into small talk."

"What do you mean, her true intentions? The woman loved me. You don't think she killed me, do you?"

Gloria had calmed herself and spoke in an even voice. "Phil, we just don't know enough to conclude one way or the other. Right now, we have to consider her claim to your property. When you died, were you searching for that Spanish treasure?"

"How did you know about the treasure? I'd only told Holly, and it sounds as if you haven't spoken to her yet."

I parked the car and turned to him. "Like I said, you may not remember everything that happened around your death. Gloria and I will talk to Holly and see if she can shed any light on your final hours. It might be best if you weren't there. She'll be sitting with her new boyfriend."

Phil's mouth gaped open. "How do you know all of this?"

"Lulu can see and hear you. She's tried to talk to you, but you've not responded to her." I put my phone back into my purse.

"That unsavory barkeep? I heard her but chose to ignore her. If she's the one who's been spreading rumors about me and Holly, then no wonder I don't remember. Because what she's been telling you are lies. Lulu was always asking questions about my dives and trying to get information that was none of her business. If anyone should be under suspicion, it's her." With his tirade over, Phil disappeared.

"Looks like we need to tread carefully. People are beginning not to be whom they appear." Gloria got out of the passenger seat and walked around to my side of the car.

Did she just use the word *whom* properly? I didn't know anyone could. "I don't know, Glo. It could be Phil hasn't remembered everything yet. My money is on Holly being the prime suspect. Still, we should be conservative with what we share with Lulu until we learn more."

Walking toward the door, I put a hand on my sister's arm. "And, Glo?"

"Yes?" She eyed me suspiciously.

"No tequila this time. Okay?"

"I hate you." She strode ahead of me and flung open the door.

Chapter 9

The same two stools we'd occupied on our first visit had a "Reserved" sign on the bar in front of them. I assumed the mismatched couple seated to our right was Holly and her new beau. She carried a few extra pounds on her short figure, while he looked almost skeletal with his gangly arms and legs. His milky pallor suggested he didn't spend much time in the sun.

Sitting across from the bar, the same patron, Hal, who Gloria had scared off last time, sipped a glass of white wine. He picked at a half empty plate of cheese slices and chunks of fresh bread. Maybe he wouldn't recognize us.

"Lulu, I'll take the tab, please," Hal called before we'd even reached our seats. The man stared off to our left not making eye contact with my sister or me.

"You want the rest to go?" Lulu asked from behind the bar.

"Not necessary." He pulled out his wallet. "Actually, this should cover it." Hal tossed a few bills on the table, gulped his wine, then hurried out the door. Yup. He remembered us fondly.

Lulu cracked up. "You certainly made an impression on him. Please don't scare off any more patrons."

"We'll try." I leaned closer. "It'll be easier if *you know who* doesn't show up."

Our bartender winked. "What're you drinking? And sorry, Gloria, but we're fresh out of tequila."

My sister huffed. "Everybody's a comedian. I couldn't possibly be the first inebriated person you've seen."

"Glo, there's a difference between inebriated and passed out on the table. Not to mention your mode of transportation home," I said.

"Yeah, Marni has a point. You're the first one who got toted out of there over the shoulder of one of the bikers. Now that was hilarious."

Gloria wrinkled her brow. "It depends on your perspective."

"Well, your perspective was hanging over Tiny's shoulder with your arms swaying back and forth across his ass. I bet he liked that part." She was so going to make me pay for this, but right now I had the upper hand.

"I'll have a glass of the house chardonnay," Gloria said. Guess she refused to be baited any further. But the night was young.

"Make mine a pinot grigio." I intentionally moved my elbow out too far and knocked Holly's purse off the back of her chair. "Oh, I'm so sorry. Let me get that for you."

Holly glared at me without so much as acknowledging my apology. Not exactly the conversation starter I'd hoped for. She flipped her long blonde tresses behind her shoulders, turned back to her boyfriend, and continued their murmured conversation.

I shrugged at Lulu as she delivered our drink order. Picking my glass up by the stem, I toasted Gloria. "Here's to surviving our girls' trip so far." We clinked glasses and drank.

"By *surviving* do you mean living through our experiences the last few days or not killing each other?" my sister asked.

"From your temperament, madam, I'd vote for the latter." Phil had reappeared, this time sitting on the bar beside Gloria, who almost dropped her wine.

"What did I tell you about doing that?" She spoke through clenched teeth, yet her enunciation was perfect.

"Wow, it must be a stressful trip if she's getting angry at a simple toast. Are you and your friend not getting along?" Holly's boyfriend asked me as he leaned over her empty seat. I hadn't noticed her getting up.

I swatted the air with my hand. "My sister and I always banter like this."

"Sisters. That explains a lot. Does she always mutter to herself?" He tilted his head.

Turning her way, I heard her tell Phil to "shut up or go away." Nudging her with my elbow, she jolted upright, then glared at me. I motioned with my eyes toward the boyfriend so she would know she had a live audience. Her lips quickly formed a polite smile.

Returning my attention to him, I said, "I hope I didn't make your friend angry when I bumped her purse."

"Not at all. Don't give it a second thought." He stuck out his hand. "I'm Lawrence by the way, and my girlfriend is Holly." Did I detect a northeastern accent?

I shook his hand. "Nice to meet you. I'm Marni, and this is Gloria." I motioned with my thumb.

Gloria nodded with the smile still pasted on her face.

"Oh, aren't we getting chummy with my replacement. What's next? The three of you exchanging friendship bracelets? Perhaps matching tattoos?" Phil crossed his arms.

"Where are you visiting from?" Lawrence asked.

Ignoring our specter would be a challenge if he didn't tone down the sniping. He completely missed the point that we were here because of him. "Long Island, New York. We came here to snorkel with the manatees and do some kayaking. Are you local?"

Holly returned from outside reeking of cigarette smoke. She slid onto her stool, forcing Lawrence to lean back onto his own.

"Holly, these ladies are from Long Island. Didn't you live there?" he asked.

She glanced our way then took a sip from her glass. "When I was a kid."

"Really, what town?" I asked.

She sneered. "Like I said, I was a kid. Don't remember much."

I put on my best meet-and-greet smile I used at book signings and held out my hand. "I'm Marni, by the way, and this is my sister, Gloria."

Holly simply nodded. Lulu's description of this woman was pretty darn accurate. I could believe her having a hand in Phil's death simply because he spilled coffee on her new shoes or had the audacity to move her toothbrush to the other side of the sink.

"Holly was always a bit shy around strangers. It'll take her a few moments to warm up," Phil said in her defense.

Who's he kidding? The woman could be in the middle of the Sahara Desert and still exude a frosty aura.

Gloria whispered, glaring at him. "I said hush."

"Pardon?" asked Lawrence. "I didn't quite hear you."

I placed a hand on her arm. "No, Gloria, that isn't a blush. You ordered chardonnay."

She scrunched her brow for a second, then her eyes popped wide. "Oh…yeah…you're right. For some reason I was thinking a rose blush. Guess all those hours in the sun these past few days are muddling my brain." She tapped her forehead.

"I'll say. Maybe Lulu should feed you more tequila to straighten things out." Phil chuckled at his own joke.

Gloria hopped off her stool and excused herself. Phil had the good sense not to follow her to the women's restroom. If he had, the whole restaurant might hear her displeasure, and she'd scare off more than just pesky Hal.

I caught Phil's attention and mouthed, "Stop it." Attempting to engage Holly in any kind of useful conversation, I fished for ideas. Food was usually a safe, non-confrontational topic. "Since you guys live locally, can you recommend a good dinner place? We were hoping for Italian food. Any suggestions?"

Holly ignored me. I could almost believe her to be a lost soul searching for assistance the way she refused to acknowledge the living.

Lawrence offered, "Mama Kettle's has amazing pasta dishes. It's about ten minutes from here."

"We'll check it out." I stifled my frustration. With no other recourse, I gritted my teeth and forged ahead. "You know, have you ever heard about lost ships from the sixteen-hundreds in these waters? I write historical romances and have been toying with the idea of my next novel being set here in this area. It could be centered around a lost treasure, possibly on a sunken Spanish ship. I'd heard a story about stolen jewels from a house in Madrid. I'm still researching it. Sound familiar to either of you?"

Lulu froze with her jaw gaped open. She may not like my tactic, but short of slamming Holly's head into the bar and shining a bright interrogation light into her face, I wouldn't get anywhere.

"That sounds very specific. Where'd you hear of such a thing?" Holly asked, her voice laced with caution.

"Just a hit on the internet. Have you heard of it? I can't remember the name of the ship that went down carrying the precious jewels, but supposedly it sank around the Florida coastline of this area."

Holly glanced at her boyfriend. I couldn't see her face, but the veins in her neck strained.

"Hey, Lulu, we're one and done," Lawrence said. "Can I get the check?"

"Sure." The bartender rang them up and slipped a tab in front of him.

He threw down a twenty. "That's yours."

"Thanks, guys. Catch you next time." Lulu scooped up the cash and waved.

"It was nice meeting you, Marni. Tell your sister the same please." Lawrence grabbed for Holly's elbow, but she'd already stormed ahead of him. No guilt there.

When they'd gone, Lulu laid into me. "Are you nuts? And I thought your sister was the pro at scaring off customers."

Phil clucked and shook his head. "Marni, you're as

tactless as a heckler at a comedy performance."

Gloria returned and looked at the empty bar stools beside me. "What'd I miss?"

Chapter 10

Lulu jerked a finger at me. "Your sister scared off Holly and Lawrence with more efficiency than you dispatched poor Hal."

"What did you say?" asked Gloria.

"Since my small talk went unacknowledged by the ice princess, I moved in for a direct hit. Lulu, you truly undersold the woman's lack of social skills. If Lawrence hadn't been here, I swear Holly wouldn't have deigned to even look in our direction."

"Yeah, but asking about the lost ship? It's not exactly common knowledge around here. You don't want them to suspect you're trying to locate it for real," the bartender said. "Might end up like Phil."

Gloria perched on her barstool. "You asked them about the ship? While you held their attention, why didn't you ask if they'd killed her boyfriend too? I'm sure they would have confessed immediately, and this mess would be cleared up before supper time."

"Speaking of which, Lawrence suggested Mama Kettle's for good Italian food. You in?" I asked.

My sister leaned on the bar. "Don't change the subject."

"I believe I already did. Lulu, can we have the bill? We're off to find pasta." I pulled my wallet out of my purse.

"That's it? You've blown your only lead, and now

it's time for dinner?" Phil materialized nose-to-nose with me.

"Everybody relax—that includes the living and the dead. We'll get another shot at them. Don't you think they're curious to know more about us, since I obviously hit a nerve? This isn't my first rodeo. Come on, Glo. I'm hungry."

"Let's hope they don't take a shot at us first." Gloria said.

I paid the bill, and we walked outside.

Phil trailed behind us. "I don't see what makes you so smug about this whole affair. And I'm not happy with any of you insinuating my sweet Holly had anything to do with my demise."

"Your *sweet Holly* could barely put two civil words together, and you're ready to nominate her for sainthood?" Gloria got into the passenger seat.

"Well, if the halo fits…" Phil snarked.

"Obviously, it didn't fit you, or you wouldn't be here interrupting our vacation. Why don't you—" My sister turned toward the empty back seat.

He'd disappeared from my rearview mirror after his last remark. I hated to mention it to Gloria since she'd been on a roll. "Are you ever going to try helping him, or do you intend to nag the crap out of him until he goes away? I mean, both tactics will work, except option two might take longer. In case you haven't noticed, your witty jabs amuse more than annoy him."

"How can you say that? I *am* trying to help him."

"Are not." Phil's head appeared momentarily by her ear then disappeared again.

Gloria whipped around, then faced forward with arms crossed.

That's it. I slammed on the brakes, and the tires squealed until we stopped at the side of the road. "Enough! Both of you. You're worse than my two kids, who won a gold medal in bickering. Now, back off to your neutral corners. Phil, I know you can hear me. Go spend quality time with your spirit mammal for the next few hours."

My sister shook until laughter spilled out of her.

"What's so funny?" I asked.

"You actually pulled the car over to chastise us."

"I did not." I shifted the car into drive and pulled out.

She turned to me. "What do you mean you did not? I was right here beside you."

"Technically, I screeched to a halt." I stuck my tongue out at her.

A few hours later, we both lay on our beds fighting off a food coma. I'd give Lawrence credit for recommending Mama Kettles. The homemade pasta and sauces took me to a level of nirvana I didn't know existed. It far surpassed Maestro's, my favorite Italian restaurant in Northport.

"We should go out. It's way too early for bed, unless we want to be wide awake at two in the morning," I said.

Gloria rolled onto her side. "What do you suggest?"

"We could walk over to Crys—"

"Don't even mention that place." She held up a hand. "And if you say anything about IPAs or tequila, I *will* hurt you."

From the glare in her eyes, I reconsidered my suggestion. Guess her sense of humor hadn't progressed that far yet. "How about the place our lunch server suggested yesterday? You know, the one with live music."

Gloria perked up. "She said they had a string quartet, right? Book Benders or Book Mongers. Something like that."

"Bookends over on Beach Avenue." I got out my phone to verify the address.

"Yes. I would love a bit of culture after last night's fiasco. Perhaps we might meet some of the more refined residents of the area. Give me a few minutes to change." She slid off the bed.

"Glo, in case you haven't noticed, this town has more of a 'come as you are' vibe. What you're wearing is fine."

She looked down at her striped, cotton capris and T-shirt. "I am not wearing this to listen to classical music."

"Trust me. Nobody else will be dressed up. Let's go."

Reluctantly, she slipped on her flip flops and picked up her purse.

****

We sat in a corner of Bookends waiting for our drinks to arrive. Gloria wore a scowl as she gazed back and forth between the well-dressed patrons and the two of us. Even the men dressed on the casual side wore pleated and pressed linen shorts with button-up shirts or polos. Maybe I could slip her a shot of tequila to take the edge off.

"Come as you are?" she glowered.

"How was I supposed know these people came straight off their yachts in perfect nautical attire?

68

You've got to admit, we made quite the entrance."

"It's a wonder they allowed us in at all. Why do I listen to you?"

"Because I'm full of fun ideas? Who cares what we're wearing? Look at what an amazing place this is. They've literally turned a bookstore into a speakeasy."

Bookshelves lined the walls interspersed with portraits of literary authors from the last few centuries. Dual metal staircases spiraled up each side of the bar reaching three levels. After giving us the once-over, the hostess had led us to the far corner of the third level. We couldn't see the small stage the quartet would play from, which didn't bother me. My sister would surely have a comment on our location once they began.

Our server, Davis, ignored our obvious lack of appropriate wardrobe. The thirty-something, clean cut man delivered our drinks in record time. The name didn't fit with his dark Asian eyes and light coffee skin, but his politeness and grace exuded an air of refinement.

"Thanks, Davis. I feared after the hostess's shock at our unsophisticated duds, we might be expected to serve ourselves," I said.

He swatted the air. "Don't mind her. She's descended of a long line of Frenchmen. Acting with utter disdain has been programmed into her DNA. Sadly, there's no cure."

Gloria's scowl eased.

"Besides," he continued, "you got put into my section. Things are looking up for you."

I raised my glass. "Cheers to that."

Gloria lifted her own drink, and we clinked glasses. Our server walked away, but the man who'd just been seated next to the rail overlooking the bar below, caught his attention. Davis returned to us.

"Ladies, your luck is improving by leaps and bounds. The gentleman at the front table has extended an invitation for you to join him. Shall I take your drinks?"

My sister let out an exasperated breath. "We're not here for a pick-up."

Our would-be host stood and turned in our direction. The large man wore black slacks and a polo shirt with his hair neatly combed back. His face broke into a wide grin as he gestured toward the other chairs at his table.

I placed a hand on Gloria's shoulder. "We're not turning down an invitation from a man who has rescued both of us over the last twenty-four hours."

My sister looked his way and smirked. "Tell Tiny we'd love to join him."

Chapter 11

"What a wonderful surprise, ladies. Please, make yourselves at home." Tiny waited for us to sit before taking his own seat. "Thanks for the assist, Davis."

"My pleasure, sir." The server placed our drinks on the table and left.

Gloria scooted her chair farther from the railing. "If I didn't know any better, I'd say you're following us," she teased.

Phil materialized in the empty chair beside me. "More like stalking. What are the odds your large friend would continue to turn up everywhere you go?"

The ghost's appearance caught Gloria mid-sip, and she sputtered out a few drops of her martini. She grabbed for a napkin and dabbed her lips and chin. "Excuse me."

"Are you okay?" Tiny asked.

"Fine. I felt a sneeze coming on as I drank." She set her glass on the table and flashed a scowl at Phil before recovering her smile.

Our host wrinkled his forehead at me, and I shrugged.

"Have you heard this quartet before?" I asked.

"A few times. They play a great mix of composers. Tonight, I believe they'll be performing Vivaldi's Four Seasons," Tiny said.

Phil leaned his elbows on the table. "I find it hard

to believe this tattooed barbarian knows the difference between a violin and a banjo."

A tall gentleman in khaki slacks and a pale yellow, short-sleeved shirt approached our table. "Hey, buddy. How's it going?"

"You made it." Tiny stood and shook the man's hand.

"Just in time, apparently. The seats at your table are filling up fast." He flashed a smile and brief nod in my direction.

"Ladies, I'd like to introduce my co-worker and riding buddy, Dodger." He gestured to the newcomer then motioned toward us. "This is Marni and Gloria. They're sisters on vacation from Long Island."

Gloria nodded at him. "Dodger. That's different, or is it your street name?"

I snorted out a laugh. "It's called a 'road name,' Glo. You make it sound like he's working a drug buy."

My sister's face flushed. "Well, I didn't mean…what I was asking—"

"Honest mistake. Unless you're familiar with biker culture, it's easy to get them confused. My given name is Max if you'd prefer." He sat down on top of Phil, who quickly disappeared.

"Pleasure to meet you, Max." I admired his athletic build, like that of a tennis player. A touch of gray at the temples accented his dark hair and eyes.

"The pleasure is all mine. How long are you ladies in Crystal River?"

"Only a few more days." Did his eyes give me the once over? "What do you do at the animal preserve? Are you one of the vets like Tiny?"

Max chuckled. "Nothing so glamorous. I'm the

head bean counter. It's my job to keep the place financially solvent." He waved at Davis, who nodded and went down the stairs.

The musicians on the first floor plucked and tuned their instruments before settling the loose music pages on the stands. A man in a beige suit walked up and shook the first violinist's hand.

When he returned to his seat, I caught a full view of his face—Lawrence. I didn't recognize the woman beside him as he threw an arm around her shoulders. *Let's hope Holly isn't the vindictive, jealous type.* The cast of characters in this unfolding drama grew longer and resembled an episode of a soap opera with switching partners. Keeping up with everyone's alliances blurred around the edges.

"I knew Holly would be loyal to my memory." Phil teetered on the railing glaring at Lawrence. It took all my restraint not to push him over the edge—not that it would have worked. "Once she finds out about her two-timing beau, she'll go back to mourning yours truly."

I'd helped souls who'd been confused about their current state, yet Phil sometimes slid into delusion with his obsession over his rude girlfriend. Some people lacked standards.

I pointed. "Gloria, isn't that Lawrence, the man we met at Libations this afternoon?" I didn't need confirmation but wanted her to get a look at who sat next to him. From her angle, she'd have a better view of the woman's face.

Her knuckles whitened as she gripped the railing and peered over. "I believe it is." She immediately retreated to the safety of her chair back.

Tiny tracked the direction of my finger. "You've

met Lawrence and his wife, Kate? The two of you certainly do get around."

My head shot up. "Wife? No, he'd been with a friend." They didn't need to know the gender of his drinking companion. A small town like this already had enough rumors without my contributing to the fodder.

"No doubt," Max said. "We rarely see Kate out with her husband. I'm surprised she's come here tonight with the place so crowded. She tends to be a bit of a recluse. You know how writers can be."

"Marni's a writer," Gloria chimed in with a smirk.

Glowering in her direction, I forced a smile onto my face.

"Sorry. I didn't mean to sound condescending. There's nothing wrong with being reclusive. Well, reclusive probably isn't the right word. Perhaps…"

I leaned back and crossed my arms while Max tripped over his own tongue. Instead of allaying any fears of his insulting my occupation, the evil streak in me took command and let him stumble. The crease between his brows deepened as his distress elevated.

Tiny smacked the table and chuckled. "Max doesn't get out much in polite society. He needs to gently slide into the water like a raft rather than blast through the waves like a motorboat. Breathe, buddy."

Davis arrived with a mug of beer for Max and checked on refills for the rest of us. The server's timing couldn't have been better, at least for our blushing table mate.

Gloria nursed her drink. No doubt shades of last night's finale swirled fresh in her mind.

"Come now, Gloria. Don't you want to order a round of shots?" Phil taunted her from his perch.

She ignored our pesky specter.

I took pity on Max before he could dig himself any deeper. Besides, he was the first male to pique my interest since my brief affair with a car thief. *Let's hope this one didn't have any felonious sidelines.* "How did you get the name Dodger?"

His shoulders eased. "It's a little embarrassing. During my teenage years my parents' marriage had been on the rocks. Like any typical child screaming for attention, I did what I could to get them to notice me. I became quite adept at sleight of hand."

"In other words, you shoplifted." I chuckled.

"Yes. My friends compared me to the Artful Dodger in that old British story. After a while, they dropped the Artful and just called me Dodger. I became a legend in my high school. Until I got caught, but luckily, the shop owner chose to let me work off the cost of the candy I stole instead of pressing charges."

Another criminal. *Do I know how to pick 'em, or what?* "Are you still practicing your *craft* as an adult?"

Tiny snorted. "Mr. Straight and Narrow? I believe he's reformed."

A tapping of a bow on a music stand rose above the din, and the quartet raised their instruments. A hush fell over Bookends as if we sat in an auditorium rather than a bar. Classical music had that effect on people. It commanded reverence rather than toe tapping and humming. Not my usual cup of tea, but the rapture on Gloria's face signaled she would enjoy this evening better than the last. Too bad. It would have been fun filming her carried rescue-style between our male companions if she became too inebriated again.

Davis made his rounds replacing empties with

refills. With my focus on the musicians, I hadn't noticed my fresh drink being delivered. Part of my attention remained on Lawrence and his wife. Shortly after the performance began, another gentleman joined them. Lawrence and the newcomer bent their heads close together in discussion. Their voices didn't carry, but if body language were any indication, the conversation turned heated. Kate glanced at the men occasionally, then shook her head and returned to the entertainment.

Before the end of the first movement, the man bolted upright. He wore his gray hair in a tight, military crew cut, and his stocky build reminded me of a bulldog—an angry one. He swiveled his head and locked eyes with me. The set of his jaw harshened his features. After pressing his lips into a thin line, he stormed out the front door.

I gulped as a cold chill ran down my spine.

Chapter 12

When the musicians took a break, I excused myself. As I stood, I caught Gloria's attention and shifted my eyes to the side.

She scrunched her face at me.

Really? My second attempt had me jerking my head toward the stairs. Tiny and Max probably thought I had a nervous tic.

This time my sister took the hint and joined me. We found the ladies room at the back of the bar on the first floor. No need for a sign—a line of women waited in the hallway before the open door. *What else is new?*

"We'll come back later, Glo. I needed to talk away from listening ears," I said.

"Why'd you drag me down here? We could've pretended to look at the bookshelves along the third floor."

"I hate to break it to you, but your acting skills aren't the best. Besides, the men might have wanted to join us." I pulled her by the arm away from the bathroom line until we stood a few tables behind Lawrence. "What do you think about Max? He's got possibilities, huh?"

Gloria crossed her arms. "We're down here to talk about your raging libido? With only a few days left to our trip, should you really be wasting time on a fling?"

I stepped out of the way to allow a server, carrying

a full tray, to get by. Glasses tinkled as he slipped past then stopped short avoiding another patron.

"How do you know it would only be a fling? Maybe we'll fall madly in love and have our wedding on the beach with the manatees frolicking in the bay." I fluttered my hand over my heart.

Gloria huffed. "Well, don't expect me to attend unless there's a boardwalk. I draw the line at wearing anything but heels to a wedding. Now, if we're done discussing your sex life, can we get in line for the restroom?"

"Get serious. Would I really ask *your* opinion on my dating habits? We're down here for reconnaissance. Did you notice the guy who sat down next to Lawrence?"

She peered through the crowd. "There isn't anyone else at the table except his wife."

"No, during the performance. An angry troll sat next to him, and from their reactions to each other, they weren't having a happy conversation. You didn't get a look at him?"

"Why would I? I focused on the players on stage not the audience. Does everything on this trip have to be about Phil?" My sister glowered at me.

As if on cue, we had another listener to our conversation. "I would say yes. Your sole purpose should be helping me."

I held up my hand. "Phil, not now. Go play with your manatee. We'll handle things here."

The kitchen door swung open wafting scents of garlic and pesto through the air. A waiter strode through Phil's body, which didn't so much as flinch.

"Marni, can we get back to why I can't use the

bathroom? The line should be shorter by now." My sister shifted from foot to foot.

"In a minute. We need to learn more about Lawrence. The other guy I told you about got up during the performance and glared right at me."

She shook her head. "How could you see him *glare* from three flights up? You're imagining things. He probably looked in our direction, and it had nothing to do with you."

"Trust me. His gaze landed directly on me as if he were searching for my face. Lawrence must've said something to him about our conversation at Libations earlier."

Phil offered, "Might I suggest—"

"No!" Gloria and I said at the same time.

"No need to be rude. If you don't want my help—"

"We don't," I insisted. "C'mon, Glo." I led my sister toward Lawrence's table.

She grasped my arm and whispered, "What are you doing?"

"Relax. We're just going to say hello and meet the wife. Trust me." I flashed an evil grin before moving closer to our target.

A tug on the back of my shirt stopped me. I spun and faced my sister. "All I want to do is see his reaction. There's more going on here than we know. Paste on a smile, and act as if we're long-lost friends of his. Got it?"

"Weren't you the one making derogatory comments regarding my acting skills not moments ago? Now you're suggesting I put them to use anyway?" Gloria stood her ground with hands on hips.

"Follow my lead and do the best you can. It doesn't

have to be an award-winning performance. Pretend you're attending one of your snooty garden parties. Everybody at those things is fake, aren't they?"

I waited for her to voice more protests using her signature style of speaking without moving her lips. She remained silent.

We strolled to the table where I caught Lawrence's eye. "Lawrence, funny running into you here. How are you?"

If we startled him, he didn't show it. A grin spread across his face. "Nice to see you again…"

"Marni. Marni and Gloria. Remember? We met at Libations this afternoon while you were with—"

"Let me introduce my wife, Kate." Lawrence's composure slipped a notch. "Sweetie, this is Marni and Gloria. They're sisters. Here on vacation. I met them at Libations today while out to lunch with one of my vendors." He held my gaze as he stumbled over an explanation to his wife.

Kate's posture stiffened. "Oh?"

I couldn't tell if she questioned us being sisters or his dining with an associate. My vote went to the latter, but I'm always suspicious of people. Especially ones who introduce me to their girlfriend *and* wife on the same day.

"Yes. It was lovely meeting Ho—" Gloria said.

"Hollis. Yes. He's a great guy, isn't he?" Lawrence winked.

Kate turned to her husband. "Hollis? You've never mentioned that vendor before."

"He's a new contact."

She expelled a noise, which resembled a snort more than a laugh. "You know, I thought she was going to say they'd met you with Holly, Phil's girlfriend. But that's not possible, is it? You told me she'd returned to Chicago." Kate placed a hand on his arm and squeezed.

"Boston. She went home to Boston," he said.

"That's right. Boston." Kate turned back to us. "Her boyfriend, Phil, died last year. Not sure why she chose to stay here with no other family or friends in the area."

"How sad for her. I guess she had her reasons for sticking around." I shifted my eyes to Lawrence, whose composure had returned.

The man leaned back in his chair and crossed his legs. "Yes, I suppose we didn't know everything about her, did we, sweetie?" He rubbed his wife's shoulder.

"Wait a minute," I said. "You're Kate Benedict. I recognize you from your book jacket. It's nice to meet a fellow author, especially in the same genre."

Kate wrinkled her nose as if catching a whiff of something rotten. "Same genre? I don't understand."

"Sorry. My full name is Marni Legend. I write historical romances too."

She bit her lip. "Really? I don't believe I've seen your work. Do you have a book out?"

Gloria squared her shoulders. "Thirteen to be exact. Surely, you've heard of my sister before? Her last three novels landed on the best-sellers list."

"Oh, look." Lawrence pointed. "The quartet is taking the stage for their next set. Nice chatting with you, ladies. You'll want to return to your seats. I believe your dates are waiting at your table."

Max waved from the third level. I returned the gesture before walking beneath the overhanging second floor.

"How did he know we were upstairs and sitting with two men?" Gloria demanded.

"It's not hard to figure out. He checked the surveillance feed." I swatted the air.

She stopped, and her mouth gaped open. "We're being watched *and* filmed?"

I didn't crack a smile or laugh. A small tilt of my head was enough.

Gloria smacked me on the shoulder. "I'm not amused."

"Sometimes it's just too easy." I held my hands, palms up. "He must've noticed when we walked in or spotted us at Tiny's table. Good one bringing up Holly's name. Or attempting to, anyway. Despite Lawrence shutting you down, wifey's tone suggested suspicion. Maybe she isn't as reclusive as hubby thinks."

"And what's with her pretending to not know who you were? There's no way she doesn't recognize her competition," Gloria said.

"Think it might have something to do with her last five books trailing right behind mine?" I swatted the air. "Nah, that can't be it. By the way, did you see what happened to Phil?"

"I guess he took your suggestion and left." She shrugged.

By the time we got back to our table, the musicians played. Our detective work eliminated further opportunity to chat with Max. I'd have to wait until the next break. Maybe this trip might include a little fling before heading home. Now the pertinent question, did Gloria understand the meaning of a towel hanging on the outside of our hotel room door?

Chapter 13

When the music stopped again, Lawrence and his wife made a hasty exit. Guess they weren't up for another cozy chat about his afternoon activities. Before they reached the door, he glanced in our direction.

I couldn't resist. My hand shot into the air, and I waved, then threw him a kiss.

His shoulders stiffened, and he hurried to catch up with Kate, who'd already stormed through the door. Someone might be sleeping on the couch tonight.

My hand dropped to the table.

"Didn't you say you just met Lawrence today?" Max asked.

"Yes, why?" I straightened my shoulders.

"Blowing kisses to strangers. I can't wait until *we* meet up again." He waggled his eyebrows.

Tiny stood. "I hate to tear myself away, but I've got an early morning tomorrow. Why don't you ladies let us take you for a ride in the afternoon?"

"A-a ride?" Gloria scrunched her forehead. "On..."

"Our bikes," Tiny said. "You've ridden before, haven't you?"

My sister shook her head. "No, no, no. I am not getting on the back of one of those death cycles. All my limbs are intact, and I intend to keep them that way for a very long time."

"Think of it as another adventure. You've already

snorkeled with manatees. Why not continue with another new experience?" If I couldn't sell her on tomorrow's outing, my chance of getting to know Max might slip away. "Do you guys have helmets we can borrow?"

"Is no one hearing my voice? I am speaking out loud, right? Hello?" Gloria waved her hands flagging our attention.

Tiny sat again. "Gloria, you'll be perfectly safe. Max and I are very responsible riders."

I gazed at Max. "Sounds like fun to me." Not too obvious, huh?

"Yes, it would be." Max returned the gesture. "You'll find it's a whole new way to experience the area."

"I've seen it by car, boat, and kayak. I'm good." Gloria folded her hands on the table, as if concluding a meeting. If she'd held a gavel, she would have slammed it down. "Besides, wearing a helmet would flatten my hair. Not a good look for me."

In instances like this, I wished our gift could've been telepathy instead of seeing dead people. Gloria needed to comprehend my thoughts this very moment. Telekinesis might've been handy too, so I could slap her in the back of the head with a spoon from across the table. I settled for mimicking her laser glare.

She didn't budge. "Marni, if you want to go careening down the blacktop on the back of a roaring motor atop two wheels, feel free. I intend to spend tomorrow afternoon poolside."

"It's about time I get to see you in a bikini." Phil appeared beside her rubbing his hands together. "Now ditch the gorillas. We need to chat."

Gloria sighed.

I recognized the tone of that sigh. The lifespan of her patience could now be measured in microseconds. Years of practice equipped me with this interpretational skill. Who knew so much could be transmitted by one simple utterance?

"Okay," I said.

"Okay?" Gloria asked.

"You catch some rays at the pool, and I'll ride with Max and Tiny. If that's okay with you guys?"

Tiny gave a weak smile. "Three's a crowd. You and Max have fun."

Score! I resisted doing a touchdown dance around the table.

The dull sheen in Tiny's eyes transmitted disappointment. I might have to pull him aside and remind him the ring on my sister's left hand came with a husband—and she doesn't stray.

"You sure, Tiny?" Max asked.

His friend nodded.

"It's settled. Marni, I'm off at one tomorrow. Why don't I pick you up at two?" He pulled out his cell phone. "Let's exchange numbers."

We did, and Tiny urged Gloria to exchange numbers with him in case she changed her mind. She insisted she wouldn't reconsider but agreed to the number swap in case I didn't return from our ride.

The men left and Phil sat in one of the empty chairs. "It's about time you gave them the heave ho."

"Marni, I hope you'll be safe tomorrow. You don't know anything about Max other than he works at the animal preserve," Gloria said. "How do you know he's not some manic thrill-seeker waiting to chop his next victim into pieces?"

"That's the point of going on a *date*. You get to know the other person through interaction. And if that interaction involves hand-to-hand combat while wrestling a weapon from his grasp, you get to say, 'I told you so' when you identify my dissected body parts at the morgue." I flagged down Davis as he walked past.

"Another round?" he asked.

"No, just the tab please." I reached for my purse.

Davis shook his head. "Tiny took care of the table. You have a good evening and come back again."

"That was unexpected," Gloria said. "He really shouldn't have paid for us. Now I feel obligated to him."

I emptied my glass and stood. "Obligated enough to come riding tomorrow?"

My sister followed me to the stairs. "Not on your life!"

"At least text him a thank you, since you have his number," I prodded.

We left the bar with our spirit in tow. Once outside, I asked, "Okay, Phil. What's going on? Have you remembered something about your death?"

"Oh, it's finally my turn to speak? I thought perhaps your social life took precedence," he snarked.

"Has anyone ever pointed out what a drama queen you are?" I asked.

"Nobody I knew would be so rude. You, on the other hand, appear to spew out any thought popping into your head." We'd reached the car, and he got into the back seat.

"Okay, okay. I'm sorry for being rude. What did

you need to tell us?" I shifted the car into gear and pulled away from the curb.

He leaned forward between the front seats. "I remembered diving a wreck. Rosie swam about while I explored, which she used to do a lot."

"Finally, we're getting somewhere. Who else was with you?" Gloria asked.

Phil leaned back. "I don't recall anyone else. Truly a shame such a magnificent vessel like that rested on the seabed. She must've cost someone a pretty penny."

"There couldn't have been much left of it. Wouldn't most of the wood have rotted away by now?" I asked.

"No, it remained mostly intact. The sleek white lines of her hull were marred by a gaping hole toward the stern."

"Wait. Weren't you exploring the wreck of a Spanish galleon?" I looked at him in my rearview mirror.

His nose wrinkled. "Spanish galleon? No. This was a luxury yacht, which had met with an unfortunate demise. From the looks of the damage, it might have been scuttled."

"Scuttled? Like sprang a leak?" Gloria asked.

"What's wrong? Too many syllables for you to understand, my dear?"

She crossed her arms. "Now who's being rude, Phil. I'm trying to understand why this is important. If you swam around the wreck, you obviously didn't die in it."

"My point of this story is diving around the yacht with Rosie is my last memory. I don't remember surfacing."

"You died because you ran out of air. Did you stay down too long?" I pulled the car into the hotel parking lot.

"Why would I do something so careless? I've been diving all my life and know when I need to surface. Besides, the ocean floor couldn't have been more than thirty feet deep. Even if I ran out of air, I still could have surfaced safely."

I turned to him. "Which leads us to believe you had help remaining below the water. Think, Phil. Someone else must've been there." My fingers drummed on the steering wheel. "Wait a minute. Didn't Lulu say you were found in the river? But you just said you were diving in the ocean."

"Didn't you check a map before traveling here?" Phil raised his hands. "The Crystal River leads to the Gulf of Mexico. That's why it's called 'brackish' water, which is a mix of fresh water and salt water. I had been diving in the Gulf near the river entrance when my untimely demise came about. At least that's what I remember."

"So, your body got washed into the river where they found you. How close did you swim to the ship?" Gloria asked. "Maybe your gear caught on something, and you couldn't get loose in time. Or maybe you went below and got stuck."

"The authorities found him floating, which eliminates his getting snagged on something. They would've found him below the surface for your scenario to work," I said.

Gloria slumped her shoulders. "You're right, Marni."

"Think, Phil. Are there any other details you

remember? Like the name of the boat you found?"

His hand noiselessly tapped his leg then stopped as he looked up. "*Sunset Dream*. The name on the stern read *Sunset Dream* registered out of Key West, Florida."

"Good. We'll look up the ownership and go from there. Maybe we can find where it went down." I got out of the car.

"Marni, how does the name of the ship help us solve Phil's death?" Gloria walked from the passenger side.

"I don't know. Not yet anyway. It could be useless, but it's still a clue. I'll research on the internet tonight and see if I come up with anything."

Gloria pulled our room key from her purse. "You do what you want. I'm exhausted and ready for bed."

"Shall I tuck you in? Tell you a bedtime story?" Phil offered.

"Good night, Phil." The icy chill rolling off her words left no doubt she did not need help even if he were corporeal.

Chapter 14

The next day we had no plans for the morning and were in search of a new adventure—at least I was in search of a new adventure. My sister was in search of a salon for a manicure. Okay, not my thing. She'd be on her own. Appointments at the local salon weren't available until later in the afternoon anyway.

We settled for wandering down to the hotel restaurant for a late breakfast and enjoyed the cool breeze coming off the bay. The tour boats bobbed on the river near the manatee sanctuary.

"Did you discover anything about the *Sunset Dream* in your search last night?" Gloria asked.

I forked a bite of egg into my mouth. "Not much. The yacht was registered in Key West but belonged to a guy in Boston named Herbert Kimpton. He harbored it here in Crystal River. Supposedly, it sank in a storm about eighteen months ago and hasn't been recovered. The crew went missing, but good ol' Herby wasn't aboard at the time."

"Sounds like Phil could've gotten the salvage rights," Gloria said.

"Maybe. Like I said, there wasn't anything about the ship ever being discovered. Either Phil didn't report the find, or he didn't have the chance before dying."

She sat back. "Didn't Lawrence's wife say Holly came from Boston? Kind of a coincidence the missing ship Phil found belonged to someone in Boston."

"Don't you think you're leaping to conclusions?" Many northeastern residents hit the Florida coast in the winter. Holly's exodus from the cold weather didn't signal anything out of the ordinary.

"Marni, what are the odds of that, though? Phil finds a ship from his girlfriend's hometown. There's gotta be a connection."

"No, there doesn't." I scraped the last of my breakfast from the plate.

"Marni, are you still planning to go riding with a guy you just met?" Gloria scrunched her brows.

I sighed. "He's a friend of Tiny's, who has proven to be trustworthy. Ergo, I can trust his friend."

"Ergo? What are you, friggin' Shakespeare?" She sat back in her chair. "Just because Tiny is a good guy, you know nothing about Max."

"He works at the animal preserve. He rides a motorcycle. What else do I need to know?" Was it possible my sister now channeled my mother? What's next? Critiquing my wardrobe choices?

Gloria wagged a finger at me. "You'll wear a helmet and text me every ten minutes."

"I'll wear a helmet and text every thirty minutes. Deal?"

"You won't reconsider this, will you?"

"Nope. You gonna reconsider and come with us? I'm sure we could convince Tiny to meet us. Why don't you text him?"

She shook her head. "I'm sorry, were you still talking?"

I nodded my head upward. "I give up. Just when I thought you understood the meaning of the word fun, you slip back into your straightlaced shell."

After spending a few hours lounging by the pool, I went back to the room to shower and change. As much as Phil had mooned about seeing Gloria in a swimsuit, he didn't appear. He probably would've been disappointed as despite her perfectly proportioned, petite figure, she didn't own a bikini and wouldn't be caught dead in anything but a tasteful one-piece. It made me believe his latest memory didn't sit well with him. Me either. There had to be something more to his swimming around the wreck of a modern yacht. And where did the Spanish galleon story fit in?

The sturdiest shoes I'd brought were sneakers. They would have to do. Gloria's mood hadn't rallied to support my going out with Max, but this vacation had been a stretch for her to begin with. My tripping across a dating opportunity might be a little much for her to accept. I didn't care. Max had a smoking, hot body I wanted to have a hands-on experience with.

After showering, I changed into jeans and a long-sleeved T-shirt. While lacing my sneakers, Phil appeared.

"Gloria's down at the pool. You'll have to hassle her there," I said.

Phil sat on the other bed. "She's really not very good at this, is she?"

Just what I needed—a spiritual intervention. "No. She's new."

"What do you mean, she's new? While she looks superb for her age, I can tell she's older than you. How can she not be more wizened?" Phil asked.

"Wizened? What do you think she is, a Himalayan monk?"

"You know what I mean. She doesn't seem too good at this whole spirit-assistance gig."

I stood and walked to the dresser. "No. By the time she was six, she was terrified all the time of seeing ghosts. She couldn't handle it. My grandmother performed a ritual which made Gloria's powers go dormant."

"But not yours," Phil stated.

"No, not mine. I took to it. Seeing ghosts felt natural. For Gloria, it felt alien. She couldn't sleep. From what she told me, seeing spirits terrified her so much that our grandmother finally turned off my sister's ability."

He crossed his legs. "How is it she can see me now?"

Did he really need to know the whole backstory? He required help, and his trust had been placed in a novice. I sighed. Yes. He had a right to know. "I had a difficult case. A spirit who put me in danger while I helped him. Our grandmother had told Gloria she would need to reacquire her powers when I came upon this case. That happened last May."

"What kind of danger?" Phil asked.

"Bullets whizzing through the air at me. Along with a healthy dose of kidnapping and threats of bodily harm by a thug in desperate need of a breath mint and a wardrobe consultant."

"Ah. That could be dangerous." He sat quietly, looking at the floor. I would have thought he'd disappeared, but he remained.

After several minutes, he said, "Treasure."

"Treasure?"

He stared off into the distance, not making eye

contact. "There was treasure on the *Sunset Dream*. Nobody else knew where to find the downed boat but me and Holly. I moved the goods. That part she didn't know."

I froze. "Treasure? What kind of *treasure*? Where did you move it? Why did you move it?"

"The booty didn't belong to the owner of the ship."

"Phil, what did you find?"

"I can't say." He vanished.

I had gotten used to spirits disappearing when being questioned. Usually because they had reached their comfort level or hit the limit of their knowledge. Phil knew more. What disturbed me was his reluctance to share with Gloria and me. Until he said the words out loud, we wouldn't be able to help him resolve his issue and move on.

My phone dinged with a text from Max. He stopped to gas up his bike and would arrive in ten minutes. I snagged my purse and a hooded sweatshirt on my way out the door. Before going to the front of the hotel, I detoured past the pool to say good-bye to Gloria.

She lay reclined on a cushioned lounger shaded by an umbrella. On a table beside her sat a plastic water bottle sweating from the heat. With her mirrored sunglasses, I couldn't tell if she read the book in her hand or shifted her gaze my way, until she turned her head. "I see you're off to relive your wasted youth."

"What are you talking about? After high school I went to college then got married, same as you. How is it I *wasted* my youth while you led a respectable life?" I asked.

"Are you forgetting the brief affair you had with

that young biker after your freshman year of college? It only lasted one summer, but you stressed Mom out every time he picked you up on his motorcycle."

I chuckled. "Glo, it only gets to be called an affair when one of us is married. Which neither of us had been at the time. And when did you begin referring to Chuck as 'that young biker?' We grew up with the guy, and he graduated and went off to college the same time I did."

"I call 'em as I see 'em."

I sat on the chair beside her. "Any more dire warnings before I leave?"

The roar of an engine echoed up the road to the hotel. My chariot approached.

My sister shrugged. "Have fun. Hopefully the authorities won't be scraping you off the asphalt."

"You don't know what you're missing. See you tonight." I gave her the princess wave as I walked away.

Chapter 15

I arrived out front in time to watch Max back his big, black steed into a front parking slot. He dismounted wearing heavy boots, and his feet smacked onto the pavement. Lucky me approached from behind, admiring how his form-fitting blue jeans hugged his body in all the right places. It took all my self-control not to applaud as he whipped off his helmet.

His black leather vest held several patches from biker rallies but no club monikers. As he slowly turned my way, I noted the front only had a patch of an American flag and his road name, Dodger.

"Hey, beautiful! Ready to ride?" Max strode up and kissed me on the cheek.

He caught me off guard, and my face warmed. *If that's how he starts a first date, we may need a dark alcove for the second. Get a grip.* "Nice bike." Wow, I'm sure he's never heard that one before. Despite being in my late forties, I'd turned into a tongue-tied teenager.

"Thanks. Sasha and I have put in a lot of miles together."

"Sasha?" Was there a wife he neglected to mention?

Max chuckled. "My bike." He ran his hand over the seat. Maybe *they* needed a moment alone.

"Got it. Is Sasha part of a harem, or does she run solo?" I asked.

"Right now, she's an only child. I had a little bar hopper but had to cut her loose due to lack of garage space."

"The poor girl," I said. "Why don't you break out the spare helmet, and we can take off."

He flipped open a saddle bag on the side and pulled out a silver half-shell. "Here you go. Hope it fits okay."

I preferred a full-face helmet, but at least I brought sunglasses to shield my eyes. Unbuckling the strap, I slipped it on my head. "I'm sure it'll be fine."

He stepped closer, his lips a mere six inches from mine, and placed his hands on the sides of the helmet.

My smile widened.

"Try to turn your head," he said.

I scrunched my forehead. "What?"

"Just a safety check to see if your brain bucket has a snug enough fit."

When I rode with Chuck in college, his spare *brain bucket* bounced around my head like a bowl of gelatin. Ah, the ignorance of youth—translated as stupidity. "Got it." My attempt to swivel my head inside while Max held the helmet steady resulted in no movement.

"Perfect. I don't plan on taking a spill, but you always dress for the slide not the ride." He flashed a sidewise grin.

Maybe we should skip this nonsense and go for a different kind of ride. I was pretty sure I didn't need additional equipment for *that*. At least Gloria didn't witness this display. She wouldn't have lasted past the safety check.

"I don't suppose you have gloves?"

"Wasn't on my Florida packing list." I shrugged.

Max reached into the storage compartment and

withdrew a pair of black leather riding gloves. "Here you go. I figured if I needed a spare helmet, I should have the whole package."

Believe me, you've got the whole package. "You don't happen to have a pair of size seven women's boots in there too?"

"Sorry. Too big of a range to carry. Your footwear isn't ideal, but we won't be doing anything crazy." He reached out and secured the strap beneath my chin. My face tingled where his knuckles grazed my skin.

I handed him my purse and sweatshirt to stow then pulled on the gloves. "Thanks for these. Where're we going?"

With his hands on his hips, he said, "If I told you, it wouldn't be a surprise."

At least he didn't say, *"If I told you, I'd have to kill you."* Then again, my sister would get bragging rights after insisting I had a date with a serial killer.

Max put on his gear and swung his leg over the seat. Resting both feet on the ground, he put the bike upright then snagged the kick stand with one foot.

Despite having ridden before, it had been a while. A long, long while. My body hesitated in a scared but excited sort of way. Or was it a scared and terrified sort of way?

Max nodded at me.

I nodded back and remained standing.

He leaned into his backrest. "You *have* ridden before, right?"

"Sure. It's just…been a coupla years. Like one or two…or thirty."

His head tilted backward, and he laughed. "Are you saying you haven't ridden since high school?"

My lips formed a straight line as I nodded.

"Shall we abort?" he asked.

Deep breath. One more deep breath. "No. I can do this. Besides, if I walk back to our room now, I'll never hear the end of it from Gloria."

"Good. Peer pressure." Max smirked. "Look, we don't have to ride if you don't want to."

"I got this." I stepped up. "You just hold on and do what you need to do so I don't tip us over while boarding."

"All righty." He sat up straight, gripped the handlebars, and planted his feet solidly on the ground.

Placing a sneaker on the foot pad, I leaned in and swung my leg over the seat and landed on the supple leather. At least he had a backrest for his passenger. Visions of careening down the expressway while a teenager flashed through my mind. Chuck, my driver, hadn't owned a passenger backrest, so I had to wrap my arms around his body and pray I didn't bounce off. Riding as an adult came with better comfort features.

"You might want to ease up. If I pass out from lack of oxygen, things could go horribly wrong for both of us." His voice lowered. "But I don't mind the back massage."

Without thinking, I'd wrapped my arms around him in a death grip with my breasts smashing into his back. "Sorry." I loosened my hold as I felt my face flush with heat. Settling my hands firmly on his waist, I forced my shoulders to relax.

"Ready?" he asked.

"Yup," my voice squeaked. I gulped. "Yes, let's roll." Way to make a bold impression, Marni.

His head turned my way. "Just a refresher. When

we take a curve, forget that crap about leaning into it. You stick with the seat and let me swing the bike. Got it?"

"Uh-huh." Maybe I should have slapped Velcro on my ass.

The engine roared to life, and we eased down the drive of the Harbor Inn. My skin tingled in anticipation of us accelerating. We took a left and the tilt of the bike forced me to slip my arms around Max's waist. Unfortunately, this time as I leaned into him, my helmet smacked the back of his. I immediately pulled back and returned my hands to his waist.

He had enough good manners not to turn and glare at me.

We rode past the Crystal Bar, where a few bikes populated the parking lot. It probably didn't get hopping until after dark. I did a double take as Lulu stood beside her ride and gave me a thumbs up with a nod of her head. No turning back now that I had a witness.

After weaving through more neighborhood streets and crossing the main drag of town, we hit a road which meandered south along the river's edge. Without much traffic to maneuver around, the tension in my shoulders eased. The memories of riding with Chuck came seeping back. Now that I recall, much of my time on the back of his bike was spent hanging on for dear life with my eyes closed. *Why didn't I remember these things earlier?*

The speed limit signs read fifty, but Max kept the bike moving at forty. I'd say he acted out of kindness, but his desire to continue breathing freely probably had more to do with it.

The warm breeze tickled my face as I inhaled the sea air. Despite being on a river, the mix of salt and fresh water still had a beachy feel to it. Another ten minutes down the road Max pulled into a parking lot. A beach stretched before us with the waves gently lapping on the shore.

He held the bike steady while I swung my leg over the back and promptly slipped off the foot pad, landing on my backside. So much for a graceful dismount. I'm sure the Russian judges would've given it a two.

Max rested the bike on the kickstand and hopped off. He tucked his hands beneath my arm pits and hoisted me to my feet. "You okay, Marni?"

"Just peachy. I'll have to work at sticking the landing next time." I viewed the surf before us. "Are we stopping here?"

"This is your surprise." He waved his arm at the sandy expanse.

"It's beautiful. We didn't ride too far though." I fumbled with the strap beneath my chin but couldn't loosen it. Duh! I pulled off my gloves and tried again with better success.

He did the same minus the awkward fumbling. "Since I didn't know your comfort level on a motorcycle, I thought it best to only go for a short hop on our first ride. I packed a snack if you're up for a picnic on the beach."

Where have you been all my life? "How thoughtful. I guess I should have come clean about my riding experience. It sounded like fun when you suggested it, and I guess my adventurous spirit got the best of me." Not to mention my hopeful libido.

"I'm glad you came. I do have a confession to

make." He scrunched his nose.

I knew it! He still shoplifts and is on parole. Do I know how to pick them, or what? I nodded for him to continue.

"Secretly, I'd hoped your sister wouldn't be interested in riding. At least this first time because I wanted to spend time alone with you." He bowed his head while peering at me through shaggy, dark bangs. On the adorable scale he rated a twelve. "Is that awful?"

"Only if you don't kiss me right now." *Oops! I didn't mean to use my outside voice.*

Without hesitating, he leaned down and planted one on my lips.

When he pulled back, I said, "Mmmm…nice. What are we snacking on? Gloria and I ate a late breakfast, so I skipped lunch. You must be a mind reader."

He flipped open the saddlebag on the opposite side of the bike and retrieved a small cooler, a canvas bag, and a blanket. "A little bit of bread, lunch meat, and cheeses. Do you like balsamic vinegar?"

"Love it." He could have said sardines on liver-coated crackers, and I would have choked them down.

Before closing the compartment, he unwrapped a towel-covered bottle of champagne. "I thought we might celebrate our first date with a little bubbly." He worked his shoulders back and forth.

Butterflies should have been bouncing around my stomach in a frantic dance. Instead, a quivering in parts lower down thrummed a steady beat. *There better be some cold water in that cooler.* I grabbed my purse and replaced it with my riding gear.

"You won't need your bag. I can lock the bike."

"I'll take my phone. If I don't text Gloria that I haven't become one with the road, she'll call out the National Guard."

He laughed. "Then you better send her a message. I only brought enough snacks for two."

I shot off a quick text verifying my presence among the living and received no response. So much for Mother Hen fretting over my antics.

Chapter 16

We stopped at the edge of the parking lot to remove our shoes before venturing across the sand. Close to the shoreline Max spread a blanket and unpacked the cooler and bag. The beach had a few other occupants farther away, but the little patch we'd settled on remained empty.

Along with the food, he'd brought bottles of water. Since I'd proven even stone-cold sober I had no balance, I thought it best to stick with one glass of champagne then switch to water. It would be bad form to fall off the bike while in motion.

Max popped open the bubbly, poured two glasses, and handed me one. He held his up. "To new friends."

I tapped mine to his. "To new friends."

He snagged a piece of bread and dipped it in the container of balsamic vinegar mixture. "Do you and your sister travel together a lot?"

"No, this is our first adventure together. I believe she decided her mid-life crisis would be to travel with me and survive."

"How's it going so far?"

I laughed. "We're both still breathing, so I'd say it's going well. Do you have any siblings?"

"One. I have a younger sister. She and I have never been brave enough to go on a joint vacation. I love her, but she can be a bit of a princess, if you know what I mean. She also doesn't make the best life choices."

A pelican soared over the water and landed a few feet from where we sat. I tucked my feet in fearing the bird might mistake my toes for food.

"I know exactly what you mean. At this very moment, instead of roaring down the road on the back of a motorcycle, Gloria's hands are soaking in moisturizer before getting her nails polished. I'd blame her husband for spoiling her, though I believe it's due to his phenomenal survival instincts."

"The man is good at self-preservation. Nothing wrong with that!" Max nodded.

"I hope Tiny wasn't too disappointed she wouldn't come today. He does realize my sister's married, doesn't he?"

Max tracked the pelican as it took flight down the coastline. "I've known Tiny almost a couple years now. He tends to fall for women who are already taken. At least he's an upstanding guy who would never take advantage of what's not his. Doesn't change his feelings though. I can tell he likes your sister."

"Maybe it's a good thing Gloria stood her ground. She isn't one to stray, and I'd hate for him to get his hopes up."

"Like I said, he wouldn't have made a move. Just enjoyed the company." His brown eyes gazed into mine.

I leaned in and kissed him. Max wrapped his arm around my back and pulled me closer. If the blanket wasn't already littered with food and drink, I'm sure he would have eased me down onto it.

When I pulled back sporting a satisfied grin, we sat silently for a few moments before it turned awkward. I asked, "Does your sister live in Crystal River too?"

He tucked a strand of hair behind my ear. "Enough about siblings and friends. Tell me about you."

I chugged a gulp of water cooling the flames rising inside me. "What do you want to know?"

"Anything. What kind of writing do you do? Any special talents?"

I jerked back. Did he know about my gift? "No special talents beyond being a writer. I've published thirteen historical romances and am under contract for the next one due in six months."

"Well, that's unexpected," he said.

"I know. Your first guess would have been ballerina or tight-rope walker from my graceful movements getting on and off the bike." I spread my arms and teetered them up and down.

"Circus performer had crossed my mind." Max laughed. "Is this trip for research on your next novel?"

I shook my head. "Not really, though I may use this location in a future book. I get a lot of inspiration from places I visit."

"My accounting background believes you could write off the trip. Am I right?"

"Of course! I have a well-paid financial consultant who does just that come tax time."

He stood and extended his arm. "Let's walk."

I grasped his hand and allowed him to pull me to my feet. Instead of letting go, he held on, and we strolled along the surf line, allowing the warm water of the Gulf to swirl around our feet. The temperature of the surf surprised me.

"Too bad I didn't know we would be at the beach. I would've brought my swimsuit," I said.

"There're a few beaches in Florida where clothing is optional. Sadly, this isn't one of them," he smirked.

"Darn." I stomped my foot in the sand.

In one quick motion, Max swept me off my feet and held me over the ocean. "I'd be happy to help you into the water if you want to swim anyway."

I wrapped my arms around his neck. "Thanks, but I'll pass. Besides, you wouldn't want to get your motorcycle seat all wet, would you?"

He gently placed me back on the ground and wrapped his arms around my waist. "True. It would be a shame to risk harm to Sasha." Max tightened his hold and pulled me closer. His burning lips met mine and lingered.

Yeah, Gloria didn't know what she missed by staying behind.

"Have dinner with me," Max said.

All my self-control had been used up, and now I struggled. "I'd love to, but I promised my sister I'd be back in time for supper."

"Text her. Tell her we broke down and won't get a tow until late." His coercion sounded good to me, but Gloria wouldn't stand for it.

"She'd see right through the lie. We're only here three more nights. I can't keep ditching her to meet up with you, unless it was a group activity. You understand?"

He sighed. "I guess. How about I check with Tiny and the four of us could meet somewhere tomorrow night. She wouldn't object to that, would she?"

Would she ever! "Let me talk to her tonight, and I'll let you know." I'd have to find a good hypnotist to sell her on the idea, but it would be worth a shot.

An engine roared and another motorcycle pulled into the lot and parked beside ours. A man and woman got off and removed their gear. This town became smaller by the minute. Lawrence waved at us, and Max returned the gesture. Holly remained in character from yesterday and didn't so much as crack a smile. If anything, her expression transmitted disgust. What a fun afternoon.

Chapter 17

Lawrence and Holly approached and extended a warm greeting—to Max. Holly barely nodded in my direction, while her boyfriend mumbled something unintelligible. I believed it to be a greeting. Of course, it could have been a "what the hell" for all I knew.

Not to be deterred, I didn't let them ruin my good time with Max. Actually, their appearance brought out the playful imp buried inside of me. Okay, I didn't have to reach far to help it surface. "Lawrence, it was a pleasure meeting your wife, Kate. Such a lovely woman."

"Hmmpf," groused Holly. Guess she wasn't a fan of Lawrence's marital status.

Lawrence cleared his throat. "I'd appreciate discretion if you happen to run into her again. She doesn't understand the fact Holly and I are simply friends."

Friends. Like Max and I were becoming friends? I wriggled my toes in the sand before looking up into his face. "Oh. I guess I misunderstood when you referred to Holly as your *girlfriend* yesterday at Libations. My mistake."

Holly glared at her companion, then addressed Max. "I didn't realize you gave personal tours of the area. Perhaps I can offer your services to other visitors?"

"Marni is the only one I've offered a sightseeing outing. No need to send out false advertisements, thanks," Max sneered.

I would have high-fived him for making the snobby woman uncomfortable, but it would have been misconstrued. Better to play nice. "Do you all ride together, Max?"

"We have on occasion. Usually, Lawrence and I go solo for a little bar hopping. Maybe the four of us could go for an afternoon ride tomorrow? I'm off all day."

"Sure," Holly said, surprising the heck out of me.

"Sounds like fun," Lawrence added. "Why don't we meet here tomorrow about eleven, and we can stop somewhere for lunch?"

"I'm sorry, Marni. I guess I should have checked with your schedule first. Think your sister will give you another pass to go riding with me?" Max asked.

Gloria couldn't possibly object to my riding with our potential suspects. I'd suggest this might be a chance to send Phil on his way sooner. It could work. "I'll find someplace for her to get a massage and pedicure to pass the time. Just get me back to the hotel in one piece today, and it would go a long way toward selling our outing tomorrow."

"Done!" Max smacked his hands together. "We'll see the two of you tomorrow then. Right now, I better get my precious cargo home."

"Nice running into you," Lawrence said. "Holly and I are off for a stroll down the beach. See you tomorrow."

I waved as they turned to leave.

Holly snorted air through her nose. Quite the lady.

Besides getting to spend time with my hunky

companion, I now had a solid excuse to talk more with Holly. Though, if my last couple experiences were any indication, I'd be doing most of the talking. Maybe we could work out a code where she blinked once for yes and twice for no. Disdainful noises might work too.

We cleaned up the remains of our picnic and packed it back onto the bike. Max agreed to deliver me directly to the hotel, since I needed to sell Gloria on my going out without her tomorrow. Plus, I had to convince her to have dinner with Max and Tiny afterward. As previously displayed, my powers of persuasion over her didn't always work. I'd have to up my game.

Our ride back went smoother than the outbound. I didn't fall on my butt during the mounting and dismounting of the bike, nor did I clunk my helmet into the back of his. I'd call that a win.

After being dropped off and enjoying one more good-bye smooch from Max, I hesitated outside our hotel room. A yelling match resonated from inside. Maybe I should have had more champagne. Sighing, I opened the door and walked in on Phil and Gloria having a heated conversation. Okay, maybe *heated* was too tame of a description. My sister wore a towel wrapped around her body and nothing else. Her hair dripped water down her shoulders and back, while her face glowed a vibrant shade of crimson.

"What's going on?" I demanded.

Both stopped shouting and turned my way before Gloria chimed in first. "Can you please explain to this jerk that it is not okay to show up in our room unannounced?"

"Madam, I had no idea you would be indisposed. Who showers in the late afternoon? Civilized people usually tackle that chore in the morning," Phil said.

"Civilized people, *Phil*, shower after swimming. Besides, what difference does it make when I want to shower? You have no right to just flit in and out as if you own the place." She squared her shoulders and swelled her chest. Bad move. The towel, tucked into a knot just above her cleavage, loosened and slipped. Her hands flew to the top edge and pulled it up, snugging the knot back in place. "Oh, for goodness' sake. Just get out!"

Phil laughed. "If that's an attempt to flash me, keep going."

"This is not funny." Gloria pointed at Phil. "Marni, explain to this Neanderthal why he may not appear in our room with no warning."

I stifled a laugh. After all, it would have been hilarious had the towel dropped to her feet. Not all of us would have thought so, but I believe I would've been in the majority. "Gloria, why don't you get dressed."

"That was the plan until I came out of the bathroom and found Mr. Ugly Hawaiian Shirt standing here drooling."

"I do not drool! All I said was 'hello, beautiful.' How can you turn that into something negative?" Phil sniffed.

While he had a point, he still stood in our hotel room uninvited. My sister hadn't gotten used to spirits appearing on their own time schedule. Some of them did it deliberately at inconvenient times, and I wouldn't have put it past Phil to be one of those.

Gloria grabbed the clothes she'd laid out on her bed and stormed into the bathroom, slamming the door behind her.

"Phil, you do need to be a little more considerate if you want Gloria to help you. Meanwhile, I have good news. Tomorrow Max and I are going riding with Holly and her new boyfriend. I might get information out of her about your final day. Isn't that great?"

He sat on the bed and crossed his legs. "I still think you're barking up the wrong tree. Holly wouldn't have harmed me in any way, but you go ahead. And your sister calls *me* a pervert. Sniffing around Holly's brother while pretending to get information is pretty low."

I did a double take. "Lawrence is really Holly's brother?"

"I have no idea who the man is, nor do I care," he spat. "Though I have to admit, the other day when I saw him at Libations, his face looked familiar. If he's local, I must've run into him around town."

"I'm confused. If Lawrence isn't her brother that means—"

"Yes, Einstein. That leaves your current paramour." Phil shook his head and disappeared.

Guess Max neglected to mention the family tie when she and Lawrence showed up today. What if our running into them at the beach hadn't been an accident?

Gloria stepped out of the bathroom fully dressed. She scanned the room, then said, "Thank goodness."

I pulled a soda from the mini-fridge and offered one to my sister.

She declined. "I'm happy to see you've returned uninjured. Got that out of your system now?"

"Funny you should mention that, Glo." I slid open the balcony doors and walked outside.

Gloria followed and flopped down in one of the

chairs with her arms crossed. "What's that supposed to mean?"

"Max took me to a beach not far from here. Right before we left, guess who showed up?"

"Marni, I'm not in the mood for guessing games."

"Fair enough." I leaned back on the railing. "Lawrence rode up on a motorcycle with Holly riding backseat. They walked right up to us and said 'hello.' Well, Lawrence acted pleasant, if a little nervous about my outing him to his wife. Holly remained aloof."

"I'm sure you're understating her sparkling personality. What's your point?" Gloria asked.

"The four of us are meeting up to ride somewhere for lunch tomorrow. You'd be welcome to join us. I'm sure Tiny could be convinced to come along. Especially since we're having dinner with Max and Tiny tomorrow night." I waited for the fallout from my last statement. It didn't take long.

"I'll check my social calendar, but I don't remember scheduling dinner with two men we just met. Remind me when I'd agreed to it?" She narrowed her eyes.

I sat in the other chair. "You can't tell me you didn't enjoy chatting with them last night."

"From what I recall, there wasn't a lot of conversation since we listened to the quartet play. And what do you mean you're going riding again tomorrow?"

She finally caught up to everything I'd said. So much for glossing over that part. "Think of it as a golden opportunity to dispatch Phil that much quicker. We need to talk to Holly. What better way than spending the afternoon together instead of hoping to run into her at Libations again. Remember how well that went? This way she's a captive audience, and with the guys there, she can't easily squirm out of talking to us."

My sister stood and looked out over the bay. "I guess you're right. We don't have a lot to go on since Phil's amnesia isn't clearing up as fast as we'd like. But I am *not* getting on a motorcycle. I trust in your skills at shaking Holly down for information. It'll have to be enough. Besides, I enjoyed lounging by the pool so much I rescheduled my manicure for tomorrow instead."

That went easier than expected. "What about dinner with Max and Tiny?" I crossed my fingers behind my back.

She turned to face me. "You really like Max that much?"

"What's not to like? He's gorgeous and legally employed." I lifted my arms in the air.

"All right. I'll do it for you. Just make sure Tiny understands I'm happily married. He's really a sweet man—if you don't look too closely at his tattoos."

"That's the spirit. I'll let Max know, and he can contact Tiny." I stood to go back inside, then hesitated. "Oh, by the way, Phil mentioned Max and Holly are siblings. No coincidences there, huh?"

Gloria put a hand to her forehead. "And yet you're going to go riding off into the sunset on his two-wheeled death machine?"

"We're meeting at eleven. A bit early for sunset." I turned and went inside.

Chapter 18

I changed out of my "riding gear" into a sundress and flat sandals. My toes wriggled with glee at being released from confinement. At the recommendation of the front desk clerk, Gloria and I set off to dinner at a local Greek restaurant.

The establishment didn't live up to the raves it'd received. While the menu touted the usual Mediterranean fare, the staff spoke English with a Puerto Rican accent. Could have been Cuban—either way, Greek did not translate well. Nothing about the place resembled anything close to having come from Greece, including their sad version of a gyro. Our order looked and tasted like a quesadilla with feta cheese—two cultures which shouldn't be mixed gastronomically.

We didn't linger after the bill had been paid and our mostly full plates removed from the table. After a short drive, we arrived at the docks where we'd set off on our manatee snorkeling tour. The sun had begun to set and wouldn't last long, so we seized the opportunity and sat on the boardwalk with our feet dangling over the water.

As the sun melted over the horizon, our scar-faced manatee rose from the river as if to tickle our toes. For once my sister didn't shrink back in fear.

"Hello, Rosie. Where's your partner in crime?" I

asked.

"Behind you. Thought I'd try a new approach rather than simply appearing as it throws Gloria into a tizzy," Phil said. "She might slip off the dock into the bay."

Gloria opened her mouth, but I placed my hand on her arm before she could protest. "We appreciate that, Phil, don't we, Gloria?"

Through gritted teeth she muttered, "Thank you, Phil."

"You're quite welcome. See how civil we can all be?" He sat beside her and reached down to pet Rosie. "How are you, girl?"

The manatee hovered with her head sticking out of the water, then slipped beneath the surface. Her tail gave a gentle wave as she swam away without displacing the water.

"Tell me, Phil, did you get to know Max well?" I asked.

"He went diving with Holly and me sometimes. She never got certified but would snorkel while I went under. Max had been qualified for years. I enjoyed his company as he was a very safety-conscious diver. Some people I never went twice with because they were sloppy in their protocols. Diving can be a dangerous sport if you don't take the proper precautions."

With the light fading, cooler air moved in, and I rubbed my arms for warmth. If Phil was as safety conscious as he claimed, his death probably hadn't been an accident. An experienced diver like him would never have run out of air. "Did Max go with you to the wreck of the *Sunset Dream*?"

"Not that I recall." He rubbed his chin.

"Tell me more about the treasure you mentioned," I prompted.

Gloria jolted up straight. "Treasure? What are you talking about?"

"Sorry, I forgot to tell you. When I got ready for my date with Max, Phil and I had a brief discussion. He remembered there'd been treasure on the boat, and he'd moved it without telling Holly. Phil, what was it you found?" I expected him to have disappeared again, but this time he stuck around.

He stared into the ripples of the river.

"Well?" Gloria asked, impatience oozing from every pore as her old habits crept back in.

"Phil?" If he could have felt it, I'd have poked him. Instead, I snapped my fingers.

He responded with his face scrunched in confusion. "Holly referred to it as *family heirlooms*. She knew the owner of the sunken boat, and he'd asked her to help locate it. He told her if she retrieved his *personal* belongings, she would be paid a finder's fee."

"Family heirlooms?" Gloria asked. "Like Grandma's French candlestick holders or something?

"Oh, don't be naïve," Phil huffed. "The case I found had been filled with jewel-encrusted crosses, gold doubloons, and an assortment of fine jewelry from the seventeenth century. I recognized the stash immediately and knew none of it belonged to her friend. He'd really sold my poor Holly a bill of goods. Had I not stepped in, she could have been arrested for not turning it over to the authorities."

"Doubloons? You make it sound like pirate treasure from a Spanish galleon. What's next in your story? A guy with a peg leg and an eye patch?" Gloria's voice elevated.

Phil clapped his hands. "Well, aren't you the clever one. Did you conclude that all on your own?"

I pressed my hands down while scanning the docks to assure we were alone. Thankfully, the only other living souls were too far away to hear my sister's hysterics. "Chill, Glo." I looked to Phil. "You recognized the treasure, didn't you?"

"Of course, I did. I'd certainly done my homework on ships going down in this area. The treasure had been lost when the *Santiago* got blown off course and went down in a storm. It had been headed for what is now Miami, but recent searches found a ship matching the description near Crystal River. Before those who discovered it could disclose the location of the wreck, their ship disappeared, never to be seen again.

I slapped the dock with my hand. "Well, isn't that a great bedtime story for the kiddies. Sounds like a cursed treasure to me. Anyone finding it winds up dead. Present company included."

"I'd like to say you're wrong, but the facts do speak for themselves," Phil said.

"Did Holly know what you'd find on the sunken boat?" I asked.

"She didn't tell me. I don't believe she knew anything beyond there being a case with valuable family items. Her friend wanted to return the valuables to an old uncle."

Gloria shook her head. "And you believed that crock of bull?"

"Why wouldn't I?" Phil asked. "Holly had no reason to lie to me."

"Except for the fact she'd asked you to fetch up

illegal contraband from the ocean's floor," Gloria said.

He shook his head.

I elbowed my sister in the ribs. "Phil, how did Holly react when you opened the case but wouldn't let her take it?"

"She didn't know about my finding the treasure. When we'd discovered the resting place of the *Sunset Dream*, it had been after a long afternoon, and my tanks were close to empty." Phil said. "I convinced her we could return the next day. While she pouted, she had to give in since I couldn't go back down without refilling my equipment."

"You went back without her because you didn't trust her friend, didn't you?" I asked.

"The hole in the ship made me suspicious because it looked as if there'd been an explosion inside the hull. I went back early the next morning by myself. If the treasure fit her description, I'd intended to surprise her with it. When I managed to drag the case onto my boat and open it, I discovered the treasure from the Santiago."

"That's why you moved it." I leaned forward to see around Gloria.

She rubbed her side where I'd poked her but remained silent.

Phil let out an exasperated sigh. "I didn't want Holly mixed up in this mess. She couldn't possibly have known the man dealt in illegal contraband. Uncle my foot. Probably some shady connection."

I snapped my fingers to get Phil to stop ranting. "Where did you put the case?"

Phil opened his mouth then clamped it shut. "I don't remember."

"Isn't that convenient?" Gloria sputtered. "If helping you locate illegal loot is your unresolved issue for hanging around, then get comfortable in limbo. We are *not* solving this one. Sounds like Holly's friends are dangerous. If they got wind we could communicate with Phil, what do you think would happen to us? I'll tell you—we'd be sleeping with the fishes!"

I snorted. "Sleeping with the fishes? I think you've watched too many mafia movies."

"She might not be far off," Phil said. "I've heard stories about present day pirates in this area of the Gulf. That's why I moved it and didn't tell her so she wouldn't be at risk."

"Did you tell her you moved it?" I asked.

"Hmmmm. Good question. I can't remember that either."

"Are you sure you moved it to keep her safe, or did you suspect she'd been in on the plan all along and had been using you?" I winced as I asked, but we needed to know.

"Now you're talking like a crazy woman. Holly loved me and would never have stooped to something so low. How dare you imply such a fallacy?" Phil stood and stormed to the other side of the boardwalk.

Gloria rubbed my arm. "Is it my turn to calm you?" She walked to Phil's side. "Look, Phil, Marni and I ask these questions to get to the truth of why you're still here. Obviously, something traumatic happened when you died. If we don't figure out what, you'll never move on. You'll continue hanging about annoying tourists with our gifts, until you go mad."

He took a step back and looked into her eyes. "You really do want to help me, don't you?"

"Of course, we do," she said. "I may not always be amiable to interruptions, but at the end of the day, I've been given this ability to help souls like you—even when I'm on vacation. Give us a chance to figure this out."

"Gloria, I appreciate what you and Marni are trying to do. It pains me to think my Holly had something to do with my demise. Maybe I'd been naïve. But until you find solid proof, I need to hope Holly loved me for who I was. Can you understand?"

"Of course, we understand your beliefs. But we need to look at every aspect of your life. Without an open mind, we can't help you," Gloria said.

Holy crap! Did my sister have an epiphany, or what? She summed up in a few words what I'd been trying to tell her for the last eight months. Maybe she really did get it. *Should I be afraid?*

"Phil, you need to recall your last minutes. Where were you?" Gloria asked.

He stomped his foot on the deck, though no sound emanated. "I told you I don't remember. Weren't you listening?" The man disappeared.

Gloria lifted her arms in the air. "How can we help him if he keeps having temper tantrums when we ask questions?"

I stood. "You know how this works. He died from a violent act or outright murder. If he'd simply made a mistake while diving, it wouldn't be hard to resolve. He's repressing his last minutes."

"Marni, you know I want to help him. What if our vacation ends and we don't? At some point our own lives matter."

I put my arm around her. "We have a couple more

days. Let's focus on what we can. Now, have you reconsidered a motorcycle ride with Tiny?"

She pushed my arm off her shoulders and walked to the car.

Chapter 19

I awoke the next morning to an empty room. Good, no snarling hyenas. As I glanced dubiously at our coffee maker, the door burst open. Gloria strode in carrying two paper cups. The scent of a dark brew wafted my way, and I inhaled deeply. Okay, I would keep her around another day.

"Good, you're up. I've taken over this girls' trip and booked a spa treatment for the two of us. I know you're riding with Max at eleven, but this morning is all about sister time on my terms."

I wanted to scream, "Who are you and what have you done with my sister?" The first sip of coffee scattered those thoughts to the wind. She'd done good.

She went out to the balcony, and I followed.

"What time is our pampering appointment?" I asked.

"Eight o'clock at the House of Primp. We get a gel manicure and pedicure, followed by a fifty-minute Swedish massage. That'll get you back to the hotel in time to change into your adventure gear."

House of Primp? It sounded like a stripper bar. "We're going riding, Glo, not hiking the Himalayas."

She snorted. "You'll be on a vehicle with no seat belts and air conditioning provided by its forward motion. It might as well be a trek through the Everglades. You know, Marni, sometimes I wonder if we're even related."

I leaned on the rail. "Of course, we are. How else could we both see dead people? Now that's a sister-bonding activity, don't you think?"

Gloria reclined back in her chair. "Right. And I thank Grandma every day for blessing me with such a lovely gift. I would have preferred she'd stopped at her china hutch." She rose and walked back into the room. "You better get a move on if we're going to make our appointment on time."

I followed her inside. "Wait, you got Grandma's china hutch?"

My sister ignored the question, grabbed her humongous cosmetic bag, and went into the bathroom. The door snapped shut.

I checked my phone. The time read seven thirty-five, and I needed to change out of my pajamas, unless the spa had a "come as you are" policy. I pulled on a pair of shorts, T-shirt, and flip flops. "You gonna be long, Gloria?" I called through the door. "We're having a massage. No need for major construction work."

She opened the door while working a toothbrush in her mouth. "I'll only be a minute. You might consider a little brushing action yourself before you melt the nail technician." The door closed again.

"I would, if someone would ever vacate the bathroom," I muttered to the empty room.

****

"Ohhhhhh." I lay on my stomach with my face planted against a donut-shaped pillow looking at the floor. A cricket waltzed across the glistening tiles. Yuck. At least it wasn't a cockroach. I'd point it out to my masseuse, Helga (not her real name, but the closest

125

I could get to pronouncing the one she offered), but for all I knew, those bugs were an endangered species in her country. Her thick Slavic accent massacred the English language so badly, I opted for silence rather than strained conversation.

The tiles, walls, and sheeted room dividers were all white. If the salon strived for a sterile environment, they'd achieved it. I preferred a smidgeon of color but wasn't consulted as to aesthetics.

The technician who did my mani-pedi, also Helga (not her real name, I don't think) wore me out as I attempted to translate our conversation into anything intelligible. I'd finally given up and resorted to smiling and nodding. When she laughed, I laughed. So much easier than figuring out if she talked about an impending typhoon or a secret recipe for dumplings handed down by her ancestors.

All four of the women working in the salon were cast from the same mold with blonde hair and brown eyes. None stood taller than my five-foot-three stature, yet their hands compared to a man twice their size. Nature could be very cruel sometimes when it came to genetics. At least two had found their calling as both Gloria and I had our muscles turned into putty beneath their firm manipulation.

"Pressure hard?" my Helga asked.

Crap! She either wanted to know if she was tearing apart my shoulders beyond usefulness, or if I wanted her to dig deeper until the bones disintegrated. I took a chance. "No, it's perfect." I stifled a groan as her palms kneaded dangerously close to my spine. Eucalyptus perfumed the space around me, but the scent didn't relax me like it should. The fear of partial paralysis consumed my thoughts.

I glanced at the table next to me. My sister appeared completely at ease with the abuse her masseuse inflicted. She even emitted sounds resembling contentment rather than agony. Maybe she'd be willing to switch Helgas with me.

I endured the remainder of our session by taking deep breaths through my nose and focusing on the classical music seeping out of the hidden speakers. About the time I prepared to confess to whatever sins I may or may not have committed just to make the pain end, a chime sounded, and the torture ceased.

The ladies left Gloria and me to relax a few minutes before dressing. They closed the curtained-off section to our shared room. We were supposed to have individual stalls, but since my sister had booked us at the last minute, this was the only space available.

As I slipped on my shorts and grabbed my top, soft footsteps padded into the stall beside us.

"This way, Miss Kate," a male voice said in a softer accent than the women in the shop.

"This isn't my usual room. I prefer the large space." A woman's haughty tone struck a familiar note.

I smacked Gloria on the shoulder and gestured toward the other stall.

"Why'd you do that?" she said as she bent down to buckle her sandals.

With my finger to my lips, I shushed her then mouthed the words, "It's Kate."

"What? Speak up, Marni. What are you saying?"

I bugged my eyes and mouthed, "Quiet."

The side wall of our space swished open, and I instinctively covered my chest with my shirt.

Kate stood beside a tall blond man wearing the same white tee and pants as our female technicians. Her fist still grasped the fabric. "Hugo, you told me the big room needed renovations. Are they part of the new fixtures?" She glared at the cringing man.

"No, no, Miss Kate. This is big misunderstanding. You were to wait here while we clean and prepare the big room for your use. See, the ladies go now." He pointed, and I stifled a laugh at his rather small hands. He definitely bore the family resemblance, at least in the hair and eyes. Yeah, sometimes genetics could be a bitch.

"Good to see you again, Kate." Not caring who saw me at this point, I straightened my shirt and slipped it over my head.

The woman did a doubletake. "Do I know you?"

I inwardly sighed. So this was how she wanted to play it. "Yes. We met at Bookends the other night. Your husband, Lawrence, introduced us?"

She scowled.

"I'm Marni Legend, and this is my sister, Gloria. Remember?"

A noise escaped her lips. It could have been a sneeze or a snort. Either way it fell short of a warm greeting. She turned to her technician. "Bring me a water. All this nonsense has left me parched."

"Yes, Miss Kate." The young man backed away. I waited for him to genuflect and kiss her ring.

She sighed and acknowledged our presence. "Are you two ladies finished? If my services are not begun promptly, I'll be late for our dinner reservation."

I picked up my purse. "Are you and Lawrence receiving a couple's massage?" I knew the answer, but there's something about needling a complete stranger that gave me warm fuzzies.

Another snort. "Hardly. He's out barhopping with the boys on his motorcycle. Not that it's any of your business."

Gloria tilted her head. "Isn't he riding—"

"Come on, Glo. Let's give the lady her privacy. She said he's out riding with the boys. End of story." I tugged at her elbow.

Hugo chose that moment to enter holding out a bottle of water to his disgruntled customer as if it were an offering. "Here you go, Miss Kate. Icy cold. Just as you like it. Why don't you change into your robe in the other room while my sisters prepare this one for you?" A bead of sweat trickled down his face. Talk about job stress.

Kate swiped the bottle from his hand and swished the curtain closed.

As we left, I patted the young man on the shoulder. "I'm sure she'll leave a big tip."

Chapter 20

"Do you get the feeling this town is shrinking by the minute?" Gloria asked on our drive back to the hotel.

"Tell me about it! What're the odds Kate shows up at the same inappropriately named salon as us?"

Gloria did a doubletake. "What do you mean 'inappropriately named' salon? House of Primp had extremely high ratings." My sister didn't possess the same caliber of imagination I did. Her loss.

For me, amusement waited around every corner. She did have good intentions though when she'd booked our treatments. "I'm kidding. But you're right about the town getting smaller. We keep running into the same people. Perhaps the universe meant it to happen that way in order to help Phil."

"It's about time someone recognized my importance," Phil huffed from the back seat.

Gloria and I turned at the same time.

"Perhaps one of you should be watching the road unless you're intending to join me here in the great beyond. Not that I wouldn't lament the company." He waggled his brows at my sister.

I snapped my head forward in time to swerve the car back into our lane. Good thing there hadn't been any oncoming traffic. That wouldn't have ended well. "Good morning, Phil. What can you tell me about

Lawrence and his wife?"

"Nothing. I told you I don't recall socializing with them. What can you tell me?" he asked.

I side-eyed Gloria. Something didn't add up, but I couldn't figure out what. "Holly appears to be involved with a married man, yet I'm not convinced there's an actual relationship. I'm riding with Max this afternoon, and Holly and Lawrence are joining us. Guess I'll get a little more insight."

"Gloria, why aren't you going? I believe that large individual known as Tiny offered to ferry you on his bike?" Phil asked.

"Ferry me? I have no desire to cross the River Styx. I do *not* ride motorcycles. End of story." She shot a piercing glare at Phil.

"Aha! I knew a woman such as yourself would have read the Greek classics." He placed a ghostly hand on her shoulder and leaned closer. "With so much in common, I would think you'd go the extra mile to help me move on," he said. "What's a little motorcycle ride?"

She held her hands up in the air. "Phil, I am willing to go the extra mile for you—just as long as it's in a vehicle with four wheels."

I pulled into a spot at the hotel parking lot. "Why don't you tag along with me this afternoon, Phil? Maybe see if you pick up on anything I might miss. What do you say?"

He looked to my sister then me. Gloria nodded her head with more emphasis than necessary. No selfish intentions there.

Phil sighed. "As you wish. I pray something can be gleaned from this romantic joy ride you're dragging me on."

Gloria faced forward wearing a smile. She deserved an afternoon off. Hopefully, Phil would give it to her.

****

Max rolled up to the hotel right on time. He'd already gotten off and removed his gear by the time I reached him. Such a loss.

"Hey, you!" He pulled me in close, his mouth covering mine with a lingering kiss.

"Hey, yourself." I breathed in his musky cologne before settling in for another smooch.

"Is this what I'll be subjected to all day?" Phil asked, his voice laced with disgust. "You're acting like a couple of hormonal teenagers."

I disentangled from Max's grasp and peered over his shoulder. Phil stood akimbo with hands on hips, a sneer across his face.

"Quiet," I mouthed.

He snorted, much like the sound Holly made whenever we met. The question remained who perfected it first?

"We should get going," I said to Max. "We wouldn't want our riding companions to get impatient and leave without us."

His arm circled my waist once more. "Then we'd have another afternoon to ourselves. That wouldn't be a bad plan either," he murmured.

My hands pressed against his chest, and I reluctantly pushed him away. "Since it was your suggestion to ride, we should probably show up. Don't you think?"

With a nod, he released me and dug into his saddle

bag for the spare helmet and gloves. "I suppose you're right, Marni. But I did change the meeting time to eleven thirty. There's a beautiful spot I wanted to show you on our way to the beach."

"I'm game." If it turned out to be a secluded alcove, we might scare Phil away from accompanying us though. I'd risk it.

After donning my gear, I managed to board the bike without any clumsy mishaps or injury to either of us. As I raised my arms in silent victory, the bike rolled, and I listed sideways. I grabbed for Max's waist and clunked my helmet against his. *Maybe I should just hold on.*

We cruised along the same route as yesterday, until a detour took us off the main road and down a hard packed, dirt trail. He parked in a small clearing overlooking a secluded beach. The view took my breath away with the ocean stretching for miles. A warm breeze tickled my face as I inhaled the fresh sea air.

I set my helmet and gloves on the seat and walked to the edge of the cliff. Well, I went within a few feet of the edge. I wasn't that much of a daredevil, and the ground looked a bit unstable. Warm hands wrapped around me from behind.

"What do you think?" he asked.

My head rested on his chest beneath his chin. "Beautiful."

"Just below and to the right is a network of caves. They're divided from the beach we were on yesterday by a huge rock formation. The only way in is by water, or the trail farther inland by a parking lot. Maybe we could do some exploring before you go back to New York."

"Caves? Like dank, dark caverns, possibly inhabited by ancient sea creatures?" *Hell no!*

"You're not afraid of the dark, are you?" He nibbled my ear. "I'd protect you. Plus, we'd have flashlights."

My foot stomped the dirt. "Darn, that does sound like fun." *Not.* "Unfortunately, my days are numbered here, and we won't have time. Maybe some other trip?" *Possibly never?*

"Exploring might not be his intention." Phil sneered beside me. His head shot up with eyes wide. "Marni, I just remembered where I hid the treasure."

Of course, he did. No need to tell me the location. Now, how to convince Gloria to join me in a little spelunking. Better yet, maybe we could hire the Helga sisters from the spa to tackle this chore. I still believed the House of Primp doubled as a stripper club at night. How else could they stay so physically fit?

"Does that mean you have plans to come back to Crystal River?"

Max's question pulled me out of my own thoughts and back to the present situation—the one in which my safety was now in question. "No plans right now." I turned in his arms to face him.

He wore a pout on his lips. Not terribly convincing on a man his age.

"Thanks for showing me this amazing place." I gave him a peck on the cheek. "We better head out, or we'll be late." Not to mention my concern for being in a remote area with a possible murderer. As I stepped toward the motorcycle, his grip tightened, and he held me fast. My body stiffened.

"Is that all the thanks I've earned for this gorgeous

view?"

Before I knew it, we were lip-locked again, his hands wandering below my waist and clutching my backside. My privates screamed for him to keep going, but my mind overruled the action, and I pulled away. "That's all for now." I forced a chuckle.

This time his grip loosened, and he released me.

I chided myself for jumping to conclusions. Our detour and Phil's hiding the stash in the caves below might not be connected. While Max neglected to mention his family tie to Holly, it may have been for personal reasons. Our afternoon outing might reveal those intentions.

Max navigated the bike back to the paved road and down the hill to our meeting spot. Lawrence and Holly watched as we parked beside them. Lawrence waved, while Holly stood with arms crossed, tapping her foot. Obviously, patience wasn't one of her virtues. I'd yet to discover anything positive about the woman in the encounters we'd had, but maybe today she'd have a breakthrough.

"It's about time you showed up," Holly snarked. "Was your date still primping when you arrived?"

Lawrence placed a hand on Holly's shoulder. "They're only five minutes late. We barely rolled in ahead of them."

"Sorry, it's my fault. I wanted to show Marni the view from Overlook Park. Guess we got caught up in the moment." Max gazed into my eyes and winked.

"I'd say you had more than a *moment*." Phil appeared beside Holly, drinking in every inch of her. "How I do miss you, my beautiful lady." Did he not hear any of the disdainful remarks *his beautiful lady* had just slung at me?

If we were closer to the shoreline, I'd find a way to accidentally dunk her beneath the waves. I'd be happy to hold her under until the bubbles stopped, so they could be together forever. It would be for the sake of true love, of course.

"Where shall we take the ladies for lunch?" Lawrence asked.

Max rested his arm around my shoulders and gave a gentle hug. "You like seafood, don't you, Marni?"

I nodded.

"Let's keep it simple and hit the Seafood Shack about a dozen miles down the coast. They have a huge outdoor patio overlooking the surf."

"Perfect!" said Lawrence. "I've been there several times, and the food is excellent."

"In case anyone's interested, I like seafood too, as long as it's fresh," Holly chimed in. "I know you landlubbers settle for fresh/frozen, but I can certainly tell the difference." She wrinkled her nose at me as if smelling something rotten.

Landlubber? Last time I checked, Long Island was surrounded by water on three sides. Geography must not be her strongpoint—along with civility, tact, and manners. My goal today should be to identify one positive trait, other than being positive she murdered her ex-boyfriend.

"We know what you like, Holly," Max said. "I didn't mean to exclude you. Does the Seafood Shack meet with your approval, m'lady?" He stepped forward giving a mock bow.

She snorted and grabbed her helmet from where it hung off the foot peg of Lawrence's bike.

The rest of us followed suit and got ready to ride.

Throughout our exchange, Phil remained silent—a first for him. His love for Holly still perplexed me, but he obviously saw something in her I couldn't. Despite her rudeness to me, I needed to find a way to look at her behavior from all sides. If I got too caught up in wanting to find her guilty, I might miss clues leading in a different direction. I'd been at this sleuthing long enough to know not everything is what it appears.

Or was it?

Chapter 21

The breeze felt good on my face as it banished the Florida heat. I could get used to this lifestyle. While I loved living in my little harbor town on Long Island, year-round sunshine and no snow had its appeal.

We rolled out of the parking lot with Max in the lead. Tension eased from my shoulders as I grew more comfortable on the bike. My hands remained on Max's waist minus the death grip from yesterday. If I rode more often, I might consider getting one of those cute leather vests with a clever road name embroidered on it. Marni the biker babe—who knew?

The road took us south along the shoreline. Pelicans cruised over the waves, periodically diving for the water then soaring back into the air. Between the growl of our engine and Lawrence's roaring pipes behind us, no other noise penetrated my ears.

Five minutes into the ride our bike swerved, and I instinctively tightened my hold. We teetered for a beat without slowing before Max got the vehicle under control. Instead of pulling over to comfort me or offer a tranquilizer, his inner daredevil emerged. Max gunned the engine, and we sped up.

I, on the other hand, did my best to hang on and not hyperventilate. If I didn't pull it together, I might fall off—or take us both down with the motorcycle on top of us. I quickly banished that happy thought before it morphed into a gloating Gloria standing over my hospital bed sneering, "I told you so." She'd probably use her signature skill of speaking without moving her lips for dramatic affect.

Forget the new biker wardrobe. I'd be happy to survive this afternoon without being fitted for a body cast. Had I really thought this would be fun? What would be his next trick, popping a wheelie while jumping a ravine? My fingers dug deeper into his waist for a stronger hold.

Phil better appreciate my risking life and limb for him. Well, there had been a teeny bit of selfish motivation when I accepted the invitation. Blaming Phil had a satisfying ring to it though.

Risking a glance over my shoulder, I spied Holly leaning against her backrest without holding on to Lawrence. She gave me a thumbs up and nodded her head. I resisted the urge to flip her off and returned the same gesture instead. It was the first act of kindness she'd shown me, so I thought it best to behave—unless her intent had been for me to lose balance and fall off when I let go of Max.

Our ride to lunch felt like hours, yet only thirty minutes had elapsed. We rolled into the parking lot of the Seafood Shack, which looked as if it had weathered more than a few storms. Lengths of rope, circular life preservers, and fish nets hung haphazardly from the walls. Despite a fresh coat of white paint, the dilapidated, wooden structure had the appearance of a building long past its expiration date. *Are there no building inspectors in Florida?*

I slid off the bike and onto solid ground, my knees still shaky from our little mishap. It took me three tries to unbuckle the strap on my helmet.

"How about that ride, Marni? I promised you the scenery would be spectacular!" Max took my helmet and stowed it away.

Spectacular? How about the part where we almost became one with the pavement? Eureka, I'd found the name for my vest—Roadkill. "Loved it!" I forced a smile. "Except for the wobbly part when the bike tried to buck me off like a wild bronco throws his rider."

Max swatted the air. "Just a bit of gravel on the blacktop. Nothing to worry about."

"Boy, I thought you guys were going down for sure," Lawrence said.

"Yeah, clean-up wouldn't have been pretty." Holly chuckled.

Sure, guys, keep talking. Convince me why I'll be climbing back on the motorcycle instead of calling a cab after lunch.

Max put a hand on my shoulder. "You're trembling. Really, we were fine. Don't let them spook you." He wrapped me in a hug.

I nuzzled my head against his neck and sighed. His strong arms soothed my nerves.

Phil appeared behind Max, clapping his hands. "Yes, you've got real spooks to deal with. What did I miss?"

My stomach grumbled. "Guess it wasn't terrifying enough to lose my appetite." I grimaced. "Maybe we should eat."

"Great, I'm starving." Holly strode off to the entrance with Lawrence on her heels.

"I second the motion." Max grasped my hand.

My ghostly friend trailed behind us.

I shifted back to my concern about the structure being sound. Would we fall through rotted floorboards where they'd splintered from wear? To my amazement we stepped through the rough-hewn doors into a newly renovated seaside restaurant. Smart, nautical touches peppered the inside walls and the spacious dining area. The ruinous facade of the outside must've been for atmosphere.

Our seating hostess led us through a half-crowded room. Tantalizing aromas of garlic mixed with butter and spices teased my growing appetite. She escorted us onto the back patio, which provided twice the amount of seating with mostly full tables. Luckily, Max had made a reservation, and we didn't have to wait.

"I guess I'll just stand here watching everyone dine." Phil pouted. Did he expect me to pull up a chair for him?

As the hostess dealt out the menus, I asked for the restrooms and excused myself. I motioned with my eyes for Phil to follow me.

He responded by rolling his upward before disappearing.

Inside the ladies' room, another patron washed her hands. After she'd left, I checked the stalls and found them empty. "Phil, get in here now," I whispered.

He appeared immediately, sitting on one of the sinks. "All right, I'm here. So, what happened on the road? Did lover boy almost wipe out and send you hurtling into the hereafter?" He snickered.

"Thanks for the heartfelt concern. I'm surprised you weren't along for the ride."

He raised his hands in the air. "And where would you have me sit? Holly's lap? Or better yet, floating alongside you?"

I sighed. "Look, I'll make this quick, or they're going to think I hopped a taxi and bolted for freedom. Keep your ears open for anything out of the ordinary or if anybody says something you know is a lie."

"Shall I blink once for yes and twice for no? Perhaps a hand signal?" He started to raise his middle finger but pulled back halfway.

"Are you forgetting I'm here to help you?" I asked.

"How much *help* did you provide back at the cliff while trying to suck your date's face off?" Phil crossed his arms.

Why have my latest spirits been so needy? "Remember how you're interrupting *my* vacation? You should be glad my sister and I are helping you at all. Besides, you remembered where you stashed the 'family treasure' while we stood overlooking the caves. Now go back out there and help me help you, because you are not following us back to Long Island like a lost puppy."

"Yes, ma'am. Aren't you coming too?" he asked.

"When I'm done in here. Now scoot." I swept my hands toward the door then entered one of the stalls. As I returned to the sinks, I found Lulu standing there wearing a big grin on her face.

"Fancy meeting you here," she said.

"What are you doing at the Seafood Shack?" Grabbing a paper towel, I dried my hands.

She shrugged. "It's my day off and gorgeous outside. Decided to hop on my scoot and ride. I spotted Max's bike in the parking lot and thought I'd crash the party. As I came in, I saw you heading this way. Was that Lawrence's bike out there too?"

I nodded. "Holly's with him."

"Really? Get anything out of her?" she asked.

"Not yet. We just arrived and haven't had time to chat. Come join us; I'm sure the others won't mind. And I could use some help sifting through any useful info. I've already got Phil on alert to keep his ears open." We went into the main dining room, heading for the patio.

Lulu did a doubletake. "Phil's here? So, your sister came too?"

I laughed. "Not in a million years would that woman be riding on a motorcycle. Phil agreed to give her the afternoon off and tag along with me. Did you know Max and Holly are siblings?"

"Who told you that?" She narrowed her eyes.

"Our friendly ghost. Phil said Max would dive with him sometimes while Holly snorkeled. She'd introduced him as her brother."

"Honestly, I don't know Max very well. We ride together sometimes with Tiny, but beyond bullshitting over a beer, we haven't spoken much."

Max flashed a questioning smile as we approached.

"Look who I found lurking about the ladies' room. Think we can squeeze in a fifth chair?"

"Of course, we can." Lawrence jumped to his feet and secured one from a vacant table. "What a nice surprise, Lulu. It'll be fun visiting without you working the bar."

"Thanks. Max, Holly, good to see you guys." Lulu said as she sat.

"Your timing is perfect. We haven't even ordered drinks yet." Max passed his menu to her, while his lips formed a straight line. "You out on the bike?"

"In this weather, do you have to ask?" Lulu grinned.

"Spoken like a true rider." Lawrence nodded.

I scanned the patio, trying not to be obvious about it. The gang was all here—except Phil. Did Lulu's presence shoot today's plan to hell?

Chapter 22

We all chatted amicably over a superb lunch, but I found it difficult to turn the conversation to Phil. With Lulu in the mix, much of the talk centered around motorcycles and places to ride. My frustration grew when she didn't curtail the bike talk and lead us in a more productive direction. Lulu knew my reasons for enduring *sweet* Holly's presence.

Lawrence insisted we all needed a slice of the restaurant's signature lemon cheesecake. At least the discussion went back to food and not bikes.

I used the opportunity. "Holly, what made you move to Florida?"

"Hmmm?" She shoved a bite of dessert into her mouth.

"Boston is a wonderful town, except for the weather this time of year. I was curious why you moved to this particular area." I speared a piece of my own lemony goodness.

She scowled. "How did you know I came from Boston?"

Oops. Did I slip?

Phil appeared behind Lulu, and my glance gave him away. Lulu turned her head, only to have him disappear before she saw him. Focusing back on me, she arched a brow.

I tilted my head as if to question her meaning. Lulu

shrugged, and I skated past my faux pas.

Phil's actions made it crystal clear he wanted nothing to do with Lulu. That would be a conversation he and I needed to have. He'd already admitted to Gloria and me he didn't trust her. I needed to know the whole backstory.

"Don't be so defensive, darling. I mentioned it to Marni when I ran into her at Bookends the other night," Lawrence said.

Holly placed her fork down as her face paled. "Why would you be talking about me?" Did I detect fear in those eyes?

"I'd merely mentioned how nice it had been to meet you at Libations." I flashed a toothy smile. "I can't remember how Boston came up. So, do you like it in Crystal River?"

"Excuse me." She threw down her napkin and stormed off.

I placed a hand to my cheek in mock embarrassment. "I'm so sorry. Was her move here predicated by a painful event?"

Max reached over and touched my arm. "Don't worry, Marni, you couldn't have known."

"Know what?" I don't have a very good poker face yet flashed my best doe-eyed innocent look at him anyway. It might work.

Max glanced at Lawrence, who gave a slight nod. "Holly moved here because she'd met a man. His name was Phil."

"*Was* Phil?" I kept up the pretense despite Lulu's stifled snicker. "Did they break up?"

Lawrence leaned in. "Phil died in a diving accident about a year ago. Holly hasn't quite gotten over it."

She hadn't gotten over his death or the fact she couldn't steal his half of the tour shop?

"I'm sorry to hear that happened to her boyfriend." I didn't react this time when Phil appeared behind Lulu again.

"Phil was more than her boyfriend. They'd gotten engaged the very day he disappeared," Max said.

I shifted my eyes to Lulu, who shrugged.

Behind her, Phil crisscrossed his hands while shaking his head and mouthing the word "no." His mute gestures re-enforced my suspicion he didn't want Lulu to know he'd joined us.

"Maybe I should go find her and apologize." I stood.

Before I could step away, Max stopped me. "Give her a few moments alone. She'll come back. It's doubly hard on her because he'd told her about a surprise he had for her and how excited he was to give it to her. Since Phil never returned from his dive, she never found out where he'd put it."

I had no doubt what the *surprise* was and why she would be anxious to locate it. Holly really spun quite a tale. How many at this table knew the truth? Or had she fooled them all? "What kind of surprise?"

Before I received an answer, Holly returned. Her face glistened with moisture, as if she'd splashed water on it. She either gave an award-winning performance pretending to be upset, or the woman truly had feelings for Phil. If she didn't have a hand in his demise, did she fear the same fate could happen to her if she didn't find the stash?

Everyone focused on finishing their dessert. Tension from the sudden cessation of talking hung in the air like a noose around our necks. The longer the quiet dragged on the tighter the rope squeezed. If someone didn't speak up soon, there'd be no salvaging the rest of the afternoon.

I hated being the chosen one. "Are we taking the same road back, or do you have a different route planned, Max?" This felt like a safe topic with no controversy or accusatory barbs.

"I thought we would ride inland and take Derringer Road. There are some great twisties which weave in and out along some of the waterways. I've got a great spot in mind where we can stop and view the local wildlife. What do you think, Lawrence?"

The tall man flashed a look at his companion, who kept her eyes glued to her plate. "Great idea. Lulu, will you be joining us?" He turned her way.

I held my breath waiting on Lulu's answer. The only hope I had of making progress would be if she bowed out. Phil pretending to be a mime didn't help.

"I wish I could, but I need to head home. Got a dinner date with a new hottie I met at Libations." She pretended to fan herself.

"Isn't it against the rules to date patrons?" Condescension laced Lawrence's voice.

"Nah. Normally I don't on principle in case things go south. It could get awkward if the guy turned into a regular. Tonight's delicious nugget leaves town in a couple days."

Max's expression darkened for a second before he grinned. "Sounds like you're in for an *active* evening. You'd best conserve your energy." Did I detect a note of jealousy? Maybe Lulu knew Max better than she let on. Perhaps they shared a bit of history.

"Well, you have fun. Maybe Gloria and I should stop by Libations tomorrow for a few of the highlights," I suggested. No way would my sister be remotely interested in Lulu's dating habits, but I needed to get the ball rolling so she would leave.

"*If* I make it into work tomorrow." Lulu winked. When she reached into her purse and took out her wallet, Lawrence stopped her.

"Lunch is on me," he said. "Enjoy your date."

"Aren't you sweet. Thanks." She stood and addressed the table. "Thanks for letting me crash your party. Safe ride." After only a couple of steps, she stopped. "Hey, Max, do you mind taking a quick look at something on my bike? I need an opinion."

After a moment's hesitation, he stood. "Of course." He held out a credit card to Lawrence. "Why don't we split the bill."

Lawrence held up his hand. "Nope. It's my treat today. I'll take care of this and the other two ladies while you assist Lulu. We'll be out shortly."

"Thanks, man. Next time it'll be my turn." Max leaned over and brushed a kiss on my cheek. "See you in a few."

Lulu took off for the door, and Max followed.

Our host excused himself, promising to return in a few moments. This left Holly and me to face off, with Phil in attendance.

"Marni, don't just sit there like a daft mute. This is your opportunity to find out what she knows," Phil said.

Gee, why didn't I think of that? I flashed him a scowl then pasted on a smile to address Holly. "I didn't mean to upset you earlier. The guys told me about Phil. I'm sorry for your loss." I sounded like a surgeon delivering a hollow apology. My skills with the living were getting as bad as Gloria's tactless outbursts.

"It's okay. You couldn't have known." Holly finally raised her eyes from the half-empty plate in front of her. She swiveled her head over her left shoulder then the right before leaning closer. "Marni, you seem like a nice person, and I'd hate for something to happen to you. Just be careful. Not everyone is whom they seem to be."

I had no idea what to make of her comment. Had it been a warning or a threat? I glanced at Phil and bugged my eyes.

"She's afraid. I've seen every emotion cross my Holly's lovely face, and I recognize fear." Phil rung his hands.

Holly jumped when Lawrence placed a hand on her shoulder from behind. He must've been in stealth mode as I hadn't noticed him return.

"You girls having a nice chat?" He eyed Holly. "Let's join Max out front. I believe he's anxious to get going."

"Sounds good." I led the way through the restaurant. Which of our dining companions frightened her?

The motorcycles were parked directly in front of the large picture window to the right of the entrance. Max stood in front of Lulu waving his hands in what looked like a heated argument. Lulu pointed a finger in his face then toward the restaurant. For two people who vaguely knew one another, their actions suggested otherwise. Holly's words slithered through my mind, which zeroed in on a possible explanation for her cryptic message.

By the time we walked outside, Lulu had donned her helmet and gloves. She threw a leg over her bike, which had been backed into the space beside us. Kicking the engine into gear, she blasted out of the lot.

I waved, even though she'd already taken off. What I'd just witnessed made me doubt her appearance today had been a coincidence. Gloria and I would definitely visit Libations tomorrow to find out how her *date* went. That is if I don't live up to my new name—Roadkill.

Chapter 23

Lawrence's phone pinged. He pulled it from his pocket, grimaced, then poked a finger at the screen. After studying the message, he tucked the device away. "Kate has a crisis. Her message didn't make sense other than she needs me at home. I'm sorry, but we'll have to cut the ride short. Holly, I'll drop you on the way."

"I hope everything's okay," I said.

"Knowing my wife, it's probably more of an inconvenience for her than a real issue. Since she hadn't elaborated, I'd best return home. It'll be easier than texting back and forth." He handed Holly her helmet.

"We'll do it again another time," Max offered. "You still up for viewing the local wildlife?" He sidled up to me and threw an arm around my shoulders.

My hormones raged, yet Holly's warning echoed louder. Since she hadn't elaborated on *who* shouldn't be trusted, I thought it best not to be alone with anyone in our party—for now. "Why don't you drop me off at the hotel?" I struggled to keep the disappointment from my voice. "Besides, I'll see you at dinner."

He nuzzled my neck. "We won't be alone for dinner."

"Why don't you throw her to the ground and ravage her right here?" Phil snarked. "We could all use some scintillating entertainment."

Heat flushed my cheeks. Instead of tamping down

thoughts of intimacy with Max, Phil's comments kicked my imagination into high gear. Damn, why did things have to be so complicated? Lulu had it down—meet a man, have a wild evening, and make no excuses to anyone.

"Holly and I need to bolt. Are you following us back to town or going solo?" Lawrence asked.

Holly's eyes bugged wide for a second, then she turned away as she buckled her helmet. Why do people believe facial expressions are self-explanatory? Did she warn me to follow them or get away from them?

I chose the "safety in numbers" theory. "Let's head back, Max. Gloria may want to have some girl time before we meet with you and Tiny tonight."

With a nod, Max unlocked the saddle bag and dug out our gear. "I keep forgetting you're not alone on this vacation. Maybe I should put a little effort into getting on your sister's good side, since I've stolen you away two days in a row."

You misguided man. We didn't have enough time left in our vacation for him to achieve Gloria's stamp of approval.

The ride back to Crystal River hummed along without any mishaps like our outbound trip. Not once did we falter or skid, nor did Max feel the need to play speed demon. Our companions branched off before we reached the main part of town.

When we arrived at the hotel, Max didn't remove his gear. He simply stowed mine and jumped back on the motorcycle with a promise to text our dinner location. His actions stumped me. One moment he wanted to get me alone and the next he displayed a total indifference to passion. At the very least, I'd expected a smooch or two. Even if Phil appeared, Max wouldn't know we had an audience.

This current lost soul's irritation at my extracurricular activities almost paralleled my deceased mother's. She'd had the bad timing of showing up at my apartment just after my previous beau and I had enjoyed a bit of bedroom fun. Her comments comparing his manhood to my father's scarred me for life. I still have nightmares. No amount of alcohol could obliterate those thoughts from my mind.

Phil stood beside me as Max rode away. "What, no good-bye kisses? Looks to me passion is waning."

I glared. "Must you render a running commentary on every aspect of my love life?"

"Love? Marni, you aren't in love. Lust maybe, but not love. Nobody falls that fast." He clucked his tongue.

"How would you know? Are you the *love* expert now?" I raised my arms. "Maybe I'd just like to go for a tumble with no strings attached. Did you ever think of that?" Over his shoulder a maid pushing a housekeeping cart stared at me with knitted brows. With my hands still in the air, I gave her a wave, and Phil turned.

The woman looked down and fumbled with her key card to unlock the next room. Before stepping inside, she glanced over at me.

I smiled and waved again.

She hurried through the door slamming it shut behind her.

"For heaven's sake, stop scaring the locals. Let's see what the lovely Gloria is up to." Phil took off for the stairs with me following. He went up the flight and through our door.

Gloria's scream reached me long before I got to the top step. I braced myself for round two of why Phil needed to make himself known before appearing inside our room. Doubts filled my brain as to how effective this discussion would be. I debated going inside or heading down to the bar. Resignation won out as I used my key to unlock the door.

At least I found Gloria fully clothed this time. She lounged on the bed with a bottle of water beside her and a book, now lying flat on the bed.

Phil held his sides pretending to belly laugh. These two needed a referee. At least with only one being alive, they couldn't come out swinging. Had Phil been in a corporeal state, my money would've been on Gloria coming out the victor.

"Hey, Glo! Have a relaxing time without me?" I asked.

"I did until this rude individual popped in and frightened me." She pointed an accusing finger at Phil.

He stopped laughing. "Tsk, tsk. Didn't your mother teach you it's impolite to point?"

Gloria huffed. "She also taught me not to enter someone's room without being invited."

I put my purse on the dresser. "The two of you, back off to your neutral corners."

"He started it," she muttered.

"Are you five all of a sudden? What's next? Shooting spit balls at each other?" I turned to Phil. "And you. Do we need to review boundaries?"

"I don't believe I have any boundaries seeing I can drift through any of them." He grinned. A paperback flew threw his head, hit the wall, and landed on the table. Phil didn't so much as flinch.

"Feel better?" I asked my sister.

"Much." She shifted back onto the pillows leaning against the headboard. "How was lunch?" I guess I could accept this progress. She'd had her fit and now moved on.

"Not as informative as I'd hoped. Lulu showed up and Phil took a powder." I sat on my bed facing her.

"Why'd Lulu tag along?" Gloria asked.

I shrugged. "She claimed to be out riding and spotted the bikes. We'd already been seated when she arrived."

My sister screwed up her face. "What did she have to say about Phil being there?"

"Good question." I stared at our spirit. "A better question is why did Phil become a mime then disappear when she looked his way?"

"What's she talking about, Phil?"

I leaned against my headboard and put my feet up on the bed. "You told us you don't trust Lulu. Why?"

Phil shuddered. "The woman is incorrigible. She asks questions which are none of her business."

He had my full attention. "What kind of questions?"

"She wanted to know if I'd hidden the treasure and where. Can you imagine? As if I'd tell her." He crossed his arms.

Gloria sat up straight. "Wait. Did she ask you before or after you died?"

"What difference does it make?" His good humor turned to indignation.

"Phil, it makes all the difference. How would she even know about the treasure? And is that the exact word she'd used?" This new twist turned everything we'd discovered on its head.

He held one finger up. "I see your point. She asked me after my demise. Of course, I ignored her. She had greed written all over her. The treasure would never be placed in the proper hands."

Gloria inched over to sit on the edge of her bed. "And you didn't think to mention this detail? How could she know you'd removed the goods from the ship and hidden them?"

"It didn't seem important at the time. I'd never liked her while alive. Why would I confide in her after my passing?" He walked to the patio doors and stared out at the water.

"Phil?" I called.

He turned to face me.

"Do you know who Holly meant when she told me to be careful who I trusted?"

"When did she tell you that?" Gloria demanded.

I filled my sister in on the brief conversation I had with Holly while alone and Phil's observation of the fear she displayed.

"If Holly feared Lawrence or Max, why would she continue hanging around them?" Gloria asked.

"Good question," I said. "From what Phil told us about Lulu, Holly might have referred to her as distrustful. We really don't have enough to reach any conclusions yet."

Gloria reached for her water bottle. "Maybe we should cancel our dinner with Max and Tiny. It feels as if we've gotten in over our heads."

"I vote we stick to our evening plan. We'll be meeting at a restaurant and driving ourselves. If either of them is suspect, we'd be in a public place and have our own getaway car." I walked to the mini fridge and took out a soda.

"I second the motion." Phil moved away from the patio and sat in the desk chair.

Gloria cleared her throat. "Not to discount your opinion, but only the living get a vote on how we proceed. We're the ones in possible danger."

"That's awfully prejudicial," Phil whined.

"Call me selfish, but I prefer to think of it as self-preservation. Marni, you do have a point. We'll be surrounded by people at the restaurant and won't be getting into a vehicle with them." She wagged a finger at me. "Just don't be sneaking off with Max for any romantic interludes leaving yourself vulnerable and me at risk while alone with Tiny."

I placed a hand on my chest. "I would never do such a thing."

She tilted her head and quirked up one side of her mouth.

"Okay, it may have crossed my mind. Fleetingly. He's a really good kisser." I grinned.

"*Fleetingly?*" Her voice remained flat.

"All right." I made a cross over my heart. "I promise not to abandon you while seeking romance with a hot guy, the likes of whom I've not had in my bed for months. Satisfied?"

She shuddered. "A simple 'I promise' would have sufficed. We don't need to know the carnal details of your sex life."

"Do I get to second *that* motion?" Phil raised his hand. "Marni does tend to overshare when it comes to men."

"Oh, and you've spent a lot of time experiencing

these conversations?" I liked it better when Gloria was the brunt of our jokes. How did I become the target?

My sister smiled. "Sucks being ganged up on, doesn't it?"

I stuck my tongue out at her.

Chapter 24

I got a text from Max asking us to meet them at the Growling Boar at six thirty. This town certainly had a flair for oddly named establishments. I didn't know a boar could growl.

Rather than offering Gloria wardrobe tips, since the Bookends fiasco sat foremost in my mind, I reserved comment at her donning a white sundress. The outfit gave off a casual yet sophisticated vibe only she could pull off. My similar cotton dress in blue made me appear more thrift store rescue. Maybe the secret lay in her stylish pumps compared to my flat sandals. With an aversion to twisted ankles, I rarely wore heels.

We arrived to find our dining companions in the bar. Both wore shorts and polo shirts, a tad more casual than I expected. Tiny immediately stood in greeting, while Max barely grunted a hello. Unease washed over me from his noncommittal welcome. I couldn't pinpoint my egregious error, other than ditching his plans to get me alone this afternoon. If he'd had a change of heart, why did he follow through on tonight's dinner?

"Welcome, ladies. You both look lovely tonight," Tiny said. "What're you drinking?" He motioned to the two other stools at their high-top table.

Gloria scooted hers closer to mine before sitting.

Tamping down the urge to kiss Max, I simply nodded before taking a seat. No way would I throw myself at him—at least not in public. I told Tiny my drink order and held my head high. Did I detect a smirk from my sister?

The large man retrieved our wine from the bar. "How'd you like the ride today, Marni?"

"Beautiful scenery. I can't get enough of this seashore." The forced enthusiasm in my voice got no reaction from Max, who stared into his beer as if uninterested in conversation.

Almost immediately the seating hostess told us our table had become available and led us through the entry into the restaurant. Gloria's color choice may have been a bad one. The seating consisted of picnic tables with red and white checkered tablecloths. Diners dove elbow deep into plates of ribs smothered in barbecue sauce. I breathed in the heavenly aroma of the smokey chipotle marinade.

Gloria grimaced as she eased onto a weather-beaten bench.

Tiny slid in next to her, forcing me to sit on the opposite side. With Max's cooling demeanor, this could turn into a very awkward meal. Both Gloria and I might need more wine before long.

Picking up my menu, I asked, "So, what's good here?"

Max gave a mirthless chuckle as he indicated the food on the table next to us. "I'd suggest the ribs."

My sister perused the selections, a sour expression never leaving her face. The next time we're invited someplace, she'll be researching it down to the last piece of cutlery before agreeing to go.

"This place has a great marinade nobody can beat," Tiny said. "Why don't we get the family-style platter with a mix of beef and pork ribs?"

"I'll have a salad." Gloria's lips formed a straight line.

I kicked her under the table, and she scowled. "Come on, Glo, why not try the local specialties? The mixed plate sounds great to me."

"I prefer a meal which doesn't require a slicker and a drop cloth, but you go ahead and sample away, Marni."

Tiny slumped his shoulders. "I'm sorry. I should have allowed you ladies to pick the restaurant. We can go somewhere else if you'd like."

With a foot, I nudged Gloria again.

She opened her mouth, then closed it. With a thin smile, she placed a hand on Tiny's arm. "Don't be silly, Christopher. We appreciate the invitation. I'm just not much of a rib person, but I'm sure this *Growling Boar Shrubs & Grubs Bowl* will be delicious." Color me amazed. She rattled off the selection without a sneer.

He brightened. "Order whatever you like. Marni, how about you?"

"I'm in on the ribs." I looked at Max as I amped up a toothy grin. "What do you say?"

"Count me in as well." He patted my hand. Not huge on the affection scale, but it was a start. Maybe by dessert his icy coating would have softened.

When the food arrived, my sister delicately picked at her salad, which looked like an explosion of leafy greens and root vegetables drowning in ranch dressing. The rest of us rolled up our sleeves and tucked into the house specialty. The zesty meat practically fell off the bones.

I struggled to swing our talk to Holly and her

deceased beau, until Max revisited our ride today. Bingo! "Did you speak with Lawrence or Holly after we parted ways? I really felt bad about upsetting her."

"Upsetting her?" Tiny asked.

Max shrugged. "Nah. She'll be fine." He looked to Tiny. "Marni asked what brought her to Crystal River, which reminded her of Phil. Same old, same old. She needs to get over him and move on."

The bench groaned as Tiny shifted in his seat. Frowning, he said, "That's a bit callous. It's only been a year."

I silently seconded his reprimand of my motorcycle man. Maybe Max's true colors began to shine through.

"Yeah, but she hadn't been with him for more than a few months. It's not like they had a life-long relationship. If you ask me, I think she wanted out of Boston so badly she jumped at the first bum to come along," Max said.

Phil appeared at the head of our table with his hands balled into fists. "I beg your pardon, sir. How dare you defame my good name?"

Gloria almost choked on a mouthful of lettuce.

Tiny glared at Max. "You'd know her better than most, but she didn't seem to be faking her affection for the man."

Whoa. This evening unraveled fast from a friendly dinner to a heated discussion. For a couple of buddies, the men didn't agree on the Holly situation.

"Why do you say Max would know her better? She and Lawrence appear...ah...close, but were you and she an item, Max?" I asked.

"Talk your way out of this one, lover boy." Phil sauntered around the table.

My sister shifted her eyes his way then back to Max.

"You didn't tell her?" Tiny had stopped eating.

Max's eyes flashed as he gave an almost imperceptible shake. He sighed before turning to me. "Remember the sister I told you about?"

"Holly's your sister?" I bolted up straight. Score one for my acting performance.

"That's the one," he replied before biting into his food.

Gloria mechanically forked salad into her mouth while swinging her head from speaker to speaker. You'd think she watched a tennis match. For once she kept her comments to herself and let the drama unfold instead of adding to it.

I stuffed the end of a rib into my mouth contemplating how to slow the building tension. After swallowing, I added a casual tone to my voice. "No big deal. Did she come to Crystal River to be near you?"

"Nah. We're not terribly close, despite her riding with Lawrence and me sometimes." Max gestured toward my plate. "How do you like those ribs, Marni?" Not an obvious subject change at all.

Phil leaned closer to the man. "Yet, when I met Holly, she'd been visiting her brother."

It took control not to snap my head in his direction. Phil's presence paid off tonight in helping sort the truth from lies—sort of. Tiny's displeasure about Max's deception added a new wrinkle. How did he figure into all this besides being Max's co-worker? Nothing added up. This evening's fact-finding mission failed royally, which Gloria would point out the moment we stepped outside.

I had more questions for Phil. Standing, I asked, "Where's the—" My head bumped into something hard.

With a yelp, the server carrying the metal tray fell forward launching a huge pile of ribs across the table. Bones and sauce tumbled down the front of Gloria's dress and landed in her lap, on the bench, and on the floor.

Her fork dropped, and her mouth gaped open. With horror, she surveyed the carnage as the white cotton absorbed the red liquid like a sponge.

Tiny's hand flew to his mouth as the waiter apologized profusely.

I laughed so hard I nearly fell backward off the bench. She looked like a victim from a slasher movie. When I caught my breath, I held out the cloth from my lap. "Need a napkin, Glo?"

Her glare set off another fit of hysterics from me, while Tiny attempted to dab at the sauce. This elicited a hand slap from Gloria as she got up and stormed toward the restrooms.

The large man reddened as he watched her leave.

Phil doubled over as his humor matched mine. She probably wouldn't speak to either of us the rest of the evening.

Throughout the fiasco, Max had sat speechless.

"Should I go check on her?" Tiny asked, half rising.

I sprang to my feet. "I got this."

Chapter 25

Gloria stood in front of the mirror wiping her stained dress with a wad of wet paper towels. "Glo, I am so sor—"

She flashed a hand in my face. "Don't say a word!"

My lips clamped shut. This would take serious damage control, possibly lasting several hours. Too bad House of Primp would be closed by now. She needed pampering on a major scale. More than I could offer.

The more she rubbed at the sauce, the farther the stain spread. After ten minutes of watching her work with little success, a knock sounded on the door.

"Ladies, everything okay?" Tiny called.

Leaning against a sink, I lifted my arms and asked, "Well?"

Gloria motioned to the front of her. "Does this look okay to you?"

"We're good, Tiny. Be out shortly." I raised my voice.

After a pause, hesitant footsteps moved away.

I looked to my sister, "What do you—"

"Just get my purse. I'll meet you at the car." She threw the towels in the trash and stomped toward the door.

"Shall I thank the boys for a nice dinner?"

She halted, her back rigid, before yanking the handle so hard it banged against the wall. Without a backward glance, she left.

"Right. I'll tell them dinner is on you," I called.

The only response was the door shutting behind her.

I giggled.

"Marni, your sister is quite angry. Should you really be goading her like that?" Phil materialized beside me. "Remember, you're still among the living—for the moment."

"Maybe I'd hoped to appeal to her playful side." Yes, my evil streak blazed in full force.

Back at the table, Max munched on his dinner while Tiny sat with hands folded. The mess had been cleared away leaving no trace.

"Is Gloria all right?" Tiny asked with a worried frown.

I sat beside Max. "She'll live. Unfortunately, we'll need to call it a night."

"I understand. Please tell her I'm sorry," Tiny said.

"For what? I'm the one who perpetrated that train wreck," I said.

"Well, not for the spill. For trying to help her clean up. I wasn't thinking when I touched her..." Tiny stood. "You know what I mean."

"Honest mistake. You meant well, but I'll convey your apologies. Thanks for a fun night." I gave a thumbs up.

Max leaned over and kissed me on the cheek. More progress. "We should do this again sometime." He snickered. "Tell Gloria I hope she enjoyed herself, before wearing dinner. I'll call you tomorrow."

I held on to what little resolve I had left after being ignored by him most of the night. "We leave in a couple days. I think Gloria is done mingling with the locals. Sorry, guys. Maybe we'll run into you again before we head home. Good night." With a meaningful gaze into my date's eyes, I left. Always leave them wanting more.

Gloria waited by the car, still fuming. Perhaps I should stop for a bottle of wine or two. We only had one at the room. If I couldn't medicate her into civility, I could at least drink it myself and tune her out.

When we returned to our hotel room, Phil lounged on my bed. If he possessed any survival skills, he would steer clear of us tonight. Guess with his already being dead, he didn't have much else to lose.

"Marni, I hope you're done chasing that mad man on the motorcycle. Now, can we get back to solving my death and exonerating Holly of any wrongdoing?" he asked.

Gloria huffed, grabbed her cosmetic bag and pajamas, then stomped into the bathroom slamming the door.

"Phil, let's take the night off. Once she comes out of there, anyone within target distance is fair game—including you. Unless you want her to completely shut down and refuse to help further, you'd better make yourself scarce."

He jumped off the bed and strode to the balcony. "I suppose you're right. Let's reconvene tomorrow morning, shall we?" Phil vanished without waiting for an answer.

With nothing else to do, I flipped open my tablet and typed in "*Sunset Dream.*" When the name of the yacht's owner came up, Herbert Kimpton, I typed his name into the search engine. The other night when I'd discovered his name, I hadn't researched further. The results listed his accomplishments as a prominent businessman and included the loss of his vessel. As I scrolled down the screen, his profile picture appeared with other promotional photos taken around the greater Boston area. My mouth gaped when I came to the final one. The fact he was a dead ringer for the short, bulldog of a man who had joined Lawrence and his wife at Bookends didn't throw me as much as the other man in the picture—Maxwell Dugan. Rounding out the trio in the photo was Lawrence himself. I took a screenshot of the photo along with the caption stating, "Local businessman and his Florida associates find lost treasure from the fifteenth century off the Florida coast." Sounded like the discovery of the *Santiago* wasn't their first rodeo.

The shower turned off, but my sister had yet to make an appearance. Would her anger keep her holed up in there all night? I might be using the facilities in the lobby if she chose to remain locked inside.

I took the opportunity to pop open the bottle of red we'd had sitting on the desk and set out our glasses. This would give me ammo when she finally appeared—provided it wasn't for breakfast.

Several minutes later the door clicked open. Gloria strolled out with her lips in a thin line. "I accept your apology."

One hurdle down. "Merlot?"

"Please."

Two hurdles down. I poured us each one and sat on my bed.

She eased onto her mattress and raised the glass. "To a memorable evening." Her lips quirked into a lopsided smile.

I clinked mine to hers. "We good then?"

"No wonder Timothy couldn't handle life with you anymore." She chuckled. "Your dry-cleaning bill must've been astronomical!"

"I guess I deserved that one. Let's enjoy our last couple of days here in Florida."

"As long as it doesn't involve any more *dates*. Agreed?" She stared me down.

I gulped. "Celibacy is my middle name."

"I believe I packed a chastity belt."

"You come prepared." Now that we'd smoked the peace pipe, I needed to guide her back into the fold of solving Phil's situation. "Let me show you what I discovered from a little research on the owner of the *Sunset Dream*. He's quite popular in the Boston business world and appears to have an eclectic group of associates." I pulled up my screen shot and showed her.

Gloria's jaw dropped as low as mine had. "Well, aren't we cozy with the Florida locals. I don't recognize Mr. Kimpton."

"I do. Remember the angry troll I told you about at Lawrence's and Kate's table in Bookends?"

She pointed. "That's him, isn't it?"

"You're getting good at this!"

Chapter 26

Our vacation dwindled to two more nights before flying home to Long Island. After all the revelations of the previous night's research, I couldn't stay sad at missing out on seeing Max again. Holly's warning might have included more than one individual at our lunchtime soiree.

After a morning of lounging by the pool, I dropped Gloria off at House of Primp for a well-deserved facial. These next steps would be better on my own. Somehow Lulu had been connected to this mess beyond seeing and trying to assist Phil to move on. Without my sister's sporadic outbursts, I might be able to get more information from our favorite barkeep.

Phil rode in the passenger seat. "Where are we off to?"

"I'd expected you earlier this morning. Off frolicking with your favorite manatee?" I asked.

"Rosie says 'Hi,' by the way." He stared at me point blank. "Don't change the subject. Where are you going without your sister?"

I signaled right with my blinker, despite the local population having an aversion to the use of this instrument. When I pulled into the parking lot of Libations, Phil nodded.

"Ah. You believe Lulu may have something else to contribute, don't you?" he asked.

"I'm not sure, but I needed a conversation without Gloria scaring other customers. With you here, at least she's getting a couple of hours off." I removed my seat belt and turned to face him. "Did you know Max and Lawrence were involved with Herbert Kimpton?"

"Who?"

"Herbert Kimpton. He's the owner of the wrecked yacht you found, and according to you, a friend of Holly's. It brings a serious question to mind. Why would ol' Herbie enlist Holly to help him find his sunken boat when brother Max lived here and was a certified diver?"

Phil raised his arms. "Perhaps she'd simply offered to help a friend and used it as an excuse to get to know yours truly. Did you ever consider that?"

"Nope, not at all."

He scrunched his face and huffed.

"Oh, pull back that lower lip. Pouting on a man your age is so not attractive."

"I am *not* pouting, madam." That line would have been more effective had he included a foot stomp. Another opportunity missed.

"Yes, you are. Anyway, from what you told me about the treasure, it's stolen booty. Maybe he wanted to distance Max from the situation. Or maybe Herbie didn't trust Max. There're too many variables."

"I have a question for you. What makes you think Lulu knows anything about this whole mess?" Phil asked.

I narrowed my eyes. "Just a hunch. When she *accidentally* ran into us at lunch yesterday, I watched her and Max through the restaurant window before the rest of us exited. They appeared to argue. It didn't look like two people who barely knew each other, which is what she hinted at."

"I told you not to trust that nosy woman. Now do you believe me? Besides, there's something suspicious about her *gift*, as you call it. While lingering about, after my death, other spirits approached her for help. Her response to them was to ask their name, then tell them to come back in a day or two. I don't know what difference it made, yet she never helped anyone immediately."

Each of us worked differently. This ability to speak with the dead didn't come with any rules. "Maybe she wanted to research who they were. This way she might help them more quickly if it were an easy case."

He snorted. "That may be, but most who returned, that I saw, were turned away. One man, who'd told me he'd lost everything and drank himself to death, she called a penniless pauper and demanded he leave at once."

Okay, maybe there were a couple of guidelines my grandmother had imparted when assisting souls. I was never to use my gift for personal gain. "Do you remember any ghosts she did help?"

He bit his upper lip. "Yes, actually. A middle-aged man who'd died in a jet ski accident. He had wanted his mother to know where he'd placed her diamond engagement ring, which he'd retrieved from his ex-wife. It had been left in a dresser drawer since he'd planned to visit her on the weekend."

"Do you remember his name?"

"Sorry, I didn't pay much attention. Now that I think of it, there had been one other very old chap she agreed to assist."

"Some old man?" I asked. "Another rich guy?"

Phil shook his head. "He wasn't old. The man looked to be in his twenties, but his clothing dated him to be from another century."

I'd never encountered any ghosts earlier than the nineteen-twenties, but it could be possible souls hung around longer if nobody helped them. "Did you speak with this guy?"

He smacked his forehead with his hand. "Good gracious, Marni. That's it!"

"What's it?"

"I had forgotten all about him. Now I remember— the *Santiago*. This young man had been a deckhand when the ship sank near Florida."

Damn. Lulu was a real hustler. "Let me guess. She asked him where the ship went down?"

He shook his head. "No, he wanted to know why she had not returned the treasure to its rightful owner in Spain. He'd given her the location so she could do what he wasn't able to in life when he disguised himself as a deckhand, despite being a son of the family whom the treasure had been stolen from. The young man had planned to steal the treasure back, before the ship sank in a storm. According to what I'd heard, Lulu had promised to fulfill his quest."

"Sounds like she had a quest of her own to fulfill— like her bank account. Guess her plan backfired when the goods ended up at the bottom of the ocean once more on the *Sunset Dream*. Unfortunately, that's where you stumbled upon it. What are the salvage rights on retrieving sunken treasure?"

"The law of 'finders keepers' applies to goods retrieved from a wreck too old for the owners to have a claim. Basically, if they're dead, it belongs to whoever finds it."

"What about the fact the stash had been on the *Sunset Dream*?" I asked.

"Technically, it would belong to this Kimpton fellow, if he could show proof of ownership. I would guess he hadn't acquired it legally. In which case, whoever ended up with the loot could keep it, claiming they'd gotten it from the *Santiago*."

I drummed my fingers on the steering wheel. "That leaves us to connect Lulu to Herbert and his merry band of thieves, which shouldn't be hard given her acquaintance with Max." I started the car and drove out of the parking lot.

"Where are you going? I thought you wanted to interrogate Lulu."

"We're going to the House of Primp. I need to bring Gloria in on this so we can come up with a plan."

"Your sister's at a strip club?"

Chapter 27

"Let me get this straight. You believe Lulu is shaking down lost souls?" Gloria stopped pacing and leaned against the rail of our balcony. "Isn't that against the rules?"

"My thoughts exactly." I lounged in one of the patio chairs crinkling the tin of my soda can. The Florida humidity had closed in, and the breeze off the water cooled us down.

"We should tell somebody."

I chuckled. "And who would that be? The paranormal police?"

"How about the real police? You know, the people who drive around in numbered cars and carry a badge?" She sank into the seat next to me.

"Unfortunately, in our business, we need to figure this out for ourselves. If we go to the police, even if we have proof, which we don't, how would we explain knowing about it?" My sister needed to wrap her mind around not running to the authorities every time we discovered a crime. I had no desire to sit in a jail cell next to real criminals. The last time she'd tried that, it took a friend in the Northport Police Department to get us out of it. I doubt a local cop in New York would have any pull within the Florida penal system.

Gloria paced again. "Do you think Lulu killed Phil?"

I wrinkled my nose. "That might be a stretch. Sounds like she's more into the snatch and grab type of crime than murder."

"I agree with Marni," Phil materialized, leaning against the side wall of the patio. "Lulu may be unsavory, but I don't believe she'd kill anybody." He turned to Gloria. "How was the strip club? Pick up any new moves?"

My sister's eyes bugged wide. "Strip club? What are you talking about?"

"Marni said you'd gone to the House of Pimp. Isn't that…uh…a place of—"

"How dare you insinuate." She glared at Phil, then at me where I sat laughing. "And for your information it's called the House of *Primp*. How do you surmise a beauty parlor could be a house of ill repute?"

Maybe I had a hand in this misunderstanding. When Phil leapt to the wrong conclusion, I didn't exactly correct his misinterpretation.

He stuttered. "But Marni…why didn't you…oh, never mind. It's none of my business how you spend your free time. If you want to learn how to dance around a pole for the bedroom entertainment of your husband, so be it. Who am I to judge?"

"I am not having this conversation. Let me know when you've both crawled out of the gutter." Gloria stormed into the room slamming the sliding door behind her.

"She does get touchy, doesn't she?" he smirked.

"Only when she's accused of practicing pole dancing. Look, we need to find a way to catch Lulu in the act."

He shot me a quizzical eye.

"Not *that* act. I'm talking about her robbing the dead. Can you think of any other souls you'd heard her offer to help after discovering she had something to gain?"

Phil shook his head. "Only the two, but it's not like I hung around her establishment eavesdropping."

I got up and gazed over the river. There had to be a way of getting a confession from Lulu, whether it would be coerced or volunteered. I had my doubts about the latter. "You said she tried to talk to you, but you ignored her. Had you ever attempted speaking with her first?"

"Of course, not! Why on earth would I?"

My hand shot out in a calming motion. "Hear me out before you go off on a tantrum. According to you, Lulu only spoke to souls after they'd contacted her, and she qualified them as a target. Right?"

He nodded.

"So, if you hadn't asked for her help, why would she try interacting with you?" I asked.

"Who knows? Maybe it'd been a slow day at the wine bar, and she needed someone to annoy."

I blew out a breath. "Follow me on this, will you? What if someone tipped her off on you possibly relocating the treasure?"

"If you're about to throw Holly under that bus, you can stomp on the brakes. She would never do such a thing." It was his turn to pace the balcony.

"Look, I'm not saying Holly told Lulu, but we can't rule her out. What if someone else in this small circle of treasure hunters, who knows about Lulu's ability, offered her a cut?"

Gloria leaned in the doorway. "I hate to admit it,

Marni, but you may be right."

"Done sulking?" Phil asked.

She ignored his comment and asked, "Phil, what if you shared the location with Lulu?"

"Why would I tell her? The whole point had been to eliminate the danger for my Holly."

"No, I see where she's going with this." I stood. "You give her a location but not the actual hiding place, which by the way, Gloria, is hidden in a cave by the ocean. How do you feel about exploring dark, dank places?"

Chapter 28

"I am not crawling around any caves. Why can't we tell the authorities where the treasure is hidden? They can return the goods to whoever is entitled to it, and we send Phil on his merry way. With his resolution complete, we'll have one more full day of vacation all to ourselves." Gloria smacked her hands together then spread them out like a blackjack dealer leaving the table.

"Aren't you the clever one, Gloria." Phil bounced on the balls of his feet. "But you've left out one teeny, tiny detail."

Her face went blank. "What could possibly be missing from my brilliant plan?"

"Oh, I don't know," Phil studied his fingernails. "Maybe finding out who murdered me?"

She expelled a breath. "Oh, yeah. I forgot about that. Would it really make a difference? You'd still be dead. Isn't returning the treasure enough?"

"Your compassion is overwhelming, madam. And no, it wouldn't be enough for me."

"He's right, Glo. Our job won't be complete until we find out what really happened to Phil on his last dive," I said. "Now, about retrieving the treasure. We'll need a couple flashlights. Did you bury it?" I looked toward our specter.

"Not exactly," he said. "I found a small cubby

hole, which I covered with rocks."

I smirked. "Then we'll need gloves, so Gloria doesn't chip a nail."

Gloria snorted. "Is no one listening to me? Sometimes I think I'm the ghost. I am not, I repeat, *not* crawling around a cave." She returned to the room. "It's sweltering out here."

I followed, waiting for Phil before closing the sliding door. The air conditioning had been cranked up to stave off the heat. "We have one other decision to make."

"Besides who will go spelunking with you, since it won't be yours truly?" my sister asked.

"You'll be fine. Just pretend you're crawling around Great-Uncle Harry's attic. Remember when we had to clean that place out after he died?" I asked.

She crossed her arms and glared. "That's different!"

"We'll discuss it later." I swatted at the air. "We need to figure out *whom* to give the treasure to. Phil, since you were the last one to retrieve it, isn't it technically yours?"

"Don't we need to turn it over to the state of Florida?" Gloria asked.

"Nope. According to the finder's laws, if a treasure is found on a sunken ship for which there is no claim by the owner, it belongs to whoever discovered it. Since I doubt Herbert Kimpton filed a claim for his stolen booty, it belongs to Phil. At least that's how he explained it to me."

Phil sighed. "You are correct, Marni. While it does me no good now, I'd like it to be split between my sister and Holly."

"If Holly is proven innocent," Gloria chimed in.

He shot her an angry glare. "Which, I am sure will happen."

"Okay, you two, back to your neutral corners." I pointed to opposite sides of the room. Neither moved, but at least they stopped sniping at each other—for the moment.

"I have another question," Gloria said. "If we can't go to the police because we have no logical explanation for how we know everything we do, how do we explain finding the treasure and knowing Phil's wishes? As far as the good residents of Crystal River are concerned, we're tourists who never met a man who died a year ago."

I picked up my phone. "Let's jump off one bridge at a time. First, we need to make sure Phil's memory of the hiding place holds true and nobody else has discovered it." I tapped the screen and searched for local hardware stores. "We need flashlights, gloves, and a small shovel in case the tunnel flooded and washed debris over the hiding spot. You coming with me, Glo?"

"No to all the above. When I agreed to begin helping souls, I didn't sign up to go traipsing about in the muck searching for gold. That's more your realm, Marni." She took her swimsuit from a drawer and walked to the bathroom. "I'll be poolside. Let me know how it all turns out."

Steam fumed from my ears. "You can't just give up now. This is part of the job."

She held her ground like a prize fighter while clearly enunciating her words. "No, it is not. Besides, with the people we've discovered to be involved, do you think it's safe to pursue? Remember, one of us here is dead, and it all circles around a lost treasure from the seventeenth century."

"Thank you for remembering the whole dead part," Phil sneered.

"Look, Marni. You go check out the cave if you like. When you're ready to confront Lulu with whatever you come up with, let me know. Talking is more my specialty." She closed the door.

"Guess it's you and me, Phil." I grabbed my purse and keys. "Let's hit the hardware store."

"You don't need me to shop." He hunched his shoulders and rubbed his hands together. "I believe I'd like to catch a little pool time myself."

I added a whistle and striped referee shirt to my list.

Chapter 29

I searched for directions on my phone and arrived at the store twenty minutes later. Instead of a regular flashlight, I found one that strapped to the head, leaving my hands free. Gloria might not budge on her decision to sit this one out, but I threw two into my basket anyway.

Three aisles over I found leather work gloves and tossed them in along with a trowel.

"Doing a little gardening while you're here?" a male voice sounded behind me.

When I turned around, Max leaned against the shelf holding a coil of steel wire. "No, I'm a failure at horticulture. The last time I tried keeping a plant alive, I found it attempting to pry open the second-floor window and plunge to its death."

He laughed. "What are you doing here?"

"Shopping. You?"

"Emergency motorcycle repair." He held up the wire. "The clutch cable on my bike snapped, but the repair shop can't get me in for a few days. This'll work as a quick fix for now." Max stepped forward and picked up one of the miner's lights from my basket and tilted his head.

I cleared my throat. "Um…it's kind of a joke on Gloria. She's been complaining how the light in our bathroom isn't bright enough to put on her makeup. I thought she might appreciate this." I forced a chuckle.

"Speaking of Gloria, has she recovered from the trauma of last night's dinner attacking her?"

This time my laughter was real. "I don't know if 'recover' quite describes it, but she did accept my apology. Since I woke up this morning without her hands wrapped around my throat, I can only assume she's moved on."

"Hey, Max, did you find..." Lulu rounded the corner. "Oh...hey, Marni. What're you doing here?" Her eyes flashed with anger before her face smoothed into a passive mask.

I might ask the same question, or better yet why was she here with a man she claimed not to know well? "Just a little Christmas shopping. Same with you?"

She wrinkled her brow. "What? Oh, funny. Max needed a ride."

"I didn't know you offered a taxi service. We should've enlisted you the other night at the Crystal Bar when my sister drank herself out of commission."

Lulu glanced at the items I carried. "Nah. I was on my way to Libations for my shift when I found this bum with a broken-down bike."

"Uh-huh." I bit my lower lip. The manure piled higher and higher. Maybe I should have grabbed a pair of fishing waders from aisle six. "Well, nice bumping into you guys. Gotta run!" I spun on my heel and made a beeline for the front register. Guess I wouldn't have to drop hints about finding the treasure.

Back at the hotel, a screaming match ensued from our room. This was getting old. I used my key to open the door and found Gloria fully clothed and about to chuck a pillow at Phil. "You know he can't really feel that don't you, Glo?"

"Yes," she said through gritted teeth, "but it would make *me* feel better."

I put my purchases on the dresser beside my purse, twisted the desk chair around to face the two opponents, and sat. "Do I wanna know what this is about, or can we skip to the part where you kiss and make up?"

Gloria threw the pillow at Phil then pointed. "That gaudily dressed individual had the nerve to tell me I looked bad in my bathing suit."

He sat up straight. "I did not!"

"Did too!"

"Did not!"

My sister reached for another pillow. "Did—"

"All right!" I stood and held my hands up motioning for them to cease and desist. "Enough."

"Marni, all I told her was she might want to consider a red swimsuit instead of orange." He shook his head. "Gloria, that color just isn't in your wheelhouse."

She balled her hands into fists. "I'll show you what's in my wheelhouse."

"Ding ding ding ding." I made a tee with my hands. "This round is over. Phil, she's right. You shouldn't be offering fashion tips to a woman who makes wardrobe shopping an Olympic sport. And, Gloria, why do you care what he thinks?"

"Well…but he…" Exasperation oozed out with every breath. She closed her eyes, and her lips mouthed the numbers from one to ten.

When she finished, I asked, "Better?"

"Much." Her lips remained a straight line, but at least she hadn't picked up any more ammo to lob at the man. Housekeeping had been here earlier, and I didn't want to clean up the mess.

"Good. Now do you want to know who I ran into at the hardware store?"

They both waited quietly.

I told them about Max and Lulu. "It could have been an innocent rescue mission on her part, but I can't know for sure. They both saw the items in my basket and may leap to the conclusion I was about to set off treasure hunting. Maybe this can work in our favor."

"How can this work in our favor?" Gloria waved her hands. "We'd agreed to have Phil spill the beans about a fictitious spot for the treasure. Now they'll believe you and I know the location." She picked up her phone and scrolled.

"What are you doing?" I walked over to look at the screen.

"I'm changing our flight to tonight. Start packing." She touched the airline app.

"Sure, bolt and run when the going gets tough," Phil said.

Without looking up from her phone, Gloria muttered, "You're already dead, Phil. We're not, and I want to keep it that way."

"Glo, put down your cell. We're not going anywhere until we figure this out. Maybe they won't put two and two together, and we can still work the angle of our friendly ghost disclosing the location."

She scooped up the shopping bag and dumped its contents onto the bed. Holding up a head light and small shovel, she scoffed, "No, these are *obviously* souvenirs. They'd never guess you were digging for something in a dark place."

I shrugged. "I did tell them I was Christmas shopping."

Chapter 30

Gloria's phone dinged with an incoming text. "Tiny wants to meet for lunch to make up for our aborted dinner."

I'd give him a ten for persistence. "A cozy lunch for two, or am I included in the invite?"

Her lips grew taut. "I'd rather decline. We've had enough mishaps with locals."

"Think about it, Glo. This might be the perfect opportunity to mention the treasure. He's gotta be in on this given how much time he spends with Max. Will my hunky motorcycle guy be there too?"

She shrugged. "He didn't say. I thought we were letting Phil deliver the news to Lulu. If you or I say anything to the guys, we'd have to tell them about our gift. My vote is no."

When did this become a town meeting? "Look, we've gotta eat, right? We won't say anything to him. Maybe he'll slip up and give us a clue."

"What happened to finishing our trip with you and me on our own? Marni, this is a horrible idea."

"How bad could it be?" I paced our room. "We'll be in a public place. Ask him where and what time he wants to meet."

"You go. I'll grab lunch at the restaurant downstairs." She held out her phone to me.

"It's you he wants to see and make amends. I'm

not the one who walked out wearing a selection of sauces."

"Marni, did your common sense leave the building?" Phil asked.

"Last time I checked, it was intact. Why? Do you want a vote too?" I asked him.

He narrowed his eyes. "Don't you think this invitation is a little coincidental arriving right after you ran into Max and that woman at the hardware store?"

Gloria pointed at him. "Yeah, what he said."

My jaw dropped. Now they're agreeing? This frightened me more than when they argued. "You're only endorsing his idea to get out of meeting Tiny."

"I'm not accepting the invitation anyway, but Phil does have a point."

"Can you repeat that, please? It's not often you give me credit for having a good idea." Phil placed a hand to his chest.

My sister scowled. Any points he'd earned got reset to zero.

"Don't push your luck, Phil. Twenty minutes ago you were at each other's throat. Let's keep this civil." I turned to Gloria. "Okay, you win this round. Thank Tiny for the offer and tell him we've already got plans. Maybe add a smiley face."

"Adults do not use emojis. I'll simply send the message." When she looked down to reply, I tilted my head and crossed my eyes at her. How could I possibly share the same DNA with this woman?

She set her phone down. "Now that nonsense is over, I am hungry. Shall we go downstairs for lunch?"

I grabbed my purse and keys. "I've got a better idea. Let's go. You too, Phil."

"Go where?" she asked.

"We can talk on the way." Without waiting for a response, I was out the door and headed for the car.

When we pulled into the parking lot at Libations, Gloria refused to get out. "This idea is worse than meeting Tiny for lunch. Why can't Phil talk to Lulu by himself? He can go with the angle of our refusing to help him any further, then give a false location for the treasure. When she takes the bait, he can follow her and see who shows up. Easy peasy. Now let's go somewhere else. I'm starving."

I opened my door. "She'll never believe we gave up on him after coming this far. If he just volunteers the information, she'll get suspicious. Remember, she saw me stocking up on search gear."

Phil appeared beside the car as I got out. "I have to agree with Marni on this one. If I show up out of the blue and disclose a location, she won't believe me."

She climbed out and slammed her door shut. "Fine."

We were earlier than most of the lunch crowd, which gave us the perfect opportunity to enact our performance. A few tables on the restaurant side had diners, but the bar area remained empty. Gloria trailed behind me wearing her trademark scowl of disapproval as we claimed our usual stools.

"Be right with you," a female voice called from the back room.

A few moments later an older woman, with dark hair pulled back in a ponytail and breasts practically spilling out of her flimsy tank top, tossed us menus. "What can I get you ladies?"

I blinked. It never occurred to me Lulu wouldn't be

here, especially since she'd mentioned driving to work earlier. Did she and Max decide to go treasure hunting on their own? "We thought Lulu would be working."

The woman grinned. "Sorry, you're stuck with me today. Lulu called out sick. I'm Trudy."

"Well, this certainly has derailed our plan. Now what?" Phil leaned on the bar.

"We'll have lunch," Gloria said.

"Would you like to narrow that down to a selection?" Trudy chuckled.

My sister blushed. "Sorry, just thinking out loud. I'll start with a glass of your raspberry iced tea."

This did throw a wrench in our plans to move forward. We might as well eat and figure things out afterward. "Make that two, Trudy."

"You got it!" She left us to peruse the menu.

"Oh, by all means, let's dilly dally around here while my body continues to molder in the ground with my demise unresolved." Phil perched on the stool next to Gloria.

"It's not like you'll be reanimated when we figure this out." She scanned the lunch options.

I did the same. "There's nothing more we can do right now."

"Fine." He disappeared, then popped back in. "Do enjoy your lunch." With a scowl, he evaporated.

Chapter 31

"I don't know if your lunch invitation was a setup or genuine, but your large friend is dining with Lulu and Max." Phil popped in onto the stool beside Gloria.

"Ahhh!" She jumped off her seat.

Trudy rushed over from the other end of the bar. "What's wrong? Don't tell me you found a cockroach in your food." She gave my sister the side-eye while the other patrons sitting nearby stopped eating to stare.

Gloria remained speechless while bouncing her gaze between Trudy and me.

"For goodness sakes, I'm only kidding." Our bartender slapped the counter.

I covered my mouth to keep from spitting out my burger as I chuckled. "Lighten up, Glo."

"I'm...I'm sorry." She pointed to a dark crumb on the bar. "I thought that was a spider. Didn't mean to startle everyone." Her sheepish grin smoothed over the situation perfectly. At least my sister got better at explaining her outbursts.

Everyone went back to their meal.

Looking directly at Phil, I said, "You need to stop doing that in public places."

He raised his arms and shrugged. "So, you're saying it's okay to scare her when we're alone?"

Without moving her lips, Gloria answered, "Absolutely not."

Phil remained mute while we finished our lunch and paid the tab. Once outside, he picked up where he left off. "The three of them looked quite friendly over at the Seafood Shack. Do you think they thought to lure you in and get information?"

"It's possible Tiny called Max when we turned down his invitation. Since Lulu played hooky today, it could be a harmless meeting," I said. "Were they on motorcycles?"

"No, I told you they were eating. What difference would it make anyway?" he asked.

"If Max and Lulu were out riding, they could have run into Tiny on the road." I chirped the lock on the car and got in. "Hey, since we know our suspects are otherwise occupied, this would be the perfect time to check on your treasure. We can swing by the hotel and get our gear."

Gloria cleared her throat. "You can leave me at the room. I'll dig out my *orange* swimsuit and lie by the pool." She aimed the last comment over her shoulder toward the back seat.

He didn't take the bait and kept any retorts to himself.

I wanted to bang my head against the wheel. Both her adamant protests about not going in the cave and throwing combative barbs at Phil made me want to dump her at the airport instead. This case had been hard enough to solve without having to cater to her whims. "Why don't we compromise? You can change into your bathing suit and sunbathe near the entrance of the cave. This way, I'll have a sentry in case anybody shows up. Deal?"

She bugged her eyes. "Why would anyone show

up? Do you expect an attack?"

"No. I'd prefer to have your help inside but short of dragging you in kicking and screaming, you could at least have my back outside."

With a heavy sigh, she agreed. "I'll need to pack my beach bag and throw some waters in a cooler. Who knows how long you'll be poking around in there?"

After waiting close to forty minutes for Gloria to change and pack what she considered to be necessities, we got back on the road. Taking a herd of toddlers to the beach would have required less gear than my sister brought. Hopefully, the entrance wasn't a long walk from the parking lot. I doubted there'd be a pack mule available for rent.

Phil directed me to the closest parking lot above the location we needed.

"Phil, you neglected to mention this beach is only accessible by boat or rappelling equipment." I peered over the edge composing a compelling argument to get Gloria down there. No words came to me.

"The two of you are quite fit. I believe you can handle the climb." He snickered.

My sister stood beside me scowling at the beach below. "I am not—"

"You don't have to say it! You'll wait by the car."

"Ladies, cannot either of you read?" He pointed to a sign labeled "Cavern Beach Trailhead." "There is a lovely walking path which gradually winds down to the beach."

Gloria shuffled to the sign and scanned the path. "This I can handle." Before she turned away, she pointed at the smaller sign below the first one. "Should we be worried about this?" The sign read, "Danger—

High Tide Can Limit Access."

Phil waved his hand. "Not at all. They're required to post that, but it really doesn't mean anything."

I bit my lip. *Let's hope it didn't mean the tide swallowed the beach when high.* We unloaded our belongings and divided them between us. Somehow, I got stuck carrying the cooler filled with ice and waters. Next time I'd divvy out the load. With Phil in the lead, we wound our way along the hill. It took longer than expected as the trail was a switchback which wove back and forth several times before reaching the bottom.

Sweat dribbled from my hairline as I trudged along shifting my heavy burden from one shoulder to the other. *How much water did she pack?* I wasn't planning on getting stranded for hours, but maybe she had doubts. I'd almost reached the end when my foot skidded out from under me on loose gravel. Down I went on my butt dropping the cooler off to one side where it landed a few feet below the trail on the sand. My bag of cave supplies fell beside me.

"Marni, be careful!" Gloria stepped over me, ran to the cooler, and unzipped it checking the contents. She pulled out and inspected three bottles of nail polish, which were nestled amid the six waters.

I leaned back on my hands, the gritty dirt digging into my palms. "I'm fine, thanks for asking."

"Sorry. I wanted to make sure none of the polish shattered and spilled inside my cooler. This is my favorite one to bring when I travel. It doesn't look like you broke anything." She put everything back inside and zipped it closed.

Under the category of not breaking anything, I checked to make sure all my limbs remained intact. A scrape on my calf bled a little, but other than that I appeared to be fine. Too bad Doc Christopher wasn't around to patch me up like he had my chin. I rubbed the scab now formed over my previous injury.

"Marni, you couldn't wait to get to the beach before taking a rest? The trail head isn't that strenuous of a hike." Phil stood with hands on hips.

"I'm not resting. I fell." I rolled onto my hands and knees to push myself up.

"Did you want a hand?" he asked with a straight face.

I tilted my head and glared.

"Oh, right. You'll have to manage on your own." He turned and continued walking.

As I rose, my sister came over and handed me back the cooler. "Are you sure you want to trust me with that, Glo? I might tumble over a cliff and your precious cargo would risk breaking again."

"You're on flat ground. I think it'll be safe," she said.

I took two steps and stopped. "And why would you bring nail polish to the beach? Besides the fact we just got manicures and pedicures the other day."

"I chipped one of my toenails and wanted to touch it up with matching polish. There'll be plenty of time for it to dry while you're playing in the mud and rocks." She followed Phil across the white sand of the deserted beach.

Thank goodness she'd just had a facial, or she might have packed several beauty products and a mirror. I probably wouldn't have made it all the way down the trail before falling.

We hadn't seen any other cars in the lot on top, and

I was relieved to find the place empty. Even still, with the climb we had ahead of us when we left, whatever Phil had buried in the cave would remain there for now.

Chapter 32

We trekked across the sand to a rock wall on the far side. The place was more like a small cove than an actual beach. Gloria went about setting up her lounging area, which would also double as a spa.

I turned in a circle scanning the beach. "Phil?"

"Yes, Marni." He watched my sister remove her cover-up and tsked. Apparently, he still wasn't sold on her color choice. He'd better withhold comments, or she'd start chucking water bottles at him.

"Correct me if I'm wrong, but didn't we come down here so I could explore a cave?" With the ocean on one side and rock walls or light foliage surrounding the others, there wasn't any place with an opening bigger than a gopher hole.

"It's right there." He pointed at the solid rock.

I raised my hands in the air. "Remember, you're the only one who can walk through walls. Those of us among the living are limited on those skills."

"So you keep reminding me. Wade around those boulders where you'll come to the mouth of the cave. You did bring your swimsuit, didn't you?"

Could this be why the sign at the top warned about tides and danger? "You neglected to mention that minor detail."

He put a hand to his cheek. "Did I? Guess I always approached from the ocean and didn't think about getting in there from the beach."

I bent to remove my sneakers.

"You'll want to leave those on, Marni. Some of the rocks are sharp, and you wouldn't want to cut your foot. You've achieved enough injuries this trip." He laughed at his own joke.

And I wouldn't want to attract sharks with my blood. "How deep is the water?"

"Do I look like an oceanographer? I told you I arrive by boat and don't concern myself with the depth."

Using my phone, I searched for the tide schedule. "According to this, high tide isn't for another three hours."

He soundlessly clapped his hands together. "Well then, you should be able to wade in and out before having to swim for it."

Walking to the water's edge, I searched for an easy way around the rocks. From this vantage, I couldn't see the cave's opening. How far was it? "I'm not so sure about this, Phil. You made it sound like the cave was accessible from dry land. We might want to rent a boat before I go out there."

Sitting on a boulder, he crossed his legs with hands sitting atop his knees. "Oh, don't be such a wuss about getting your feet a little wet."

"A little wet?" My voice escalated. "How do I know there's not a huge drop-off just beyond those boulders?"

"Now who's the drama queen?" Gloria said, studying her nails. "I've got an extra towel you can use when you get back. If you keep whining about the situation, which you thought was a grand idea, the tide will be in, and you'll get stuck."

From Phil's smug look, I could tell backing out now wouldn't be an option. I handed Gloria my phone, strapped the light to my head, and carried the trowel and gloves in the plastic grocery bag they came in. "Fine. I'm going."

"Great," Gloria called. "I'll wait here, ready to dial the Coast Guard if you don't return."

"Swell." I trod to the water's edge. Looking back at my sister, I called, "If I'm not back in an hour, come find me." Or at least send out a search party for my body.

"I'll send Phil in to check on you."

We both looked Phil's way, but the rock where he'd sat was empty. *He'd better be waiting inside the cave, or this would be a very short exploration.*

Gingerly, I stepped into the ocean as my shoes filled with water. *Well, isn't that a pleasant sensation? If I'd known what I'd be in for, I would have worn my water shoes. It'll take two days for these to dry out.* I glanced back at Gloria for moral support, only to find her concentration focused on polishing her toenails. *Thanks for the concern, Sis.*

As I moved through the water, it remained ankle deep. Working my way around the boulders, the ground beneath me gave out, and I splashed below the surface landing on my backside. After a second of panic, I pushed off the rocky bottom. It didn't take long to surface, and I sputtered salt water from my mouth. Standing up, I found it only reached my waist. *Did I really need to take a dunking to discover this?*

Once I'd rounded the bend and a few more large rocks, the mouth of a large cavern gaped before me.

About ten feet inside, the sunlight dimmed, and I couldn't see beyond. *My headlight better be waterproof, or this exploration wouldn't achieve lift off.*

Right now, the entrance sat about two feet above the water line. My shoes squished with each step as I trudged onto shore. Inside the cave, dried seaweed crunched beneath my feet, while the stench of dead fish assaulted my nostrils.

Phil appeared beside me. "It's low tide. Why are you all wet?"

"It's such a lovely day I thought I'd go for a swim first." I yanked the light off my head and squeezed the water out of the elastic band. "By the way, thanks for introducing me to this lovely smell. What's it called? Eau de Fish Heads?"

"Sorry, my olfactory no longer functions." He tapped his nose before walking deeper into the darkness.

"Lucky you." With a press of the button, the light remained off. I banged my palm against the flashlight, which flickered before staying on. "Wait for me," I called, while slipping the band around my head and aiming the beam straight ahead.

The uneven ground wasn't ideal for stumbling around in the dark. The pathway curved to the left, and I could no longer see Phil. "Where'd you go?" As I came around the bend, the walls narrowed on both sides before opening into a large cavern. My light didn't go far enough to see the ceiling.

I turned my head to the left and screamed. A scruffy, young man, dressed in the ragged remains of a tunic and pantaloons, stood nose to nose with me.

Chapter 33

"Are you trying to wake the dead?" Phil materialized.

I staggered back two steps. My vocal cords struggled to utter a noise. After several deep breaths, I tried again. "I...I believe I already have."

"Why are you with this woman? Is she another treacherous whore who wants to steal my family's gold?" The young man balled his fists and anchored his feet in a battle stance.

I'd been called many things, and most times deserved the insult, but never a whore. Guess I could add it to the list. My hands raised in a defensive move. "Calm down, sir. I'm not here to steal anything."

"Yes, young man, you really need to contain your temper. Believe it or not, this woman is here to help. I know she looks a bit worn and bedraggled, but she is not a swindler. I promise."

"Thanks for the glowing endorsement." Usually, the sudden appearance of a spirit didn't faze me. However, tromping around in a poorly lit cave not knowing what to expect throws a wrench in the whole calm acceptance scenario.

"What's your name?" I asked.

With his nose stuck in the air, he said, "I am Felipe Velazquez." He swept an arm out and bowed. It would have been more effective had he worn a cape and a sword.

Besides the tattered pants, which stopped at the knees, he wore a loose, beige tunic, and nothing on his feet. His scraggly beard and unkempt hair added to his boyish charm. He couldn't have been more than twenty-five.

"Were you aboard the *Santiago* when it sank?"

He glanced at Phil, who nodded. "Yes. When the captain stole from my family's house in Spain, my father secretly arranged for me to be one of the crew on the ship. My quest had been to secure our fortune and return with it. Before that could happen, a great storm swept our ship to the bottom of the sea."

This young man must've told Lulu where the *Santiago* sank, thinking she would do as he asked. No wonder he didn't trust me.

"Your English is very good. I hardly detect an accent." From his garb I couldn't discount who he claimed to be, but his grasp of our language surprised me.

Felipe relaxed his shoulders. "I have been here many, many years. There has not been much else for me to do but talk with passing spirits and listen to the living. Almost all speak English in this land."

While his death had been tragic, it wasn't a mystery. His resolution wouldn't be so easy given his family died three centuries ago. "Since you recognize time has gone by, then you know how you died. Why haven't you asked for help before?"

"It has been many years since I found a living person who could see and hear me. Unfortunately, those before were unwilling to help. Then I found the horrible woman who promised to retrieve the gold and return it to my family. Except she did not return it to Spain."

The soggy band around my head slipped down my forehead shifting the beam toward the ground. I removed it and wrung more water out before replacing the light. "My name is Marni Legend. I can't promise to return the treasure to your descendants, since the family you left behind are long dead I'm afraid, but I'll do my best not to have it fall into the hands of the woman who betrayed you."

"Thank you for your honesty, Marni Legend." He glanced at Phil. "I remember you to be the man who buried the treasure in this cave. You could not hear me then."

Phil shook his head. "Yes, at the time I still breathed. I didn't have the gift to see dead people like our lady-friend here."

"Why did you take my treasure?" Felipe asked. "Was it your intent to return it to my people...ah...I do not know your name, sir."

"Call me Phil. And no, I didn't know what to do with the treasure. All I know is the sunken yacht where it had been moved to put a dear friend of mine in danger, and I thought if I took the goods, she'd be safe. Turns out it was myself who wasn't safe." He shrugged.

"What will you do now, Marni Legend?" the young man asked.

Good question. Now there were two souls to help into the great beyond. Gloria would be thrilled. "It's just Marni. First, Phil will show me where he buried the gold, so I can make sure it's still there. Next, we'll set a trap for the people we believe murdered him."

Felipe's hand flew to cover his heart. "My God! You were murdered? I am very sorry to hear that, Sir

Phil. How do you not know by whose hand the deed had been committed?"

"Marni, I believe your expertise is required." Phil gestured to me.

At this rate, I'd never make it out of the cave before high tide. "Short version, when a person dies violently, his spirit doesn't always remember what happened. It takes someone like me to help him sort it out. Okay, Ghostbusting 101 has ended, and we need to get moving. You're welcome to tag along, Felipe, but my time is short if I want to avoid swimming for shore." I turned toward the open cavern. "Phil, lead on."

"Why would you be breaking ghosts?" Felipe trailed behind.

How do I explain twenty-first century sarcasm to a seventeenth century ghost? I didn't have time for that now. "Never mind, Felipe. You'll catch on if you hang around me long enough. Phil, slow down. Remember, I actually have to tread on the ground."

Chapter 34

The light beam bobbed with every step I took through the cavern. We walked across the huge expanse and turned right into another tunnel. "Phil, how much farther is it?

"Not very. We're almost there." Because he drifted rather than walked, he moved faster.

I quickened my pace and tripped on a rock. My hand shot out to steady myself against the side of the cave, except I grasped nothing but air. Visions of plunging down a crevasse to a rocky death flashed through my head. Before I visualized myself splattered at the bottom, my knees connected with the ground. When I turned my head to what I thought would be a dark abyss, I found the tunnel had simply widened by a few feet.

With a sigh of relief, I pushed my hands against the ground and stood.

"You certainly pick the oddest places to stop for a rest." Phil silently tapped his foot.

"Sir Phil, the lady had fallen. I reached to help, yet my hands went through her body." Felipe's face scrunched.

A smug grin spread across Phil's lips. "Marni, perhaps from now on you can call me—"

"You can forget that 'Sir Phil' crap. I am not addressing you with a title unless it's one of *my* choosing." Like smart ass or butt head.

"I suppose our young friend hasn't quite grasped all the nuances of our language. After all, he referred to you as a lady."

I glared at Phil, which he probably missed with the bright light shining from my forehead. "Perhaps you should teach him a few synonyms for the word whore. While you're at it, instruct him on the use of jackass in reference to you."

"You're beginning to get as sensitive as your sister. Perhaps I should check on her while you take a few moments to cool down."

"Don't you dare leave me here alone." I brushed the dirt from my knees.

"I'm sure our gallant young man will keep you company. Won't you Felipe?" Phil asked.

The Spaniard flitted his eyes from Phil to me and back again. We probably confused the hell out of him. I'd suggest he go check on Gloria, except it'd be more fun to witness her first exchange with Felipe rather than speculate. I chuckled to myself. Even under stress I had the ability to torment my older sister.

"What are you laughing at?" Phil asked. "A moment ago, you were ready to read me the riot act for leaving you alone in a dark, scary cave." His fingers and voice wavered.

I huffed. "Private joke. Can we get on with this expedition already? I think I hear waves lapping at the receding shoreline."

He tilted his head as if listening. "You're imagining things."

"I will remain here with you, Marni." Felipe finally found his voice.

Great, I'd have company as the waterline rose, blocking my exit. Maybe he could serenade me with a Spanish lullaby while I drifted beneath the water.

"No need, Felipe." Phil looked to me. "Marni, we're here."

Scanning the walls with my flashlight, I failed to find anything looking like a hiding place.

Phil pointed to where I'd fallen. "You practically tripped over the stash."

I moved in closer to examine a pile of rocks forming a small mound where the floor met the wall. The stack didn't look naturally formed. Reaching into my grocery bag, I retrieved my soggy garden gloves and pulled them on.

"I thought you bought those for Gloria?" Phil watched over my shoulder.

Ignoring him, I pulled at the rocks on top. They moved easily—definitely not put there by Mother Nature.

My two specters watched as I removed the pile.

"Can't you go any faster?"

"Phil, I'm a writer not a laborer. I don't even garden, so, no, I can't go faster. Some of these things are heavy." I grunted as I reached for the stones on the bottom. "Did you haul these last ones in with a crane?"

Felipe fidgeted beside the pile. "I wish I could help you, Marni. My muscles are strong."

"I appreciate the sentiment. My muscles are weak, and I'll probably need a nap when we're finished."

"Oh, stop whining. They aren't that heavy. Remember, I'm the one who put them there to begin with, and nobody could ever accuse me of being a body builder."

Dragging the last one out of the way, I expected shiny, gold coins to be reflecting the light. Instead, a layer of dirt covered the spot. I plopped down with my arms resting on my knees. "Is this your idea of a joke?" I looked over my shoulder at Phil.

He straightened and took a step back with his hand rubbing his chin. "I could've sworn that was the place. I wonder if we took a wrong turn."

"You have lost my family's treasure? Sir Phil, how could you do such a thing?" Felipe paced back and forth. "Now I shall never be at peace."

That would make two of us if I couldn't finish up with Phil and send him on his way. Felipe would have the good manners to leave me alone. This badly dressed Floridian would haunt me until the end of time.

Chapter 35

Phil pointed at the ground closer to the wall. "Marni, what's that sticking out of the dirt?"

I yanked the light off my head and aimed the beam at the spot. Something protruded from the floor ever so slightly. Brushing dirt away, I exposed a piece of heavy canvas. With the light back on my head, I used the trowel to dig around and uncovered a strap. After further digging, the strap was attached to a bag. "I guess after a year of sitting in this cave, the ground settled covering your stash."

With a smug grin, Phil said, "I told you I remembered where I'd left the treasure. That's the satchel I transferred it to after retrieving the case from the *Sunset Dream*."

Wiping all the soil away, I pulled open the zipper. Inside, darkened coins filled the bag like a pot of gold at the end of the rainbow. The lack of shine disappointed me, but I should have expected them to look dull and dirty after sitting in the ocean for so long. I scooped one up for closer examination. I was no expert, but they certainly looked like Spanish doubloons to me. From the pile inside, there'd be no way I'd be dragging the satchel out without help.

"My family's wealth. *Gracias, Dios.* What will you do with it now?" Felipe pressed his hands together.

I zipped the bag closed and stood with hands on

my hips. "Nothing for now. I'll cover it back up and work on the next step of our plan setting up Lulu, Max, and whoever else was involved."

"You would leave it here?" Felipe's voice rose. "What if someone should find it?"

"Felipe, this stuff has been buried for over a year. If no one found its hiding place by now, I'd say your family's fortune will be safe a little longer." I scooped the loose dirt over the canvas. "I've got an idea though." I took the three largest stones in the pile and set them on top of the treasure. They covered the loose dirt completely. Unless someone examined it closely, you'd never know the area had been disturbed. With the rest of the rocks, I made a stack beside the opposite wall and closer to the large cavern. By the time I'd finished, sweat dribbled down my cheeks and my arms ached from the exertion.

Phil nodded his approval. "Good thinking. Now all we need do is lure Lulu and her cohorts to the fake spot, then nab them."

"That's the idea. Let's get out of here before I'm trapped by the tide." I took off toward the cavern at a faster pace this time. Almost two hours had passed. Gloria would be frantic by now since I'd told her it would only take an hour. I might be greeted by a patrol boat at the entrance.

I jogged across the wide, open space and came to a halt. Two tunnels opened off this side. I hadn't noticed the second one when we came through here the first time. Felipe had made his appearance the moment I'd emerged, which distracted me from looking around.

"Phil, which way…"

He wasn't behind me. I spun in a circle flashing the

light around. "Phil? A little help please."

Silence surrounded me. "Felipe? Are you still here?"

Great. When I actually needed my ghostly companions, they decided to take a powder. I looked from one opening to the other. Yes, I had a fifty-fifty chance of picking the right one, but how much time would I waste if I chose wrong?

Shining the light into the left tunnel, I couldn't see very far before it curved to the left. With a glance into the right, my beam carried farther as this one went straight. My flashlight flickered and dimmed. *Why didn't I think to bring extra batteries? Oh yeah, because I expected this trek to be a quick in and out trip.*

Crossing my fingers, I went into the opening on the right. About ten feet in, my light grew dimmer and went out. Darkness closed in, and my hand shot out to the wall. At least this time I felt the solid rock and as a bonus, water wasn't swirling around my ankles. My progress went slowly, as I didn't want a repeat of tumbling to my knees, which still smarted from the first fall. The pathway angled up, which I didn't remember when I came in, but without any light, turning around wasn't an option. If I got lost and died in here, I'd nag Phil through eternity. No way would I go to my sister so she could utter, "I told you so" while refusing to help my sorry ass. My brother might be more sympathetic. At least he'd only have to listen to me since his abilities were limited to hearing spirits and not seeing them.

While I cussed *Sir Phil* under my breath, I inched along the corridor. After ten minutes of rubbing my hand along the wall, praying I wouldn't find any spiders or other crawling creatures, a faint light cut through the inky blackness ahead. Fresh air seeped into my nostrils, and I breathed deeply. My steps grew confident as I moved faster toward the sound of crashing waves.

When I rounded the last bend, I came to a dead stop. Instead of the boulders I'd been forced to skirt around, the opening filled with blue sky. Approaching the mouth of the cave, I looked down and to the left. The tunnel from which I'd originally entered this maze sat roughly twenty feet below. The gap between ocean and cave had not only been eliminated, but sea water flowed into the entrance I should have crawled out of.

Before doing a happy dance at having saved myself from the flooded tunnel, reality set in. *How would I get down from here?*

Chapter 36

Directly below my exit, a sheer rock wall dropped to the ocean. I definitely wouldn't be going that way. Even if I survived the jump into the water, I had no idea how deep it went and if there were rocks waiting to pierce my body to shreds below the surface.

Since no rescue boat floated near the cave below, Gloria hadn't panicked yet and called for help. Her nails were probably still wet.

Not a huge fan of heights, I clung to the edge of the cave and leaned out far enough to see on either side. To my left shrubs and brush poked out from the soil, but it sloped too steeply to get out that way. The right side looked more promising.

The ledge I stood on wrapped around the hill and extended out about three feet in width. It connected to a steep, but walkable trail. This must be how people explored these caves without getting their feet wet. It would have been nice if Phil had filled me in on the alternative entrance.

Above the opening, pitons stuck out of the rock at strategic locations. *This area must be popular with rock climbers as well.* I preferred solid ground rather than dangling by a thread off a cliffside.

I peered straight down at the crashing surf below. With a gulp, I pressed my back against the wall and sidled along the protruding shelf. Sharp edges poked at my skin through the fabric of my shirt, but that was preferrable to slipping off into thin air. Pebbles crunched beneath my shuffling feet.

To my relief, I approached the dirt path, which widened slightly, but more importantly had land and foliage on either side. A two-foot gap lay between me and safety—piece of cake.

As I stepped from the ledge, Phil appeared before me. I gasped, and my damp sneaker skidded out from under me while my other foot remained on the stone walkway. With my arms flailing, I dropped the bag with the gloves and shovel and caught hold of the nearest bush. My back foot slipped into the gap, threatening to drag the rest of my body with it. The roots of the branches I held loosened from the dry soil. Muscles in my shoulders and arms screamed from the abuse I'd already heaped on them earlier in the cave. Panic set in as adrenaline coursed through my veins. With the last of my strength, I heaved myself forward, propelling my body through Phil, and onto solid ground.

The wind got knocked out of me, but at least I wasn't plunging toward the rocks below. My forehead rested on the dirt with my eyes closed.

"I wondered where you'd wandered off to. Had I known your aversion to getting wet, I would have suggested you go in this way."

"If you weren't already dead, I'd be going for your jugular right now," I threatened through gritted teeth as I rolled over to a sitting position.

He clucked his tongue. "No need for violence, Marni. You appear quite safe."

If only I possessed the laser-beam glare Gloria

could achieve. He'd feel the heat as I bored a hole through his chest.

"Are you going to sit around all day? I believe your sister is ready to go. She acted quite impatient when I popped out to check on her."

"You abandoned me in a dark cave with no flashlight or directions to check on my sister as she sunbathed?" I stood.

Stepping away from me, he asked, "What do you mean 'no flashlight'? It's on your head."

I ripped the band off and held it out. "The batteries died. And why didn't you tell me about this other entrance?"

He set off down the trail. "Because your sister wanted to sunbathe. She couldn't have done that from up here."

With a glance back at the location of my near-death experience, I shivered at the thought of not reaching the bush. There had to be a safer hobby I could take up like sky diving or shark wrangling. Perhaps the treasure from the *Santiago* was cursed since nobody seemed to be able to either hold onto it or remain alive.

The trail zig-zagged up the hill until it ended at the other side of the parking lot. It would have been great had Gloria thought to pack everything up and haul it to the car. No such luck. Ours remained the only vehicle, and my sister wasn't waiting for me there. A cold bottle of water would have been welcome right now, but they were in the cooler at the bottom of this hill.

My shoulders sagged at having to trek down and back up again, but I had no choice. Without my phone, I couldn't message Gloria to come up or even meet halfway. I would send Phil, except he inconveniently disappeared again. Resigned to another jaunt down the switchback, I trudged along until reaching bottom.

"Please tell me you didn't drink all the water?" I struggled to catch my breath.

Without a word, my sister pulled a bottle out and handed it to me.

I held the icy plastic against my cheek before cracking it open and taking a long drink. "Thanks."

"It's about time you showed up. I thought about calling for help but didn't want to cause a fuss," she said. "Why were you coming from the parking lot? I thought the cave entrance came out there." She pointed to where I'd gone into the water, except the tide had moved in so high it covered most of the smaller rocks I'd waded past.

To think my drowning might cause a stir with the local search and rescue team. So considerate of her not to disturb them. "I wanted to give you enough time for your nail polish to dry. Ready to go?" I chugged the rest of the water and put the empty bottle back into the cooler.

Gloria gathered her things and stuffed them into her beach bag. "Yes. I need a restroom. I've been holding it for the last half an hour."

I pointed at the ocean.

"Oh, that's disgusting." She wrinkled her nose.

"Just giving you options, Sis."

She handed me her bag, which weighed a ton. "It's only fair I carry the cooler this time." Slinging it over her shoulder, she walked toward the trailhead.

Of course. We wouldn't want to risk my dumping her polish bottles on the trail again.

Chapter 37

Gloria practically sprinted to the top, ignoring my labored pace. I'd be renewing my gym membership when I got home.

Her screech echoed across the bay.

When I reached the top, Phil comforted Felipe while my sister picked up the cooler she'd dropped. At least it stayed closed with her polish safely inside.

As I approached, Gloria aimed her fury at me. "Why didn't you tell me we'd picked up another spirit? You took so long to catch up, I thought I was about to become a victim of a mugging with no help in sight."

I set her beach bag on the ground. "I see you've met Felipe."

"Met him? He's as creepy as Phil with his popping in without notice. Marni, I'm washing my hands of this mess. Phil, Felipe, have a nice death." She yanked on the car door, which hadn't been unlocked yet. "Arghh!" Flipping her hand over, she examined her nails for damage.

"I am sorry, Marni Legend. Sir Phil told me to introduce myself." Felipe kept his distance from my sister.

She spun to face them. "*Sir Phil?* When did you become royalty?"

He chuckled. "This young man is the only one here who acknowledges my proper status."

I chirped the car remote.

Gloria threw her stuff into the back, got into the passenger seat, and slammed the door.

"What did I do wrong?" the young man asked.

Wagging my finger, I said, "You did that on purpose, Phil."

He gave a sheepish grin. "Did what?"

"Felipe, your only error was to trust this old bugger. He gets off on tormenting my sister whenever he can, despite still asking for our help." I removed the light I'd forgotten still rode on my head and chucked it into the car before getting behind the wheel.

Both ghosts appeared in the back seat.

Confusion covered Felipe's face. "What did Sir Phil get off of?"

Gloria's head whipped around. "Why are they in our car? And who is this other guy?"

"Okay, boys. Time for you to give my sister and me some alone time. Gloria, I'll explain everything on the way back to the hotel." I started the ignition then looked into the rearview mirror before backing up. "I still see you."

"Come on, Felipe. Apparently, our hosts are being rude and kicking us out." Phil placed a hand on the other man's shoulder. They disappeared.

She sighed. "Thank goodness! Marni, is this how your whole life has been?"

"Not all the time. Well, most of the time. At least I've only been shot at once, but today I got to add hanging off a cliff."

"What?" She braced her hands against the dashboard.

With a shrug, I said, "Never mind."

After driving a quarter mile on the main road, I caught sight of a black motorcycle coming from the same turnoff we'd used. It went in the opposite direction. A braid of red hair waved below the shoulders of the passenger. From what I remembered of the map as we drove to the cave, that road didn't lead anywhere else. There must've been a second place to park not listed and possibly another secluded beach—if sunbathing was the pair's objective. The roar of the engine dulled as the bike grew smaller in my rearview mirror.

For the rest of the drive, I filled my sister in on finding the treasure as well as another tunnel leading out. I omitted anything incriminating, like being left in the dark without directions to the entrance. My explanation about Felipe's appearance didn't go over well, but he did play a part in all of this. Had he not gone to Lulu in the first place, the treasure would still be with the *Santiago*, and Phil would be alive, leaving our girls' trip to be spook free.

"How do you expect to catch Lulu now that you know the treasure exists? I still don't know why you needed to verify where Phil left it anyway?" she asked.

"I believe part of his resolution to move on involves getting the gold to the right people. Solving his murder is only part of why he's still here."

The second I parked the car, Gloria bolted for the room, fumbling with her key. I gathered our stuff from the back and hauled it up the stairs.

When I entered, she came out of the bathroom. "I could have stopped somewhere if you had told me it was an emergency."

"Where, a gas station? Those places are usually

filthy." She took a soda from the mini fridge and offered me one.

I gestured to the sliding glass doors. "Let's relax on the balcony while I tell you my plan."

"You mean the plan where Phil leads Lulu on a wild goose chase while getting her to confess to his murder?"

"That's the one. Except you're not going to like it."

Chapter 38

I walked into Libations with Phil at my side. A quick phone call earlier got me the information from Trudy that Lulu would be filling in for a couple hours between shifts. Perfect timing for my plan.

Lulu looked up from where she tended bar. "Hey, Marni. You and Gloria here for a late lunch?"

"Just me this afternoon. We decided to take a break from sister bonding, so she's eating at the hotel. I needed to get away." My usual stool was available.

She tossed a coaster in front of me. "You two had an argument, didn't you?"

"I'll say," Phil sat on the bar. "It was like having a ringside seat to the fight of the century." He swung his fists through the air ending with a one-two punch.

"Thanks for the assist, Phil, but I got this," I whispered. The place didn't have a ton of patrons, but there were enough within earshot.

"Glass of cab?" Lulu asked.

Placing my arms on the bar, I leaned closer. "This wasn't our usual sibling tiff. I'm gonna need something stronger. Do you have any double IPAs?"

She reached for a frosty pint glass. "I got you covered."

"Uh-uh. Go big." I nodded toward the thirty-two-ounce mug.

The bartender hesitated. "You sure? The double

packs a real punch. Remember how well your sister handled it at the Crystal Bar."

"She's a lightweight. Besides, I don't intend on following it up with tequila shots." I laughed at the memory of Tiny carrying my sister back to the hotel over his shoulder. Definitely a classic.

Lulu pulled the tap and filled the mug to the rim, allowing only a thin line of foam at the top. Quietly, she asked, "Did Gloria kick you out too, Phil?"

"Let's just say she didn't invite me to stay. I thought it safest to stick with Marni," he said. "Besides, I have unfinished business she needs to attend to since Gloria refused to assist me any further." He glanced my way.

"Oh?" She shifted her eyes back and forth before centering on Phil. "Do tell."

He stiffened his back. "Madam, this is between me and her." He pointed a thumb in my direction.

"Well, excuse me for trying to help." Lulu set a menu in front of me. "Let me know when you're ready to order." She walked to the other side of the bar where a man twirled his empty wine glass.

I sipped my beer and read the menu. Wow. For being high in alcohol, this IPA went down a little too smoothly. "Nice play, Phil," I muttered quietly.

"I have my moments." His smug grin told me he enjoyed toying with our target.

"Just don't go overboard, or we'll lose her." I took another long draught.

He hopped off the bar. "And you be careful with the drinking. You're only to give the *illusion* of being too tipsy to drive."

I ignored his nagging. As casually as I could, I

glanced over the edge of the bar and found a sink to the left and within reach. "Go distract her."

With a slow gait, he sauntered around to where Lulu chatted with a customer. He walked behind the customer, forcing Lulu to look at him.

The two seats beside me were empty and the other diners focused on their drinks and food. I quickly dumped over half of my beverage down the sink. If anyone noticed, they didn't react. I nodded at Phil, who returned immediately.

Lulu tracked him as she walked back to me. She eyed my glass before asking, "You decide on dinner?"

I ordered food and another thirty-two-ouncer.

"You might want to wait for something in your stomach. Those are pretty high in alcohol," she said.

"Don't worry about me. Go ahead and pour it because this one won't last much longer."

Reluctantly, she picked up an icy glass and filled it. Tossing down another coaster, she set the IPA in front of me before going to the kitchen to put in my order.

The second she left I gave a quick glance around then poured the remainder of my first into the sink. When I turned, a man sitting a couple stools down stared at me. "It had a fly in it." I shrugged.

He gave a half-hearted smile and returned to his conversation with the woman beside him.

When the same man turned at the opening of the front door, I sloshed a third of my new beer down the drain as well. Just as I pulled the glass back, Lulu walked into the bar, so I lifted the mug to my lips. "This is really tasty. I see how Gloria easily chugged it."

Lulu knit her brows. "Your burger will be up shortly. Wanna talk about what happened between you and your sister?"

The plan had been for Phil to disclose the fake location of the treasure, but Lulu handed me the perfect opening. I looked left then right before saying, "Well, Phil gave us some info about where to find some kind of buried treasure. It sounded off to me, like he hadn't reclaimed his full memory, but I wanted to check it out. Gloria refused to help and has washed her hands of anything further to do with Phil."

She leaned in closer looking from me to Phil. "What kind of treasure?"

I took another fake sip of my IPA. Drawing my hand across my mouth, I wiped the foam tickling my upper lip. "Well—"

"Marni! I told you the location in confidence." Phil soundlessly slapped the bar.

"Phil, I can't do this alone. If Gloria won't help me, why not let Lulu in on it so we can do the right thing and send you on your merry way?"

He gave me the side eye.

"My responsibility to the dead is the same as Marni and Gloria. I've been given this gift to help lost souls. Let me help make this right for you, Phil." Lulu's voice cracked. *No anticipation there.*

Phil shifted from foot to foot. "I don't know if I'm comfortable with this, Marni. You and I have developed a rapport, as strained as it has been at times."

I leaned against my seat back. "It's your call. Excuse me." Rising off my stool, I intentionally tripped and grabbed the edge of the bar for support. Righting myself, I shuffled to the restrooms inside the main dining room.

When I returned, my food sat at my place next to a

refilled glass. My friendly specter had disappeared.

"I topped you off, Marni." The bartender indicated my drink. "Look, on second thought, maybe you should heed your sister's warning. You leave the day after tomorrow and this local stuff should be left behind."

"Where'd Phil go?" I asked.

"Don't know. Look, enjoy your food and beverage, then I'll drive you back to the hotel. I'm only covering for a couple of hours, and the shift is almost done. We can arrange to get your car later."

I didn't know what Phil had told her, but it sounded like she'd taken the bait and tried to cut me loose. The question remained, would I be delivered to our hotel or over the edge of a cliff. *Maybe I hadn't thought this plan through completely.*

Chapter 39

I finished my burger while taking conservative sips of the beer. When Lulu got busy with other customers, I looked around. Drat! Hal sat at his usual spot, toasting me with his wine. With Gloria absent, he must've felt safe enough to venture inside.

Forced to drink my beverage rather than dump it, I looked for an alternative. Channeling my inner klutz, I reached for a napkin from the stack behind the bar and knocked over my glass. "Oh, damn! Sorry, Lu…lu." A fake stammer reinforced my sloppy drunk façade.

She rushed over with a rag. "No worries, Marni. I probably shouldn't have given you more." As she mopped up the liquid, a puddle seeped toward me.

Luckily, the edge of the bar had a raised finish which halted the beer before it drenched my lap. Despite Gloria knowing about our plan, I didn't need to arrive reeking like a brewery—that is, if Lulu delivered me to the hotel as promised.

I dug out my credit card and handed it to her. "Jus' run it."

She returned a few minutes later with the bill and my card. I gave her a generous tip, scrawled my name, and shoved it across the surface.

The door behind me opened and the barkeep smiled. "Just in time, like a knight in shining armor."

I turned and found Max grinning at me.

"I hear somebody needs a ride." He approached and kissed me on the cheek.

"Hel...hello." I scrunched my face as I turned to Lulu. "I thought you—"

"The night barkeep called off. Seems to be going around." She smirked. "Anyway, I need to work the dinner shift, so I called Max to play taxi service for you. Hope you don't mind."

I forced a laugh. "Why would I? Wanna join me for a drink?"

Max leaned on the stool beside me. "Maybe next time. Let's get you back to the hotel." He grasped my arm and helped me to my feet.

His touch sent a tingling sensation throughout my body that I couldn't deny. Despite my doubts about which side of the law he resided, I still wanted to drag him into the nearest dark corner for a little one-on-one time. Taking a step, I leaned hard into him.

He wrapped an arm around my waist and half walked half dragged me to the exit. "Steady there. I don't want a detour to the ER."

"I'm fine, Max. I don't know why Lala is making such a fuss over my having a couple beers."

Max glanced over his shoulder toward the bartender. "Yeah, *Lala*, I don't know why you're making such a fuss."

She burst out laughing. "Me neither. All the same, since you're here, you should escort our tipsy friend home."

He looked down at me. "Guess I have my orders, Marni. You're stuck with me. Shall we?" With his free hand he motioned to the front door.

I bobbed my head and staggered forward.

Once outside, Phil joined us. "As you told me earlier, don't over play your part, Marni. He already thinks you're inebriated. Now the question remains whether he's in on the scam or if he will safely deliver you to the hotel. You should have listened to Gloria when she said the plan had flaws."

Now he agrees with my sister? Honestly, this could blow up in my face, and I'd only have myself to blame. Gloria hadn't been keen about me putting myself at risk. Just one more opportunity for her to say, "I told you so." Let's hope it wouldn't be over my lifeless body in the morgue.

I looked at Max. "Where's your bike?"

"Do you really think you're in any shape to hang onto the back of a motorcycle? Besides, it's in the shop. They had a cancellation this afternoon, so I dropped it off." He snickered and led me to a black pickup.

Why do men drive vehicles requiring a step ladder to get into the passenger seat? Had I really been buzzed he would have had his hands full shoving me up onto the seat. As it was, he still gave me a push on the backside. *Did his hand linger longer than necessary? Perhaps I should slip back to the ground for a repeat performance.*

Max reached across me, pulled the seat belt in place, and buckled it. "You are so irresistible right now, but I won't take advantage of your condition."

Condition? Which one—being drunk or horny? Don't start being an upstanding guy on my account. I'm too drunk to remember, right?

By the time he'd walked around the truck and gotten behind the wheel, I'd formulated a new plan. Well, sort of. I leaned my head against the window and shut my eyes.

He let out a soft chuckle before starting the engine. As we pulled out of the parking lot, I cracked one eye open to make sure we turned toward the hotel. I muttered a brief prayer and sat up straight, rubbing my eyes. "How long was I out?"

"Moments, if that. I thought I'd be driving home a comatose tourist." He reached over and squeezed my hand. "Lulu said you and Gloria had a fight. She still angry about wearing dinner the other night?"

"Nah. She got over that pretty fast. This something else entirely."

"Like where Phil hid the treasure from the *Santiago*?" he asked.

Chapter 40

The crunching of glass and metal drowned out everything else from the immediate world. My body strained against the safety belt before knocking back into the seat cushion. Before I could process Max's question about Phil hiding the treasure, our vehicle had been pushed off the road into a ditch and came to a stop. Silence returned as the engine cut off.

A trickle of blood slid down the side of Max's head as his body slumped over the steering wheel.

Through my hazy vision, the back end of a dump truck rolled away down the road. The guy had slammed into us and didn't even stop. "Max...Max...are you okay?" I reached out a trembling hand and gently shook his arm. "Max?"

He emitted a low moan and shifted his body as he struggled to sit upright while keeping his eyes shut. At least he remained among the living.

The passenger door flew open, and a hand grabbed my arm. "Marni, you need to get out of here. Now!"

Holly tugged at me, and I shook my head trying to process what was happening. She leaned in and unfastened my seat belt. Had she been the one to ram into us? No, I'd seen a truck drive away. It couldn't have been her behind the wheel. I protested as she pulled me from the truck. My purse, which remained slung across my chest and shoulder, caught on the buckle. I pulled on it without any luck.

Holly reached in to untangle the strap, while urging me to go with her. A small red sedan, parked at an angle behind us, had the driver's door standing open.

"Holly, what's going on?" I looked toward the cab of the truck. "Max. We need to help Max. He's hurt."

"He'll be fine. It's you they want." She flung open the passenger door and tried to push me inside.

I braced my arms against the frame of the car and refused to budge. "What are you doing? What do you mean it's *me* they want? Who are *they*? And why are we leaving your brother?"

"Dammit, Marni, he's not my brother! Now will you get in the car before someone returns to inspect their handiwork?" She stood with fists balled at her sides.

My mouth gaped open. If I were a bass, I'd be ripe for the picking from the next hook to come my way. The dull throb in my head escalated into a pounding drum as my body swayed ever so slightly. I didn't know if I'd hit my head during the impact or the barrage of information caused the jumbled thoughts swirling inside my brain. With another glance at the truck, I got into the passenger seat of Holly's car.

She slammed the door and ran to her side. In one swift motion she closed her door, started the engine, and shifted into drive. Gravel spun beneath the tires as she gunned the gas pedal propelling us onto the road. She sped past my hotel and continued straight until we turned onto a side road, practically tilting the vehicle up on two wheels. The foliage became dense as the road curved to the left, where she turned onto a dirt track and pulled up in front of a small bungalow. The car skidded to a halt.

I turned to my driver. "Do you drive race cars in your spare time? My life passed before my eyes even faster than when Max almost wiped out with the two of us on the bike the other day. Explain why we left him behind."

"Get out." She jumped out of the car and stepped onto the porch, which wrapped around the house on both sides. Without waiting to see if I followed or made a run for the road, she went inside, leaving the door open.

From inside the car, I took in my surroundings. No other houses were visible. If she were going to kill me, it would have been easier to leave me in Max's truck, unless the river gave better access from here to dump a body. *I should be writing murder mysteries instead of historical romances.*

On the other hand, she didn't take my phone. What kind of assassin would she be if she left me the means to escape or call for help?

"Are you going to sit here all day or go inside to thank Holly for saving your life?" Phil appeared beside me.

"Jury's still out on whether she saved me or threw me into deeper water without a life jacket." I rubbed my temples. "So you saw the accident?"

"No. I sat in the seat behind you and got distracted when your boyfriend told you he knew about me and the treasure from the *Santiago*. Where do you think he got that information?" Phil placed his hands on the wheel.

"First of all, he's not my boyfriend. Second, he's not Holly's brother either, or at least that's what she claimed. Third, he said he knew you hid the treasure not anything about you still hanging around. My instincts are pointing toward the one who called him for a ride in the first place—our favorite bartender."

"You finally believe Holly has good intentions in this whole scheme? It's about time!" He gestured toward the porch.

I took the hint and got out of the car. Pulling my phone from my purse, I scrolled until getting to Gloria's number. My finger hesitated over the contact. What could I tell her that wouldn't send her into a packing frenzy and racing for the airport? I locked my phone and tucked it away. Eventually I'd have to fill her in on how badly my plan went south but now wouldn't be the time.

"Where are we anyway?" I asked Phil.

"Not a clue. I've never seen this place before. She must've moved in after my untimely demise. She probably wanted complete isolation to mourn my passing." He went through the front doorway.

Yeah, I believe that one. There's probably a shrine erected in his honor covering most of the living room. When I stepped inside, dishes clinked from the back of the house. I followed the sound and found Holly setting teacups on the table.

"Do you take milk and sugar in your tea, or perhaps a shot of whiskey?" She gestured to a chair on the other side of the table.

What's next? We'll find some newspaper and start cutting out paper dolls?

Chapter 41

Holly poured hot water into two cups. She pushed one toward me and sat by the other. "I bet you have a lot of questions."

"Can't think of a one." Holding the string, I bobbed the tea bag up and down.

"It's better if you allow it to steep on its own."

I leaned on my elbows. "Enough with the tea trivia. Mind telling me what the hell is going on? Why did you drag me away from a traffic accident, which is illegal by the way, and leave behind not-your-brother Max?"

She folded her hands and rested them on the table. "I saw him move so knew he survived the crash. Honestly, I shouldn't have told you what I did. But I thought you wouldn't come with me if I didn't give you a reason to leave him."

I tilted my head. "So he isn't your brother, or did you just say that to get me out of the truck?"

Her voice got quiet. "No."

Risking the wrath of the tea gods, I dunked the bag up and down a few times then set it on the saucer. If I were going to hell because of bad manners, it certainly wouldn't be over this. "No, what? I asked an either-or question."

The sadness in her eyes tugged at my resolve to bully her for answers. "Marni, leave it alone. I don't want to see any more good people die over this thing.

Can you just believe me when I tell you you're in over your head? Walk away. I'm in over my head, but it's too late for me."

Phil materialized in the chair beside her. I'd almost forgotten he came with us. His hand covered hers, yet she gave no reaction. I knew she wouldn't sense him. Those without the gift never do no matter how much they want to believe.

"Holly, I have an obligation to see this case through."

"Lawrence was right about you. You're just another treasure hunter trying to steal what isn't yours. I've read up on you. You're a very successful author who doesn't need the money. Why would you pursue this?"

I got up and strolled to the other side of the kitchen before turning around. "Let's set aside the fact that ownership of the *Santiago*'s treasure is in question. I'm not in this for the money. Neither is my sister. Believe me, there's more going on here than a simple heist. But you knew that already, didn't you?"

She held her head in her hands. "I don't know what to believe. Lawrence told me Lulu can…I can't believe I'm saying this. Lulu can see ghosts. She's seen Phil, but he won't talk to her. She also told Lawrence that you and your sister can see Phil, and he's spoken with you." Her eyes darted around the room. "Is that true? Is he here now?"

Leaning against the counter, I asked, "What do you believe, Holly?"

"I believe there is an afterlife and good people go to heaven. That's where Phil should be. He was a good man. The best I've ever been with."

"You have to tell her I'm here," Phil pleaded. "Please, Marni. Do this for me." In the few days I'd known him, the man had never sounded so desperate.

I struggled with situations like this. It wasn't necessarily a good thing to put the dead in touch with their loved ones. It didn't always bring the closure both parties hoped for. With a slight shake to my head, I ignored him. That would be an argument for another day. My first priority was to figure out who I could and couldn't trust. My current playbook didn't look too promising.

"Tell me who ran us off the road?" I asked.

"I know who was behind it, and I won't tell you. Marni, you and Gloria seem like nice people, and I don't want you ending up like my boyfriend." She spooned sugar into her cup and stirred as if her life depended on getting the mix just right.

Phil stood in front of me with eyes blazing. "Tell her I'm here! Tell her I love her and want her to be safe."

My hands rose up. "Okay!"

"No need to shout." Holly dropped her spoon. "Does this mean you and Gloria will leave?"

I pushed out a breath. "I wasn't talking to you."

Her face scrunched and her eyes narrowed. "Huh?"

Sitting in the chair next to her, I said, "Phil is here. He has been the whole time"—I glared at him—"badgering me to tell you."

She glanced in the direction I'd aimed my gaze. "Phil, baby, is that you?"

He walked to her and went on one knee. "I'm here, my Holly. I'm right here."

I covered my face with my hands and shook my

head. "I am so gonna regret this." Looking up, I said, "He's kneeling in front of you. And he says he's here and called you 'my Holly.' "

Her gaze shot forward. "Who did this to you?"

"He doesn't know. When people die violently or by the hand of someone else, their memory tends to be fuzzy. He'll remember in time." I crossed my arms. "Tell me something. If you knew Phil had been murdered, why didn't you go to the police?"

She hung her head. "I suspected but didn't know for sure." Her face formed a scowl. "How do I know he's really here and *you're* telling *me* the truth?"

Oh joy. The whole "prove to me my dead boyfriend is present" scenario. Did she read that in a book? *Now she'll ask something dumb like what did she wear on their first date or how many shoes does she own. I need a new hobby.*

With a sigh, I asked, "What's your question?"

"My what?"

I jumped up and waved my arms around. "Your question. You know, the one thing only Phil would know so I can prove I can really talk to dead people. C'mon, let's get this over with. Apparently, I've got murderers and thieves to outmaneuver."

"Way to be sensitive, Marni." Phil stood. "Why don't you simply tell her I came back looking like a decaying corpse and moaning until all hours of the night?"

I stood toe to toe with Phil. "Hey! You weren't the one dragged from a truck after it got battered off the road, leaving behind a man who either wants to kill me or take me to bed."

"No. I'm just the dead guy who may or may not

have been murdered by the man you want to do the horizontal mambo with." He puffed out his cheeks.

"I…Phil…okay, you have a point. Putting it all in perspective." I looked back to Holly. "Sorry. So what was your question?"

The woman braced her hands on her knees while puffing small breaths in and out. *Please don't swoon and faint. I've got enough to deal with.* I nodded encouragement.

"Well…um…ask him what the name of my cat was?"

Phil took a step back. "She never had a cat. The woman's allergic to them." His voice faltered as he shook his head. "Wait a minute, did she have a cat?" He placed a hand to his cheek.

Yeah, she might as well have asked him to name her favorite brand of toothpicks. I relayed his response anyway.

Holly's face lit up. "That's right. I am allergic to cats. Oh, Phil, I miss you so much. I'm so sorry you got mixed up in this. I never would have involved you had I thought it would end in tragedy."

"Better me than you, my sweet. I only wished we'd had more time." He moved closer to her.

Before I could relay his answer, the table buzzed as Holly's phone vibrated. She snatched it up and read the incoming text. "You need to leave, Marni."

"I don't know where I am, remember? You're the one who drove me here with still no explanation as to why." Another thought struck me. "Earlier you said it was me who *they* wanted. Since I escaped, will *they* go after Gloria?"

Chapter 42

Holly tucked her phone into her back pocket, shoved my purse at me, and ran to the back door off the kitchen. Slamming it open, she motioned for me to follow.

I trailed her onto the back porch and across a small patch of overgrown grass ending at a dirt path. I peered over the top of the hill. A weed-choked trail led to the right, then zig-zagged down to the bottom of a steep incline ending on a beach. *Aren't there any trailheads in Florida which start and end at ground level?*

A diesel engine rolled up to the front of the house and cut off. "That'll be Lawrence's jeep. Take this trail to the beach and head north along the river. Your hotel is about a mile."

My toes wriggled in the leather sandals I wore—not exactly the best hiking shoes. I glanced back at the house when more than one car door slammed shut. Two muffled voices argued. "Sounds like he's not alone. Maybe you should come with me."

"Get out of here now!" She spoke in a hushed voice then hurried toward the house.

"Holly," I called as quietly as I could to get her attention.

She stopped and turned.

"The teacups. Get rid of the second one, or they'll know you had company."

Panic crossed her face before she scurried into the house.

Without wasting another moment, I dove down the path as quickly as my flimsy footwear would allow. Whoever arrived with Lawrence didn't sound happy and certainly wouldn't want to have any discussions over a cup of tea—properly steeped or not. As I rounded the first switchback, my foot caught on a root. With nothing to grab onto, I fell, landing on my right arm, before rolling over the edge onto the next switchback, then sliding on my butt to the following one. At least I'd traversed the trail quicker than I thought possible in these shoes. Not waiting to take inventory of any injuries, I sprang to my feet and finished off the last two turns before voices from above caused me to throw myself against the bottom of the hill, praying anyone standing at the top couldn't see me. A slight ledge angled over me.

"See anyone?" a gruff voice yelled.

"Not a soul," Lawrence replied. "Whoever came for tea is long gone."

Pebbles skittered down the hill, probably dislodged by the men at the top. I held my breath hoping they wouldn't venture onto the trail to check for Holly's visitor. Afraid to make a move for fear they still watched, I stayed put pressing my body tighter against the loose dirt.

I counted my escape a success, at least until my sister's ringtone sounded through the thin leather of my purse. "Shit!" Even though we'd been getting along better over the last several months, I'd left her distinctive ring as the music from my favorite horror movie murder scene. It fit her. I struggled to get the zipper open and snake my hand inside searching for my cell. Finally locating the device, I hit the side button silencing the call. I bet she waited on the edge of her seat to discover how well my clever plan played out. Biting my lip, I listened for any movement down the trail.

After another few minutes, I leaned out far enough to scan the landscape above me. It remained deserted and the voices had ceased. As quickly as I could, I backed away while hugging the embankment until it rounded out of sight of the hill. Gingerly I stood and assessed the damage to my body. I'd torn the nail on my big toe and a spot of blood bubbled at the edge. Nothing some ointment and a bandage couldn't patch up. New scrapes on my calf blended with the old ones from the spill I took on the way to the cave, and a red mark blossomed on my elbow. By this evening it would be a pretty shade of purple. So much for a relaxing, sister-bonding, girls' trip to Crystal River. *Maybe I should let Gloria plan our next expedition—that is if we survived long enough to make it to the airport after this one.*

I set off at a brisk pace. My toe throbbed as I skirted the edge of the river. The path disappeared in places where foliage met the shore. I trekked through the water and muck at these spots while muttering obscenities to no one in particular. Between the heat and humidity, the mud at the shoreline gave off a peaty odor. Not the most pleasant smell, especially when bordered by skunk weed. To my surprise, Phil hadn't made an appearance at my side. Since his conversation with Holly got interrupted, he may have hung around her place.

Holly neglected to mention the one-mile span had private residences. About a quarter of a mile from the Harbor Inn I came upon a stockade fence blocking access to the river, which forced me away from the shoreline.

Once on the street, I followed it to the main road leading me to the hotel parking lot. The river had washed away the blood from my toe, but it hurt worse than before. I couldn't wait to collapse on my bed after this afternoon's ordeal.

When I arrived at our hotel room, the door stood ajar. My sister would never neglect a detail like that. Looking about for a weapon and coming up empty, I took my purse from where it hung over my shoulder and held it high. It wouldn't be as effective as Gloria's arsenal-sized cosmetic bag, but it would have to do.

I nudged the door with my foot and let it swing open. Jumping through the doorway, I yelled, "Aha."

My entrance was met with silence. I didn't find anyone inside, even when I glanced into the bathroom. Our belongings lay scattered about the room, and the mattresses had been yanked from their frames and left askew. This looked way more than my sister pitching a fit at Phil while chucking pillows in his direction. I went through the open balcony door where one of the chairs rested on its side.

"Please, God, no." I lowered my purse and peeked over the railing. A sigh of relief escaped my lips when I didn't find Gloria's beaten and battered body lying on the sidewalk below. The only things down there were a couple of cigarette butts and a toddler-sized shoe with tangled laces.

Inside our room, Gloria's purse sat on the carpet

beside the nightstand with the contents scattered around it. A chill wound up my spine sending icy tendrils throughout my body. Her wallet was among the items. She never would have voluntarily left it behind.

Chapter 43

Retrieving my phone from my purse, the screen read a missed call and a voicemail. I'd forgotten Gloria had called me about forty-five minutes earlier when I hid from Lawrence and whoever he had with him.

I played back the message. "Marni, I thought you'd be back by now from your drunken performance. Hope all is going as planned, and Lulu is on her way to dig for treasure in the wrong spot. I'm down at the pool, and I forgot my room key. The dolt in the front office won't give me another without ID, which is also in the room. Like I'd burgle a room wearing nothing but a bathing suit and sunglasses. I am so going to rate this place a two for customer service on the review site. Anyway, let me know when you'll be back. Hopefully it'll be before I turn into a lobster from the sun."

Tearing down the steps two at a time, I raced to the pool at the back of the hotel. Gloria lounged in a recliner beneath one of the straw umbrellas. At least she lived to gripe another day about my hotel choices.

I knelt down and threw my arms around her. "Oh, thank God. You're all right." I held her at arms' length. "They didn't hurt you, did they?"

"Oh, Marni. It's so good to see the two of you getting along." Phil appeared on the lounger next to us with his hands pressed together. "By the way, I love the redecorating job in your room."

Gloria's gaze bounced from me to Phil then back to me again. She pulled her arms from my grasp, pushing my hands away. "A little space please. First of all, the idiot at the front desk didn't harm me in any way other than to refuse to give me a key. I'm sure his next job will involve asking customers if they want fries with that."

Too much time in the sun obviously didn't cause her any harm. "I'm not talking about you being refused a room key. Has anyone suspicious been hanging around here? Did you see anyone you recognized like Lawrence or Kimpton?"

"I've been sitting by the pool reading and haven't noticed anyone in particular." She adjusted the sunglasses on her face. "What's Phil talking about regarding our room decor? It had the same awful shag rug and drab walls when I left."

With no easy way to break it to her, I filled Gloria in on the condition of our room. Before I could tell her about my adventures over the course of the afternoon, she bolted for the stairs.

I sauntered behind her, babying my sore toe. In my haste, I'd left the door wide open, so she wouldn't need my key card to get in. When I got there, I found her in the bathroom rooting through her cosmetics. She inspected a tube of lipstick. From the looks of her purse contents on the floor, she hadn't touched those yet.

"You raced upstairs to check on your make-up bag?" I waved my arm at the bedroom in disarray. "Do you really think somebody did all this in search of your favorite pink lipstick?"

She glared in my direction. "It's a discontinued color." With a shake of her head, she asked, "Do you think we should call the police?"

"Nah. Nothing appears to be missing. By the way, my afternoon didn't go as planned." I closed the door leading to the hallway outside. "Just in case you're wondering."

After a few minutes, Gloria joined me where I picked up our clothes and made two piles on the dresser. I'd already put the drawers back where they belonged.

"Now do you think we should change our flight and leave tonight? This whole Phil situation is getting much more complicated, not to mention dangerous, than either of us believed." She folded her shirts and shorts.

"Not yet. We have one more day to wrap this up, and I intend to see it through." I slid the box spring in place and lifted a corner of the mattress. "Help me with this, will you?"

Gloria huffed but grabbed the other corner and we shoved the mattress in place. We did the same with her bed before straightening the sheets and comforter. By the time we'd gotten everything put back together, I'd filled her in on my afternoon adventure.

"Thank goodness you weren't hurt in the accident. Do you think whoever did this to our room believes we found the treasure? And why would they risk hurting Max? Maybe they don't trust him." Gloria walked into the bathroom to change out of her bathing suit.

I rubbed my sore elbow as I relaxed against the headboard. "Of course, they believe we've found the treasure and were searching for clues. This certainly wasn't a robbery attempt with your wallet still intact. Did you notice anything missing?"

She came back wearing shorts and a tank top. "Not a thing. Should we—"

My cell phone rang. She picked it up from the dresser and looked at the caller before handing it to me. "It's Max. Do you really think it's a good idea to talk to him right now?"

With a shake of my head, I waited to see if he'd leave a voice mail. Instead, my phone pinged with an incoming text. —*Call me*— was all he sent. I set it down on the nightstand without responding.

"Marni, how do you propose to wrap this all up?" Gloria dumped her purse onto the bed and went through the contents again. *Did she expect things to have disappeared since she examined them five minutes ago?*

"Yes, do tell how you plan to wrap this all up?" Phil sat in the desk chair.

"I've been wondering when you'd show up again. After I bolted from Holly's did you stick around and see who arrived with Lawrence?"

He shrugged. "I didn't know the man, but Holly called him Herb. I'm assuming he's the infamous Herbert Kimpton whom you discovered owned the *Sunset Dream*."

I sat up straight. "What did they say to her? Did they know she'd pulled me from the accident?"

"Now we're concerned about Holly? Marni, I'm still not sure she's really on our side." Gloria put her bag back together and set it aside.

"I have to admit, I'm beginning to come around to Phil's way of thinking. She may be an innocent victim in all this who's trapped by her connection to these guys."

Phil snorted. "It's about time. Why else would she

rescue you? The men asked who had been there, and she lied, telling them she'd had a girlfriend visiting. Herb acted as if he didn't believe her, but Lawrence smoothed things over before discussing the accident."

"So they knew Max and I had been run off the road?" I glanced at my phone. No more messages had come in since the first one.

"Oh, they knew about it. Herbert groused about you not being in the vehicle like he'd been told and how the idiot driver should have checked before hitting Max's truck. Lawrence claimed it had been a bad idea risking injury to one of their partners without warning him first. Sounds like your boyfriend is in on this whole robbery plan." The smug grin on his face annoyed me.

We all froze when a knock sounded on the door.

Chapter 44

With a finger to her lips, Gloria quietly shushed me.

It could be any number of people on the other side of that door. I agreed not answering would be the smart play right now until we figured out our next move.

The gentle knock turned into heavy rapping. "Hello? Ms. Legend? This is Lenny from the front desk. I have a message for you." He banged again.

I got off the bed, but my sister reached over and grabbed my arm. Her eyes bugged wide as she shook her head.

Before I could move, a folded slip of paper got shoved partway under the door. The height of the shag carpet stopped it from going farther. Footsteps moved away and pounded down the cement stairs.

We remained motionless another moment before I retrieved the paper. A handwritten note read, "Meet me downstairs in ten minutes. I'll explain everything." With no signature, I didn't have a clue who wanted to meet with me and what needed explaining.

"What does it say?" Gloria reached for the note.

"Somebody wants me to meet in ten minutes. Maybe I should have a chat with Lenny about who asked him to deliver the message."

She jumped off the bed. "You're not going, are you? This could be from the guy who ran you and Max off the road. Or it could be from Max himself, wanting to finish the job Holly deprived him of."

I looked to our ghost. "Phil, could you zap down to the office and see who's around?"

He bobbed his head and disappeared. Minutes passed before he returned. "The only one around is the pimple-faced adolescent, who I'm sure is the idiot who denied a key to Gloria."

"There's no one waiting in the parking lot?" I asked.

"Not that I could tell. None of the parked cars had anybody inside." He leaned against the dresser. "I believe Gloria is correct, and you shouldn't go. What about hiding nearby until you see who shows up?"

"Phil, that's actually a great idea." I slipped my sandals back on and tucked my phone into my back pocket.

Gloria formed her hands into a tee. "Hold on. Time out. Are you even listening to what you're saying?"

"It's a great plan. I'll hide behind one of the parked cars and see who shows up. What could go wrong?" I lifted my arms into the air.

"What could go wrong? Are you forgetting how fast your last plan went careening off the tracks?" She pointed at my bruised elbow. "Why can't Phil wait for whoever might show up? Nothing can hurt him."

"What if it's somebody I want to talk to? By the time he zips back here and I get downstairs it could be too late." I stuffed my room key into the other pocket. "Trust me, I know what I'm doing. I won't be going anywhere with anyone. If this mystery person has something to say to me, it'll take place in the parking lot." I vaulted through the door before my sister could lodge any further objections.

She had the good sense not to follow me. If she chased me while continuing to argue, we might scare off my visitor before I had a chance to discover his or her identity. Phil came beside me and reiterated my sister's concerns. At least nobody else could hear him.

At the bottom of the stairs, I skirted the building until reaching the front. "Phil, do you see any new cars in the lot since you checked?"

He looked around and shook his head. "Actually, there had been a blue sedan over there, but it's gone now." He pointed to an empty spot in the corner. "Everything else looks the same."

"Okay." I hurried over to a white SUV with tinted windows parked next to a large shade tree. The vehicle would be between me and the entrance from the street with a clear view of the front office. Sitting on the raised curb beside the front tire, I watched for moving vehicles. My phone vibrated twice in my back pocket. When I pulled it out, I saw messages from Gloria. I'd give her credit for persistence. Before I could unlock the screen, two more messages came through, also from her.

I read through them. "Phil, can you please go tell Gloria to chill the hell out. I can't focus on this while contending with her."

"As you wish, madam. How I ended up being a messenger boy in this plan eludes me." He sighed before disappearing.

With my phone still in hand, I reread Max's two-word text. Lawrence's and Herbert's conversation left no room for doubt that Max was one of the bad guys. His interaction with Lulu made me suspect they did more than ride motorcycles together. How could I continue to be so clueless when it came to men? At least my marriage to Tim lasted a couple of decades before he called it quits because of my paranormal heritage.

A stick cracked beside me, and a hand covered my mouth. I dropped my phone as the barrel of a gun shoved into my back. My hands froze in position as fear surged through my body like a serpent.

"Don't do anything stupid. Remember, you're not the only sibling we can get our hands on," Lawrence hissed into my ear. "Is your ghostly friend around?"

I swallowed.

He eased his hand off my face. "Answer me!"

I shook my head.

"Then call him."

"It…it doesn't work that way. He needs to seek me out." I kept my gaze focused ahead and didn't move.

Lawrence grabbed my arm and dragged me to my feet. "Then we'll just have to wait while he comes to us." He opened the back seat of the SUV I'd hidden next to and shoved me inside where Lulu held a small pistol of her own. Holly sat on the bench seat in the back, her pallor whiter than snow.

Seriously? I'd picked the one hiding spot next to the villains. It didn't look like my day would be improving by any stretch of the imagination.

Chapter 45

"Did you really think I didn't see you dumping your beer down the sink?" The smug grin on Lulu's face told me she'd had no intention of working the dinner shift. "If Max had done what he'd been told, we would have had this wrapped up by now."

"And what would that be?" I spat, feeding off my anger to tamp down the sour taste of fear. Wrapped up might have meant my body in a canvas tarp with an anchor tied to it.

"Oh, don't be so naïve, Marni." She pointed at my seat belt. "I suggest you buckle up. We're going for a little ride as soon as you give Lawrence a destination."

I crossed my arms. "Sure. Do you guys want Mexican or Italian? I'm leaning more toward pasta myself."

"Just shoot her, Lulu. We'll get Gloria to lead us to where Phil buried the treasure. I'm sure seeing her sister's dead body will inspire her to talk." Lawrence carped from the driver's seat.

"Marni, please tell them where he hid it, and this will all be over." Holly gripped the back of my seat.

"It won't do you any good grabbing my sister. Phil never showed her where he put it." That part wasn't exactly a lie. Since Gloria refused to follow me into the cave, she'd have no idea where to dig.

"But he told *you*, didn't he?" Lulu grabbed my sore

255

elbow causing me to wince. "From your little field trip to the hardware store, I'd say it's buried somewhere dark. Unless you already moved it?"

No need to tell me who had tossed our room. They left me no option but to cooperate. I might not make it out alive, but as long as I still breathed, I'd have a chance at keeping my body and spirit on this side of the great beyond. *If only Phil would appear, he could assess the situation and get my sister to call the police.* However, there'd be two possible drawbacks to that plan. Lulu would spot him first and threaten Holly. From the fear covering her face, I was sure Phil's girlfriend had been dragged along as leverage and not a partner.

The second flaw in my plan would be Gloria actually listening to me for once, leaving the authorities out of the mix.

Lawrence started the vehicle and shifted it into gear. "You have thirty seconds to give me a location, or we'll be going with our back-up clairvoyant. Which will it be?"

My shoulders slumped. "Cavern Beach. The treasure is buried in the caves at Cavern Beach."

"Now was that so hard?" Lulu waved her weapon in the air. "Let's roll."

I reached for the door handle. "So you don't need me anymore, right? I'll just head out now."

"You open that door, and it will be your last act on earth in your corporeal state. Don't test me." Lulu pointed her gun at my chest.

Such big words from a relative petty thief. Releasing the handle, I buckled my seat belt. I wouldn't chance us being run off the road by another one of their "partners."

Holly settled back and did the same.

The SUV pulled out of the parking lot onto the main road. Driving with one hand, Lawrence used his cell phone with the other. "It's inside the caves at Cavern Beach." He listened for a beat. "Yeah, that's the place. Grab a motorboat from the harbor and meet us on the beach. If the tide's high, we'll need it to get inside." He ended the call.

A block later, I heard the roar of a motorcycle. Turning in my seat, I recognized Max as he tailed our vehicle. So much for his bike being in the repair shop.

Our driver glanced into his sideview mirror and nodded. "Had you answered Max's call, you could have had one more motorcycle ride together." His eyes met Lulu's in the rearview mirror. "Oh, but you'd be jealous again, wouldn't you, Lulu. These love triangles are so tedious."

"Just shut up and drive, asshole," Lulu barked with her eyes blazing. "Maybe Kate and I should have a talk about all the time you've spent with Holly. It may have been innocent, but who do you think your wife will believe?"

My assumption about Max and Lulu being a couple hit the target. Somehow, I couldn't picture them going on romantic dinner dates. From the way Lulu spoke about her pending conquest the other day, I'd guess theirs to be more of a physical satisfaction than an actual relationship. My picker was definitely broken when it came to potential love interests.

We rode the rest of the way in silence until we parked in the lot above Cavern Beach. Phil had yet to make an appearance. Surely by now my sister would have wondered where I'd gone off to and maybe found my phone on the ground. Either that or she'd decided on another treatment at House of Primp if she could ever get a taxi. I'd left our car at Libations.

Lawrence hopped out of the vehicle and whipped open my door. "Everybody out!" He'd tucked his gun into a holster on his hip. Chances were good he'd have it in hand before I reached cover if I made a run for it.

Max parked his bike beside us, his eyes never leaving my face. Did he regret pulling me into all this or was he as cold and calculating as his partners? Which one of them killed Phil, or was it a group activity?

After Max stowed his gear, Lulu sauntered over and planted a long kiss on his lips. His arms remained at his sides. When she didn't pull back, he pushed her away. "Enough! Quit claiming territory. We have work to do."

"I've already laid claim to *my* territory." She turned to me with a sneer. "I wanted to make sure everyone knew about it."

"Save your carnal antics for the bedroom, Lulu. Max, get out the flashlights and shovel," Lawrence ordered.

Max did as he'd been told and unloaded the gear from the hatchback.

Lawrence looked into the SUV. "Holly, get out here!"

She climbed over the flipped down seat and out the door. "Please don't make me go into the cavern. I don't like dark places."

I couldn't believe the personality change in her compared to the rude and demanding woman I'd met earlier. Had it all been an act? Did she really want to warn Gloria and me off after all?

Lawrence herded us to the trail head like a bunch of stray sheep and took the lead followed by Holly with Lulu bringing up the rear.

My big toe ached at the thought of hiking in my flimsy sandals down the switchback. *What's another few injuries to add to my current list of wounds?* By the time I made it home, *if I made it home*, I'd be one big scab. I didn't think it possible, but I began to hate the scent of the ocean and the caw of pelicans.

Max walked behind me. "Marni, I'm sorry about all this. I never thought—"

"Thought what?" Anger sizzled beneath the surface of my skin. "That pretending to date me while your *girlfriend* encouraged me to see you would end badly?" I'd stopped walking to face him.

"She's not my...I mean we aren't..." He raked a hand through his hair.

"I'm sorry, is girlfriend too cliché for you? How about lover? Partner in crime? Co-murderer? Jump in when I hit the right term that won't offend your sense of propriety."

"Keep moving!" Lulu nudged Max on the shoulder, who glared at her in response.

I continued down the trail picking my footing as carefully as possible.

"I'm not a murderer, Marni. You've got to believe me," Max pleaded.

A puff of air escaped my lips. "Yeah, I suppose Phil really did run out of air by accident." What difference did it make to him whether I believed him innocent of murder or not? I had my doubts there'd be five of us trekking back out of here. His conscience would be the least of my worries.

Chapter 46

When we reached the bottom, Lawrence led us toward a small motorboat beached on the sand. The rocks I'd waded past the other day were completely underwater. Apparently, they had no intention of waiting until low tide.

Herbert Kimpton stood on shore with hands on his hips. I'd say he scowled, but since that was the only facial expression I'd seen on him, perhaps this was his excited face. Either way, I'd prefer not to experience his angry face.

As we approached, he barked, "It's about time." The gravel in his voice made his speech more guttural than human. With that harsh tone, he must've ruled the playground by five years old.

"It takes a lot longer to get here by road than it does boat. Besides, you didn't have to hike down from the parking lot above." Lawrence exuded the same impatience he'd received as trickles of sweat laced his forehead and cheeks.

Kimpton nodded in my direction. "She tell you exactly where that idiot hid my treasure?"

I held up a hand. "Ah, excuse me? I don't believe the treasure belongs to you. As I understand it, Lulu scammed a poor lost soul from the *Santiago* into revealing the location. It belongs to his family in Spain."

Kimpton's eyes opened wide, as if he couldn't believe I'd actually spoken to him with such insolence. "You do know the law of finders keepers, don't you?"

"If that's the case, then Phil *found* it and gets to *keep* it. Since he's not here for a discussion on the dispensation of the wealth, I guess we're done here. Nice meeting you, Herbie. Come on, Holly, we have a long trek ahead of us."

A gun cocked behind me as I spun to walk away. Looking over my shoulder, Lawrence held his weapon at the ready. So much for bluster.

"Pissing us off isn't a good tactic," Lawrence said. "Now get in the boat and show us where he buried it."

I splayed my fingers and gestured for him to calm down. "Point taken. Look, the truth is I don't know exactly where to find the booty. The cave was dark, and Phil led the way. I'm not sure I could find it on my own."

"Then our tour guide better appear soon, or we're going to start removing excess players from this game." Lulu took a step toward the boat. "You know, I can just as easily follow Phil's directions as you can. We really don't need you, Marni."

"Except Phil doesn't like you. At all. I find it hard to believe he'd show you anything but his middle finger." I shifted my weight from one foot to the other.

Max stepped beside me. "Look, everyone, settle down. Nobody needs to get hurt. Let's all get in the boat and motor into the cave before it's as dark outside as in. Maybe by then our spiritual guide will make an appearance and speed up this hunt." He placed the flashlights and shovel on the floor, and, with Lawrence's help, pushed the craft farther into the water.

Before it completely got off the sand, he held it steady.

Kimpton jumped in first and manned the engine at the back of the craft. Six people on board would be tight, but even at high tide I didn't imagine we'd be traveling far before having to walk.

Lulu leaned on Max as she boarded, her hand lingering on his shoulder as she gave him a pointed stare. Next, he helped Holly, then me, and she and I sat side by side in front of our captain.

After Lawrence climbed in, Max shoved the boat into the ocean. His athletic prowess showed when his feet didn't touch the water once as he launched himself onto the front seat.

We backed away from the shore and motored forward around the rocks to the mouth of the cave. Since I'd exited via the entrance above on my last visit, I never saw how far the water intruded inside. A shiver ran through me at what might have happened had I come out this way. Thoughts of being sucked under by the current weren't far from my mind. Phil had done me a favor by disappearing that day in the cave. His lack of presence now, however, put me in a precarious position.

The boat sat low in the water from the weight of so many passengers. Waves lapped at the sides and spilled into the bottom tickling my feet. Sitting in the bow, Max shone a light as we traversed what would have been a pathway with the walls closing in tighter. After a full five minutes, we hit dry land. I couldn't be certain how far we'd come compared to when I'd walked in, but I'd guess we were close to the large, open cavern.

Every ounce of my being focused on Phil materializing. Our gift didn't work that way, but my desperation left me running out of options.

"The carnival ride is over," Lulu said. "Everyone out of the boat and switch on your flashlights."

Max held out a hand to assist me, which I ignored. The thought of his touch sickened me.

Flashlights were passed out to everyone except Holly and me. Another bad sign. Lulu and company may have already determined who wouldn't be leaving once the treasure got dug up. *Damn it, Phil, where are you?*

Holly gripped my arm. "Marni, please, tell them where it is." Fear consumed her voice and exuded outward. Too bad she couldn't channel anger like me. Where was the snarky woman who could dismiss my presence with a sneer?

My toe caught a rock, and I pitched forward against the wall of the tunnel. *Thanks for the light, guys.*

Max hurried over and grabbed my elbow. "Are you okay?"

Focusing a glare at his face Gloria would have been proud of, I asked, "What about any of this is okay?"

"I meant…Marni, I never wanted—"

"Never wanted what?" I snapped. "To be involved in an abduction? Theft? Murder? Are you a murderer? Or will you be? I'm a little confused about where we stand. Maybe you can clarify the situation for me." I wrested my arm away from his grasp.

His voice lowered. "I won't let anything happen to you. Please believe me."

Lulu shined her light in Max's face. "What are you doing? Don't tell me you're going soft now. Remember who warms your bed." She aimed her beam at me. "Get moving!"

I turned to head farther into the tunnel and came face to face with Felipe. Maybe the universe had thrown me a bone.

"Marni Legend, what are you doing with these horrible people?" Felipe asked.

"Why are you still here, Spaniard?" Lulu asked. "In case you haven't noticed, you're not needed, unless you can show us to the treasure. Did Phil share his hiding spot? Marni's life depends on us finding it. So, if you care for her wellbeing, you may want to speak up."

Felipe's eyes widened. With Lulu watching him, I shook my head once and mouthed the words "get Phil."

He disappeared.

Lulu whipped around. "Where the hell did he go? I'm not kidding, Felipe. If you don't help us, your good friend, Marni Legend, will be joining you in the hereafter."

I shrugged. "Maybe if you worked on your social skills he might stick around. Then again, he knows you're just a bitch and probably won't bother coming back."

She shoved me against the wall and placed her gun under my chin. Reality shivered through me. *How is it that guns came into play with my helping a lost soul? Actually, Gloria was the chosen one, how did I end up here? Not that I'd want her in this place either.*

"Do you see him?" she asked.

"What the hell is going on?" Herbert stormed up beside Lulu.

"Nothing apparently," she said. "That Spanish sailor popped in and then left."

He pointed a finger in her face. "You told me we didn't need him anymore. Why would he be hanging around?"

A smug grin covered Lulu's face. "Because he'd want to be near his family's precious belongings. We must be close if he's hanging around." She stepped back and waved her arm in a grand gesture. "After you, Marni."

How long would it take Felipe to find Phil and convince Gloria I needed help? Even if Phil showed up, his lack of a corporeal body did me no good as far as wrestling me away from this band of modern-day pirates. By the time my sister convinced the authorities to come to my rescue, Holly and I could be fish food. *Why didn't I take Gloria's suggestion when she picked Hawaii for our trip?*

Chapter 47

"How do you expect me to find anything in the dark?" I glared at Lulu.

"Oh, for heaven's sake, take mine!" Lawrence thrust his flashlight at me. "Now let's get a move on before we all die of old age."

I took the weighty instrument and shone it on the path ahead. Once we reached the large cavern, I searched left and right. I longed to dash into the tunnel on the left, which led to the opening on the cliff. While Lulu stood close enough for me to smash her in the head with the flashlight, Lawrence also had a gun. So much for a brilliant escape plan. With a sigh, I searched to the right and found a tunnel. Since I hadn't paid much attention when Phil led me to the spot, there could be more than one tunnel on this side of the cavern. I took a chance and strode inside.

Slowing my pace, I didn't want to arrive too quickly, giving them a chance to dispose of Holly and me before help arrived. *If* help arrived. Having my sister as backup didn't instill a warm, fuzzy feeling of confidence. Knowing her, she'd dissolve into a panic attack and not surface until this episode ended. Something told me it wouldn't have a happy ending.

My steps took me farther into the inky blackness ahead, abated only by my light beam and those from the people behind. Max, the ever-persistent lap dog, walked beside me. His feigned concern led me to believe his acting skills had been honed, and I didn't believe for a minute he would protect me from the rest of the crew. I knew how these stories go. The innocent bystander, who knew too much, never made it out alive.

"Marni, are you sure this is the way? Herbert is losing his cool, and I'm afraid he'll hurt you or Holly," Max said.

"Well, golly gee, let's hope my memory serves me better than my choice of friends," I snapped. We rounded a corner, and I caught a flash of a Hawaiian shirt.

Lulu lagged behind with Lawrence and wouldn't see him until they caught up.

Phil spread his arms wide. "It's about time you showed up. I've been hanging around this dank place forever."

I flashed the specter an angry look. "Tell me what's going on."

Max did a double take. "You know what's going on. Phil hid Herbert's treasure before he died, and the man wants it back. Just give it to him, and we can all walk out of here."

Ignoring Max, I stopped moving so Lulu wouldn't round the corner before I got an answer.

"You need to stall," he whispered.

"What do you think I've been doing?" My voice elevated a notch.

Max raised a hand. "Calm down. I know you're trying, but we have no time for false leads." He glanced over his shoulder then back to me.

Lulu shoved him aside and pushed past me. "She's not talking to you, Max. Isn't that right, Phil?" Her light illuminated his presence but only to herself and me. "Get over here, Holly!"

The frightened woman shuffled to the front of the group.

Judging by Phil's surprised reaction, he hadn't anticipated his old girlfriend being here. "Please tell me she isn't truly involved with all of this and my demise."

"Well, now, Phil, that depends on how you answer my next question." Lulu brought up her gun and stuck it against Holly's side.

"Is that thieving bastard here?" Kimpton caught up to us. "Where the hell did you stash my treasure?" He looked down the tunnel.

"Isn't that the pot calling the kettle black." Phil snarked. "You steal from innocent people and have the nerve to accuse me of taking what isn't mine? I suppose living all those years looking like a disgruntled bulldog can sour a person."

"He's there." Lulu indicated the spot where the ghost stood.

"Did he say anything?" The man's face reddened.

A giggle escaped my lips at Phil's accurate description.

Herbert snorted. "What's so funny?"

I shrugged. Relaying Phil's comment wouldn't help my situation any. "Nervous laughter. Give it another few minutes, and the tension may elevate me into a full belly laugh."

Lulu smirked. "Show us where the treasure is. Maybe it will give you closure, so you can move on."

Phil narrowed his eyes. "Closure, madam, would see you and your cohorts in prison."

"Perhaps you need a little persuasion." In one swift

move, Lulu shifted her gun and shot Holly through the arm just above the elbow.

The boom echoed through the tunnel in a deafening crescendo, accompanied by the injured woman's screech. Blood spurted from the wound as she covered it with her other hand. Max moved toward Holly, but Lawrence was quicker and aimed his weapon at the man.

"I wouldn't do anything foolish right now. You're the reason we're all here since you botched the operation this afternoon." He held the gun steady on Max.

"Oh, my Holly. What have they done to you?" Phil ran to her side, unable to do more than reach for her, his hands slipping through her body as she dropped to the floor whimpering.

My hands shook at my sides. I opened my mouth to protest Lulu's actions, but no sound came out. Swallowing, I mustered my voice. "Please, there's no need for violence. Give us time to locate the spot. This is the tunnel. We're heading in the right direction, and I can show you where the gold is buried."

"Let's hope so," Kimpton said. "Otherwise, we'll need to offer more *encouragement*."

No encouragement needed. I preferred to keep all my limbs intact, as well as Holly's remaining extremities. He definitely proved to be in charge, letting his underlings handle the dirty work. The problem had escalated, and Lulu enjoyed her role too much. Would she back down if commanded or go off on a rampage until she held the loot.

"Max, get her on her feet," Kimpton growled. His harsh tone grated on my nerves.

Holly winced as Max helped her stand. Blood seeped from where she pressed her hand on the wound.

With Phil willing to do anything to keep Holly safe, I worried the boss man would decide they no longer needed me. Since our ghost could show Lulu where we'd really hidden the loot, they wouldn't need two ghost whisperers.

Phil glared at Lulu. "I need your word you will not hurt Holly any further or Marni. Both are innocent in this mess you all created."

"And what is it you have to bargain with?" she asked. "If you don't lead us to the *Santiago*'s treasure, Holly dies. Are you willing to risk her life? It's not like you can spend any of the gold yourself."

His shoulders slumped as he walked farther into the tunnel. "This way."

I quickened my pace and caught up with him. "Phil, try not to annoy that woman any further. I don't know a lot about guns, but I'd say there're plenty of bullets left to do more harm."

"That's the smartest thing you've said all day, Marni. Now try heeding your own advice and stay quiet until we need you." Lulu waved the gun in the air.

How I'd love to lob my flashlight across her skull. I'd bet the men in this group were a lot less trigger happy than she was. I might stand a fighting chance of making it out alive—might being the operative word.

What happened to Felipe all this time? Did he go off searching for Phil not realizing the man had been here all along? With his steadfast dedication to right the wrong done to his family, I would have thought he'd want to be present at this little shindig.

With one more twist in the path, we came upon the

pile of stones I'd placed as a decoy. Phil stopped beside it and pointed. He had wanted me to stall but steering them in the wrong direction would only make Lulu angrier. Had he not listened to anything I'd said?

"Why are we stopping?" Lawrence asked.

"This is the spot." She indicated the stones.

He dropped to his knees and began removing rocks. His pace quickened as he got closer to the dirt. "Give me the shovel." The excitement in his voice resonated through every word.

"Crap!" Max muttered.

"What?" Lawrence turned toward him.

He shook his head. "I left the shovel in the boat. I'll have to go back for it."

"You moron," Kimpton yelled. "Hurry up before the tide comes all the way in and swallows the whole cave. We don't know how high the water will rise."

Lawrence ran his hand over the ground. "It won't come this far. The ground is too dry, but I would like to get out of here before nightfall. It's bad enough traipsing around in the darkness inside."

With a glance in my direction, Max hurried back the way we'd come. As much as I didn't trust him, his was the only level-headed presence out of my group of captors. At least they wouldn't find out Phil led them astray until he returned.

Since I couldn't ask Phil what great plan he and Gloria had schemed up to get me out of harm's way, I struggled to find a way to get the attention off of Holly.

"So how does this work? I mean, Herbie claims the treasure is his, so where do you all come in? Ten percent to the hired hands and the rest to him? Seems so unfair if there isn't an even split." I edged closer to the darkness of the continuing tunnel. Fleeing might be an option, as long as there wasn't a dead end around the bend.

"Well, Ms. Legend, it appears I've underestimated you. Since we've never been introduced, I assume you've done your research based on lies Phil told you. That is if you really can talk to the dead. You might be running your own scam. And the name is Herbert."

Was it my imagination, or did he sound a little impressed? "Sorry, you don't strike me to be that formal, Herbert. Oh, and that whole ghost talker thing is real. A family inheritance passed down from my dear old granny. How much do you trust your current employee and her so-called abilities?"

"Shut your mouth!" Lulu snapped. "Don't listen to her. I have the same skills she does, except I know how to use them to my advantage."

In a low voice, he asked, "Don't you mean *our* advantage?"

For the first time she hesitated. With a nasty glare in my direction, she said, "Of course, *our* advantage. Just remember none of this would have happened without me. I'm the one who found the treasure of the *Santiago* by my contact with the sailor. You never would have discovered the ship with it being so far off course."

"True enough." Herbert nodded.

Lawrence sighed. "Don't you see what that woman is trying to do?" He pointed at me. "My wife creates these scenarios all the time in those stupid romance books she writes. Marni is trying to pit us against each other. I can't believe you're falling for it. Maybe we do need her on this team instead of Lulu. At least she appears to keep her temper in check."

Lulu stepped up nose to nose with him. "My temper is not the issue here. For now, finding the treasure and getting our fair share needs to be a topic for discussion. Yes, I do see how Marni is attempting to put us at odds with each other, but she does have a point." She narrowed her eyes at Kimpton. "Just how much of a cut are we all getting?"

Footsteps sounded in the tunnel leading toward us. Both Lulu and Lawrence swung their guns in that direction. Max appeared carrying a shovel.

"Whoa, it's just me. Put those things away before someone else gets hurt." He held out the shovel to Lawrence.

"Why don't you do the honors?" The tall man stepped aside to make room for Max. "After all, you were hired for your brawn, remember?"

Apparently, I didn't need to instigate any in-fighting since angst among the group already existed. It wouldn't hurt for me to throw a little salt on that wound just to amp it up a little.

"Herbert, maybe you should answer Lulu's question. Perhaps I could make a better deal for future explorations of this type. My personality is way more conducive to chatting up spirits compared to your existing member. She has a little too much vinegar in her sting, don't you agree?"

Without warning, Lulu fired a shot over my head.

Chapter 48

My ears rang from the explosion as shards of rock and dust rained down on me. Instinctively, I crouched and threw my arms atop my head shielding me from the debris.

"That will be your last warning. Next time I'll prove just how dispensable you are to this operation. Got it?" She stood with a hand on her hip.

The others had frozen in place.

Herbert found his voice first. "Put that thing away or our agreement is terminated!"

"Do we know how stable these caves are?" Lawrence backed toward the way we'd come. "For all we know she'll bring the whole hillside down on us."

"Please," Lulu snorted. "These tunnels have been here for hundreds of years. If the pounding of the ocean hasn't tumbled them, one tiny bullet won't do any damage. Quit acting like a scared little girl."

Her assessment didn't instill confidence in me. Unless she whipped out a geological engineering degree, I'd guess her comments weren't based on facts. It never occurred to me we'd be in danger of getting trapped if there was a collapse. Thanks, Lawrence.

Throughout these exchanges, Holly remained quiet. I flashed my light in her direction, where she sat on the ground slumped against the wall. Her face had paled, and a small puddle of blood formed beside her.

"She needs a doctor. Can't you see she's losing blood?" I pointed to the small red pool.

Max stopped digging and pulled a bandana from his back pocket. "Tie this around her arm. It might slow the bleeding until we can get her out of here."

Snatching it from him, I pulled Holly's hand off her wound and tied the bandana around her arm, cinching it tight. "Keep pressure on the hole. You'll be all right," I said quietly.

"Marni, do something before she passes out," Phil pleaded.

"Oh, isn't this a touching scene?" Lulu put her hand to her cheek. "You know, Phil, if she doesn't make it, you'll be together forever. Isn't that what you'd want?"

He rushed her, and she put up her hands as he dove and went straight through her. It had the same effect as when my sister threw stuff at him.

She recovered her composure. "Really? What do you think you can do to me in your ghostly state?"

Max continued with the shovel until he'd gone down about two feet. "How deep did he bury the gold?"

An uneasiness spread through me as our ruse grew near the end. They wouldn't believe Phil had dug too much deeper since the location itself had been hidden in darkness. Now what?

"Is he certain we're at the correct location?" Lawrence inspected the hole.

Spearing the ground, Max scooped out more dirt before the metal rang as it hit something hard.

Herbert moved closer and shone his light. "Did you find it? Is that a chest or case with my gold?"

Lulu joined the search with her own flashlight

beam swinging back and forth.

I whispered to Holly, "Can you stand?"

When she gave a slight nod, I tucked an arm beneath her shoulders. Gently, I helped her rise, and we skirted the wall as we plunged deeper into the tunnel.

"Marni, you're taking her the wrong direction. The exit is that way." Phil pointed past our abductors.

"And how do you propose we slip past them. We don't have an invisible mode like you, remember?" I hissed. "Now hush before Lulu hears you."

Holly leaned heavily on me. I'd turned off my flashlight and carried it in the other hand. We'd need it once we put enough distance between us and them.

As the tunnel curved toward the left, we crawled along putting us out of sight of the four standing around the hole. Two more steps and Holly tripped and fell, taking us both to the ground.

"I'm sorry, Marni. My arm hurts too bad to keep going. Just leave me and get yourself out before they notice we're gone," she whined.

"Well, that's not going to happen." I sat against the wall of the tunnel and helped prop her up.

A bright light blinded me. "No, that's not going to happen." Lulu's voice sounded from behind the tunnel. "Is this your big escape plan? I expected a little more creativity from you, Marni."

I put my hand up to block the glare. "Holly needs help now. She practically passed out, which is the only reason you caught up to us."

"It's a good thing we no longer need her. Do as she asked and leave her behind, or I'll remove her permanently from the equation."

Rising to my feet, I handed the injured woman my

flashlight. I hated to relinquish my only possible weapon, but I couldn't leave her sitting alone in the dark. At least with her away from the crew, Lulu would focus on me and leave her alone. By now they should have discovered Phil gave them the wrong location. Since his fear for Holly's life didn't result in a correct location, they'd try a different tactic.

I trudged back to my other captors, risking a glance at Holly before rounding the bend. The three men waited, with Max leaning on the handle of the shovel.

"This is the wrong place, isn't it?" Herbert groused. "We will give you one more opportunity to get this right."

Time had run out. Whatever plan Gloria and Phil hatched had failed. Nobody would be coming to my rescue. My only shot rested on convincing Kimpton he needed me for future jobs. I slumped my shoulders and pointed at the large rocks covering the treasure. "It's under there."

Lawrence motioned Max to do the honors this time. He must've had enough of getting his hands dirty.

Max hefted the large rocks as if they were made of feathers. As he reached for the shovel leaning against the wall, he never got to dig.

"Federal agents! Freeze!" A voice boomed from the tunnel entry. "Drop your weapons." A brightness illuminated the tunnel, blinding me until I saw spots before my eyes.

Lulu wrapped an arm around my neck and placed the muzzle of her weapon against my head. "Either I leave safely, or Ms. Legend has written her last chapter."

"Don't be a fool, Lulu." Lawrence called as he

threw his gun to the ground and kicked it away. "I have no desire to wind up dead. Surrender."

She dragged me toward the back of the tunnel.

"Lulu, believe me, I am so not worth it. Let me go, and I'll put in a favorable word with the authorities. They could use your gift on the force," I pleaded.

"Well, I'm not sticking around to find out if they'll make that bargain. Cooperate, and I'll let you go once we get out of this cave." She inched closer to the bend in the path.

"Treasure hunting isn't a crime," Herbert stated. "Believe me, if we aren't allowed to walk out of here freely, my lawyers will have us sprung within the hour. Let the woman go, Lulu."

Her grip on my throat tightened as her body twisted to see behind her. The gun left my temple. This would be my chance to break free.

Before I could act, a loud clunk sounded behind me, and Lulu's hold eased as she dropped to the ground. Turning around, I found Holly teetering over her ready to deliver another blow with the flashlight. *Damn, I wish I'd gotten to do that!*

I slipped an arm around Holly's waist and led her toward our saviors. Except Max now held a gun in his hand aimed at Lawrence and Herbert. I judged the distance between me and the shovel before giving it up as a lost cause.

With his light aimed at the ground, Tiny strolled onto the scene. Was he really law enforcement, or was this a scheme set up between Max and him to steal the treasure for themselves?

Chapter 49

Max stepped forward to retrieve Lawrence's gun. He tucked it into the back of his waistband then retreated before looking at Tiny. "Federal agents? Freeze? You watch too much television, my friend. But all the same, thanks for the assist. How on earth did you know to come here?"

With a shrug, Tiny stood by Max's side holding only a flashlight. "It got their attention. Everyone good?"

"No. Holly needs a doctor. Lulu shot her in the arm," I said. "Anybody care to tell me what's going on? You're not really an officer of the law, are you?"

Tiny pursed his lips and tilted his head toward Max. "I'm not, but—"

"You scum!" Lulu stumbled closer with her weapon raised.

I'd forgotten to disarm her when Holly knocked her out. How could I have been so stupid? *Oh yeah, I don't do this for a living.*

Two shots rang out and this time, when Lulu fell, she didn't get up.

Max held his gun at the ready, but two bullets were enough to put her out of commission. He hurried to her side, scooped up the weapon, and checked for a pulse. With a shake of his head, he looked back to Tiny, now scuffling with Lawrence, who'd tried to make a run for it. The gangly character was no match for the large biker and got taken down easily. Tiny pinned Lawrence to the ground with a knee on his back and meaty hands restraining the felon's wrists. Lawrence quit resisting and laid his cheek on the dirt.

"Marni! Thank God you're all right." Gloria plowed through the tunnel with her head light catching me in the eyes. She threw her arms around my shoulders, almost knocking Holly over.

"Gloria, what are you doing here? You hate dank places," I said. "Not to mention gunplay."

Tiny released Lawrence and stood. "I told you to wait outside the tunnel entrance. You could have gotten lost or worse."

"And miss all the action? Not on your life!" She stomped her foot. "Besides, Felipe showed me the way."

The young Spaniard stood behind my sister with a huge grin on his face. "Not to worry, Marni Legend, I would never let harm come to Miss Gloria."

Astonishment didn't begin to describe my sentiment at Gloria's presence. "Since when are you afraid of missing the action?"

"Since someone nabbed my little sister and dragged her off to find stolen treasure." Gloria crossed her arms and bobbed her head.

"Tiny, what did you mean about you not being law enforcement? Please tell me you're not part of this heist?" I asked. "Is this a double-cross?"

Max pulled a leather folder from his back pocket and flipped it open. "Tiny's just a loyal friend." He held the wallet out to me. "Officer Max Fielding at your service."

"You're a cop?" I helped Holly ease to the floor before taking the credentials from his outstretched arm.

"Like he said, I'm a federal agent. We've been tracking cases of stolen goods taken from loved ones of the recently departed. Treasures from sunken ships added another layer to the spree when the provenance of who originally discovered the downed vessels became obscured, yet the goods landed in Kimpton's possession. We suspected foul play by him and his associate, Lawrence. Tiny had also contacted the bureau in relation to Phil's death. He never believed the reports about a simple drowning of a skilled diver, but local authorities deemed the case closed. It took a while to find the psychic connection, if you will, until Lawrence introduced me to Lulu. Then pieces began to fall into place."

"I'm confused. So you aren't Holly's brother?" I asked.

He grinned. "No. She's an old family friend who got roped into something over her head. When she came to me for help, I convinced her to introduce me as her brother, so I could gain the trust of Herbert and Lawrence, which worked like a charm. Didn't it, guys?"

Lawrence had rolled to a seated position, while Kimpton stood motionless with hands at his side. His trademark sneer rested smugly on his lips.

"I'd worked as Herbert's personal assistant until I discovered his criminal activity." Holly's voice came out weak, almost a whisper. "I worried about being arrested too if he got caught. When I'd heard Lawrence speaking about the beauty and tranquility of Crystal River, I decided it would be a good cover for me to get away and think. As far as my boss was concerned, coming here gave me the appearance of taking an interest in the business. Max got himself set up at the wildlife preserve and settled in as a resident before I introduced him to Herbert and Lawrence."

"How did Phil get mixed up in this?" I asked.

A sad smile crossed her face. "Sheer coincidence. I booked one of his manatee tours and fell in love with the tour guide—Phil. When I tried to quit my job a couple weeks later, Herbert suspected I knew too much and threatened me harm if I didn't help him when the *Sunset Dream* sank. He'd kept tabs on me and found out about Phil having a boat and diving skills."

"I don't mean to break up this cozy reunion," Lawrence said, "but shouldn't we be getting out of here before the tunnel floods?"

Tiny chuckled. "You really don't pay attention to where you live, do you? High tide peaked an hour ago. We're safe from having to swim for our lives."

Gloria walked to Phil, who sat quietly beside Holly. Her eyes had compassion, a quality she rarely displayed openly. "All this treasure hunting doesn't tell us the main reason why we're here."

"You mean where the treasure is buried?" Max pointed to the area where he'd cleared away the rocks.

"Uh uh." She shook her head. "How did Phil really die?"

Chapter 50

I suspected the two men would like to blame Lulu for Phil's murder except she didn't dive. The odds of the woman having enough strength to overpower a man almost twice her body weight didn't add up. If he'd been shot, I would believe our trigger-happy bartender had been the culprit.

"Marni, is this really the right place to dig?" Max asked.

"Yes. I created the decoy when we'd originally thought to trick Lulu into going after the treasure and tipping her hand. Phil secured the doubloons in a canvas satchel. It still rests in his original hiding place."

He held the shovel out to Tiny. "Mind doing the honors while I keep an eye on these guys?"

"My pleasure." He dug into the soil where the rocks had been removed. Before long the tan canvas came to light. Tiny pulled it from the dirt and zipped it open before letting out a low whistle. Rays from the lights reflected off the coins and other finery, which had lain at the bottom of the ocean for centuries. "So this is what all the fuss was about."

Gloria moved closer to examine the stash. "Never in my life did I ever expect to go digging for pirate treasure, let alone find it. You sure do know how to plan an interesting trip, Sis."

I spread my arms wide. "All part of the tour."

We shared a laugh before Max interrupted us. "Ladies"—he turned his head toward the two men— "and felons, it's time to go." He gestured with his gun for them to walk ahead.

Lawrence hesitated and raised his nose in the air. "You know we're innocent until proven guilty."

"You're kidding me, right?" I waved my hand at our surroundings. "You've been caught with two kidnap victims, one stolen treasure, and one dead body. Do you really think a jury of your peers will find you innocent?"

Herbert huffed. "Lulu didn't die by our hands."

"I didn't mean Lulu." I turned and offered a hand to Holly.

Once on her feet, she scanned the tunnel. "Is he still here?"

"Right beside you." I gestured to her side.

Her voice cracked. "Phil, I'm sorry I got you into this mess. I miss you so much. If only we'd had more time, we could've had a real life together."

If ghosts could cry, Phil would've had a stream running down his cheeks. A forlorn look of loss covered his face instead. "I don't blame you. You were forced into a bad situation by horrible people. Move on and be happy. I'll always love you, my Holly."

I repeated his response word for word. Corporeal beings do shed tears, and Holly's came in buckets as she moved away.

Tiny hefted the bag to his shoulder and looked at my sister. "Ready to go home, my beautiful adventurer?"

Gloria swatted the air. "Need I remind you, *again*, I'm a happily married woman who doesn't stray?"

"You know I'm kidding. Friends?" He offered his free hand.

She clasped both hers around his. "Friends."

"Awww. How touching. Can we go now?" I asked. "And what does he mean by 'adventurer' anyway? Just because you got your feet dirty by trekking into a moldy cave doesn't qualify you as daring. Wait, are those *my* shoes?"

She shrugged. "Maybe…"

I turned to go then stopped. "Hey, where'd Felipe go?"

Gloria looked around. "He does that a lot. The young man isn't as social as our buddy, Phil."

"Hey, Tiny. What'll we do about Lulu? We can't just leave her body here." I cringed at the thought of crabs and other sea creatures feasting on her.

"Max will send a crew back for her with a litter after they process the scene." Tiny shifted the weight on his shoulder. "Let's catch up before the boat leaves without us."

You didn't have to tell me twice.

Once we reached the entrance to the cavern, the place hummed with activity. Two small Coast Guard boats were beached near ours, and a mixed cadre of uniformed officers and other personnel milled about. The tide had receded since we'd arrived, and our skiff now sat completely out of the water. Two uniformed officers led Lawrence and Herbert in hand cuffs toward one of the vessels. The younger officer recited their rights.

Holly rested on a rock with two medical personnel tending to her injury. The tears on her face had dried, but her dour expression remained. Phil had disappeared, but his business wasn't finished, and he'd be back.

Max pulled me aside. "Can we talk when this is all over? I'd like to explain."

"I suppose we'll have to so I can find out who I really went riding with." I smirked. "How'd the cavalry get here so fast?"

"Remember when I came back here for the shovel?"

"You forgot it on purpose, didn't you?" I asked.

He nodded. "I had a radio stashed in my pocket, which I hid in the boat. There wasn't an opportunity for me to notify my backup with a location until we'd gotten to the cave. I needed time alone to call them. Sorry to have gotten you involved."

"You didn't. Lulu did. And look how that worked out for her. You sure you want to see me again? The last guy I was with didn't fare well either."

He laughed. "You'll have to tell me about it some time."

"Maybe."

"Hey, you two love birds, where do I dump this load?" Tiny strode up with Gloria.

I burst out laughing. "You'd better not be talking about my sister. She won't need any bullets to tear you apart for a crack like that one."

"Really, Marni? I knew he referred to the treasure. Honestly, sometime your humor is going to get you into trouble." Gloria stood with hands on hips.

I spurted, "Because the last few hours have been a sedate picnic?"

She sighed. "You have a point."

"I've got a question. How did you and Tiny get into the cave without running into all those people?

They never would have let you go in alone and unarmed." My gaze bounced from Tiny to Gloria and back.

"Oh that." Gloria studied her finely manicured nails. "Tiny knew about the upper entrance that didn't involve water and boats. So much easier than slogging through the surf."

I narrowed my eyes at her. "By the way, how did you end up arriving with Tiny anyway?"

"His was the only number I had for someone in the area. You'd told me not to involve the police. When Phil and Felipe told me what had happened to you, I took a chance believing a man so kind to animals had to be one of the good ones."

Tiny pointed at my sister. "Don't ever underestimate this woman, Marni. She refused to tell me where you'd gone without taking her along. I almost didn't, until she told me about Felipe and how he would have to lead us to you once we'd reached the cave. If I hadn't met Max, who'd informed me of what he worked on, it might've taken her a lot longer to convince me she could really talk to spirits. You must have some peculiar family gatherings if you all can see them."

Max relieved Tiny of the bag. "We'll have to log this in as evidence until the case gets sorted out."

"Will Phil's family see any of that wealth?" I asked.

"I really don't know. Since the discovery of the *Santiago* came about as a tip from a long-dead seaman, I'm not sure how the bureau will proceed." Max handed the bag over to a uniformed officer who punched information into an electronic tablet.

Two men from the Coast Guard led Tiny, my sister, and me to a boat and took us back to the beach. More personnel waited on shore to assist us to the upper parking, where we were given hot coffee and blankets while agents took our statements.

After an eternity of questions, we were offered a ride back to our hotel.

"Tiny, would you mind driving us?" I asked.

Gloria bit her lip. "Um…he wouldn't have enough room. One of the agents can drive us."

I laughed. "Don't tell me he drives one of those fancy, two-seat sportsters?"

"Well, the vehicle does only have two seats." She shuffled her feet.

A huge grin spread across his face. "Remember when I referred to your sister as an adventurer?" He motioned toward the back of the lot where his motorcycle sat parked.

My eyes widened. "No way you got her on the back of that thing. Glo, tell him you'd never get on the back of a 'death-machine' as you call it."

She blushed. She actually blushed! It took a monumental force to get my sister to turn any shade of red, let alone the crimson blossoming on her face now. "His truck was in the shop, you were in mortal danger, and this town has no cabs. What else could I do?"

"Did you at least take a few selfies?"

Chapter 51

We spent our last evening in Crystal River sitting on our balcony dining on delivery pizza and sipping merlot. "Our girls' trip kinda spiraled out of control, didn't it, Glo?"

She held her thumb and pointer finger an inch apart. "Just a tad."

"Do you regret allowing me to plan the whole thing?"

Gloria leaned back in her chair. "Not for a moment. Well, I take that back. There were a few moments I could have skipped completely, but I only have one real regret."

"We didn't help Phil." I sighed.

"We didn't help Phil." She nodded.

The next morning I received a text from Max asking to meet him in the hotel restaurant. We had a noon check-out, and our flight didn't take off until five in the evening. The packing could wait.

Max sat in a far corner closest to the river. A waitress set a pot of coffee and two cups on the table as I approached. The scent of fresh brew drifted through the air on a light breeze. He stood and gestured to the seat across from him. "Coffee?"

"Please." I pushed my cup closer so he could pour.

We stared at each other for a long moment over the steam rising from our beverages. I waited for him to speak first.

"I'm not sure where I should begin," he said.

"Why don't you start with your real name," I suggested.

He laughed. "I told you last night it really is Max, and my last name is Fielding."

I tilted my head. "And Dodger?"

"That wasn't a lie. My road name and the story behind it did come from my youth. When working undercover, I try to stick as close to the truth as possible. There's less chances to slip up and tip off my mark."

Crossing my arms, I sat back and studied his face. "What about your involvement with me? Was that just part of the job to get to Phil? Since you and Lulu were quite…friendly, I assume she filled you in on my abilities."

His face reddened. "I'm not proud of that part of the assignment—sleeping with Lulu or conning you into thinking you and I could be…well…together. At least when I first met you, it furthered the job when Lulu pushed me into seeing you to get info about Phil."

I looked away. Here I thought he would have lied to spare my feelings, but he blazed through giving sheer honesty. It made me want him more knowing he could be so upfront. Yet I was only an assignment to him. Merely a means to an end. "How could you know we'd be at Bookends? Gloria had only suggested it right before we went."

"I followed you. When I saw Tiny enter after you, I took a chance and sent a text asking what he was up to that night. At work that day he'd mentioned meeting you and your sister, and he'd escorted you to your hotel. As expected, Tiny invited me to join him, and I figured somehow I'd bump into you. To my surprise, you'd already been seated at his table."

I smirked. "It seems we were destined to meet, if only to help Phil."

He ran a hand through his hair. "Like I said, it began as another piece of the job. Until I got to know you. Then it became personal. As Lulu turned unstable with her jealousy once she guessed I'd fallen for you, I backed away. Since Phil had lost his life due to his association with that crew through Holly, I didn't want anything to happen to you or your sister."

I did a doubletake. Did Max say he'd fallen for me? My heartbeat quickened like a lovesick teenager about to get asked to the prom. Until reality bounced back in—*he lives in another state. How could this possibly work out for us?* Did I even consider there could be an *us*, or had my sex drive taken over believing a quick romp upstairs would suffice? Would Gloria agree to wander off for a couple hours and leave me to my carnal desires? I needed to check how early House of Primp opened. She could always get a facial or her eyebrows waxed.

Rosie's head popped above the surface of the water behind Max. When I jumped in my seat, he turned around, but of course, saw nothing. I stood and went to the ghostly creature with my hand reaching out as if I could stroke her face. "I'd forgotten about you girl. We may never know what happened to you or Phil."

She bobbed her head then slipped under the water. Whether she understood or not, her soul hadn't moved on.

"Marni?" Max stood beside me. "Who are you

talking to?"

I gazed at him. "Did Lulu ever mention Rosie to you?"

He shook his head.

We sat back at the table, and I told him about the manatee whom Phil had rescued.

When I'd finished, Max said, "Your world gets crazier by the minute."

"Want to reconsider that whole falling for me statement?" I asked.

Placing a hand beneath my chin, he leaned in. "Uh uh. You?"

"Uh uh." My lips met his before pulling back. "The only problem now is you live about six states away. I don't do long distance relationships well. Unless, of course, you're only thinking of having a fling. In which case, we might be able to come to an agreement before I board the plane this evening."

"When did this become a business transaction?" He laughed. "You may want to revise your assessment of the situation. With the culprits apprehended, I won't be staying in Crystal River. I'm set to head home in a couple of days."

"Where's home?" *Please don't say California.*

He clasped my hand. "Let's just say it's a lot closer than six states away. Now, it's against the rules for me to talk about a case before the investigation is complete and it's gone to trial. Since you have unfinished business in the spirit world, which some at the bureau can't quite wrap their heads around, I'll give you what you need to put Phil to rest."

My whole body perked up. Here I'd thought we completely failed at our current soul assignment.

After we packed the car and checked out of the hotel, Gloria and I walked along the river's path behind the building. We stopped at the public dock next door and sat on the end with our feet dangling close to the water's surface.

Phil appeared beside my sister.

"There you are," I said. "We'd hoped to find you before we left so we wouldn't have to come back searching for you."

"I hate long good-byes and didn't want the two of you to get all mopey. After all we've been through together, I'm sure you'll miss me terribly." He swung his legs back and forth off the edge of the dock.

"Believe it or not, Phil, I will miss you. While you added a little too much spice to our trip, maybe I need more adventure in my life," Gloria said. "Maybe not bullets flying through the air, but you get my meaning."

He clapped his hands. "Well said, madam, well said. I guess people can change. What about you, Marni?"

"What about me?"

"Will you tone down your life as Gloria amps up hers? There could be a happy medium." Phil tilted his head.

I waved my hand through the air. "Not a chance. Besides, most things that happen to me are beyond my control. I'm just one of those targets that attracts trouble, no matter how hard I try to avoid it." Glancing at my sister, I asked, "Glo, since you were the chosen one at the start of this mystery, do you want to give Phil the news?"

"Oh, Marni, you haven't known motorcycle man that long. Please tell me you're not planning nuptials or anything else drastic." He placed his hands on his cheeks.

"Phil, it'll be a long time before I walk down that aisle again with anyone. Have you been visiting Holly?"

He smiled. "Yes, I couldn't help myself. She's been released from the hospital and home resting with her arm in a sling. With that wretched Lulu gone and the two of you going home to New York, I suppose we won't be able to communicate anymore."

Gloria flung an arm around my shoulders and smiled at Phil. "That's what we wanted to talk to you about."

Chapter 52

Phil shifted so he could face both of us. "Do tell."

"Max has sworn us to secrecy, but who are you going to talk to?" I grinned.

Gloria spun her head toward me. "I thought I was telling him?"

I nodded.

"It seems Herbert isn't as loyal to his associates as they'd like to think." She released me and laced her fingers together. "The day after you and Holly discovered the location of the *Sunset Dream*, you went back. Lawrence joined you because your girlfriend had told him and Herbert the yacht had been found. Do you remember any of this?"

With an elbow to his knee, Phil rested his chin on his hand. "That's why he looked familiar, but I couldn't place him. It had been the first time Holly had introduced any of her coworkers to me. He dove with me so he could help retrieve the loot."

I raised my eyebrows, prodding him to go on.

He shook his head.

"Holly remained at home, feigning a headache, per Herbert's instructions. You and Lawrence were alone when you dove the wreck for a second time," Gloria said.

"That's right." Phil slapped his forehead. "I wanted to wait until she felt better, but Lawrence insisted we not waste a minute in case somebody else found the boat." He looked out across the river. "I swam into the cabin first to grab the case I'd replaced earlier. When I handed it through the hatch, Lawrence snatched it and locked me inside." His voice lowered. "He left me there to die."

Gloria bit her lip and tears glistened in her eyes. "You might never have been found, except when Lawrence got the case ashore and opened it, he found rocks weighing it down instead of gold and jewels. By the time he dove in again and pulled you out, you'd expired, taking the secret with you."

"I'm sorry, Phil, but at least you know for certain Holly had nothing to do with it." I moved to sit on his other side. "When Lawrence found he'd arrived too late to get the location of the treasure out of you, he set you adrift. Somehow the tides pushed you into Crystal River where they found you."

He looked to me. "What made them so sure I'd taken it? It could have been stolen before it reached the *Sunset Dream*."

"They weren't completely certain, until a week later. Felipe appeared to Lulu one more time. He told her the man in the flowered shirt had hidden his family's treasure where she'd never find it again. If she wouldn't return it to his family, at least it would remain lost," I said.

My sister picked up the tale. "Herbert insisted that Holly claim to have been engaged to you and wanted half of the tour shop. She confirmed her part in the story to Max. Kimpton and friends could search the grounds without suspicion if she were part owner."

"What does he get in exchange for this morbid

revelation?" Phil asked.

"Leniency. Nothing more. He wanted absolved of everything, but kidnapping me nixed any kind of favorable deal he could have made. Kimpton will do jail time, just not be convicted for murder. That's all on Lawrence. Herbert claimed to have never ordered your death. Of course, Lawrence will contradict that to save his own hide, but that'll be up to the judge and jury to sort out." I pulled my phone from my back pocket. We needed to leave for the airport soon since we had a two-hour drive ahead of us.

"I hope you said your good-byes to Holly, because now it's time for you to leave for good." I stood and brushed off my pants.

Before Phil got up, Rosie rose out of the water in front of him. He smiled as he patted her nose. "What about you, my sweet friend? Will you be coming with me?" He looked my way.

I shrugged. "Ghost animals are a whole new realm for me. Rosie is my first. I'd like to think she died of natural causes but stuck around for you. Maybe she'll follow you."

"Oh, I hope so." With one more pet, she disappeared instead of sinking back into the river. Phil stood and faced my sister. "As for you, my beautiful Gloria, it truly has been a pleasure sparring with you. I'd kiss your hand if I were able."

My sister let out a laugh. "Yes, it was fun—some of the time. I'm glad we were able to help you in the end."

"Farewell, Sir Phil." Felipe appeared beside him.

"So you're still here?" Phil asked. "I'd hoped last night's actions had resolved your presence on Earth."

The young sailor shook his head. "While the treasure has changed hands, it still has not been returned to Spain. I cannot yet rest."

"I'm sorry, Felipe," I said. "Maybe I can speak with Max and see what the authorities can do about returning it to your country, if not your descendants. I believe that's the best you can hope for all these centuries later."

After a brief smile in my direction, he reached out a hand to Phil, who shook it. "Journey well, my friend." Felipe walked down the boardwalk and vanished.

Phil turned to Gloria again. "Perhaps I'll see you up there someday."

"And what about me?" I asked, but the question came too late. Phil's ghost faded to nothing, leaving Gloria and me alone on the dock. "Rest in peace, Phil."

"I second the motion." She jerked her finger toward land. "Shall we hit the road?"

"If we want to fly out of Tampa tonight, we'd best be going."

Motorcycles roared into the parking lot as we rounded the side of the hotel. Tiny and Max rolled their bikes to a stop beside our rental car and got off.

Tiny spread his arms wide. "You weren't thinking of leaving without saying good-bye, were you?" He stood decked out in blue jeans torn at the knees and a black leather vest over a red, sleeveless T-shirt. His boots pounded on the ground as he neared.

Gloria set her purse on the front passenger seat and extended her hand. "Christopher, it was truly a pleasure meeting you. You are quite a unique individual."

With a glance at her hand, Tiny pulled her into a bear hug, dwarfing her small stature with his bulk.

"Friends don't shake hands around here."

When he released her, she placed a hand on his chest. "I can see that."

"Someday, I hope to meet your husband, so I can tell him what a lucky man he is." Tiny grinned down at her.

"Oh, he knows." I stepped up and got the same farewell embrace. "She never lets him forget it either."

"Marni's right. The man spoils me, even when I don't deserve it," she said. "Though, I can't ever think of a time when I didn't deserve it."

Max wrapped his arms around Gloria. "Thanks for coming to our rescue at the cave. You surprised us all."

"Yeah, well, nobody messes with my baby sister's life." She held him at arms' length and narrowed her eyes. "Or her heart."

He nodded. "Point taken."

I nudged Gloria out of the way. "My turn." Slipping my hands around his waist, I put my forehead against his. "I'm going to miss you."

"Only for a week or so. Boston isn't that far away, and remember, I do a lot of work with our New York City office too. That's a forty-five-minute train ride at most." His lips met mine. After a minute, someone cleared her throat behind me.

Expecting it to be Gloria, I found Kate wearing a serious expression on her face. Her rose perfume gave off a delicate aroma, making her seem almost civil. Max released me, and I scrunched my brows at her.

"Ms. Legend, I'm glad I caught up with you. When I called the hotel earlier, the clerk told me you'd just checked out, so I'd hoped you might be here still. I wanted to apologize for my behavior when we first met.

Lawrence, my soon-to-be ex-husband, had been putting a tremendous amount of pressure on me to raise my ratings and sell more books. Meeting a compet…fellow author in the same genre pushed me over the edge a bit." She took a deep breath, as if a weight had suddenly slid from her shoulders.

"Please, call me Marni. Did you say soon-to-be ex-husband?" Now that warmed my heart almost as much as her apology.

"Lawrence had dug himself into a hole with bad investments. Lucky for me, I never let him touch my inheritance from my parents, so my fortune is intact. My books are more of a hobby that I enjoy, and I'd foolishly allowed him access to the royalties. I suppose I should also add my gratitude for your part in removing him from my life."

"I suspect he'd have landed in jail eventually without my help. But you're welcome."

She stuck out her hand. "I'd hoped we might do a book signing together when next you visit Crystal River. It would be an honor sitting with someone as talented as you."

I debated whether she abided with the "friends don't shake hands" theory before returning the shake. "I'd love to." Digging into my purse, I retrieved a business card. "Let me know if you're ever in my neck of the woods."

"I will. Thanks again, Marni. And you too, Gloria." She walked back to her car and drove away.

"Think we'll have any more surprise visitors before you ladies leave?" Tiny asked.

"Considering we've probably said so long to most of the town, including the deceased, I'd say no. Ready,

Glo?"

She jumped into the passenger seat. I took that for a yes. With one more quick peck from Max, I got behind the wheel.

****

Back in Northport, Robert and Gloria dropped me in front of the bakery below my apartment. It had snowed while we were away, but the streets had been cleared and sidewalks salted. I trudged up the stairs lugging my suitcase, ready for a hot shower and a night in my own bed. A glass of wine would be a relaxing touch. Tossing the keys on the table in the entry, I flipped on the kitchen light.

"It's about time you showed up, young lady. Where have you been?" My mother's spirit sat at the dining table with arms crossed.

"Ma, think of the pearly gates as a turnstile at the subway station. It's a one-way trip not a revolving door. Everything is resolved in your life. Say hello to Dad for me." I set my purse on the table, turned off the light, and walked toward my room.

"That's what you think," she called after me. "Fine, I can wait."

Why couldn't Gloria be the chosen one this time?

A word about the author...

Terry Segan, originally from Commack, NY, now resides in the desert where she'll never require an ice scraper or snow shovel again. The beach is her happy place, but any opportunity to travel soothes her gypsy soul. The stories conjured by her imagination while riding backseat on her husband's motorcycle can be found throughout the pages of her paranormal mysteries. Growing up immersed in sarcastic humor and science fiction, Terry's goals are to cause her readers to laugh out loud, cry with joy, or cower beneath the covers wondering if the noise under the bed was real or imagined.

http://terrysegan.com

www.ingramcontent.com/pod-product-compliance
Lightning Source LLC
Chambersburg PA
CBHW051141030726
47504CB00004B/974